Chasing the Wind

Gill Wyatt

CW01496421

2

& blessings

Gill Wyatt

16. 12. 12.

Heartsease Publishing

Acknowledgements

The biggest thanks go to my family who have supported me throughout this venture. Special thanks go to my husband Barrie, and my son Joel, who painstakingly formatted the book for publishing. I truly could not have done that myself. Many thanks to Dan and Steph, who did the final edit for this edition. You have greatly improved it. Thanks to Vikki and Tom who designed my website and used their musical knowledge to check out the guitar playing in the final chapter. Thanks too, to Ruth who made fliers for marketing and to Geoff whose idea of using thenewboston.com helped Barrie and Joel with the formatting. Thanks to Carole Davies for checking out a folk scene to make sure that I had the details right.

Thanks to Ned Hoste of 2h Design Consultancy for the cover design.

Thank you to all my friends and family who supported and encouraged me along the way. You believed in me when I didn't believe in myself.

1

Seconds before it happened, Bobby Barron sensed his father's temper was about to explode. It still startled him as his father's fist collided with the dining table. Crockery and cutlery, and his mother, jumped.

'This conversation isn't over,' his father said as Bobby got up, shrugged and walked out. It was pure bravado; his breathing was fast and shallow and his heart pounded in his chest as if it was beating time to an African war cry. He kept his pace slow; if he slammed doors or stormed out, his father would give chase like a threatened animal. He picked up his leather jacket and crash helmet from the hallway, and let out a sigh as he shut the front door behind him. As he reached the bottom of the steps, he put on his jacket, lit a cigarette, and leant against the wall in the dark, inhaling deeply.

By the time he started up the motorbike and rode off towards town, his pulse and breathing had returned to normal, but his mind was scrambled. He pushed the argument to the back of his mind, and thought ahead to the folk club. Considering that he was only in the first term of his foundation year at art college, he felt a measure of pride at being asked to be President of the folk club.

Reaching the Cotswold town of Brockton, he passed by his dad's Graphic Design Studio. "Barrons" the notice said. The name was synonymous with perfection, unlike the relationship with his father. His mind returned to the argument. He replayed it over and over again, becoming angrier with each action replay. By the time he reached the art college, his heart was thumping again and his breathing was fast and shallow once more.

He screeched to a halt outside the entertainment block,

heaved the motorbike onto its stand, and threw the crash helmet into the top box, slamming down the lid with more force than was necessary. As he walked quickly down the concrete steps to the basement folk club, he ran his fingers through his shoulder length, blond hair as if, by doing so, he could gain control and restore order.

He glanced back up the steps at the grey, pebble-dashed walls as he opened the main door to the folk club. It was reminiscent of a rundown council estate youth club. *Such a pity that nothing has been done to improve this place,* he thought.

As he swung open the inner doors and entered the room, he adopted a confident air. He looked around briefly; it would need changes. The posters on the walls no longer concealed the flaking paint, and a slightly musty smell of stale beer hung in the air, but it gave it atmosphere, and having a bar of its own made it a good room for a club.

His best mate, Jerry, strode towards him. 'At last' he said, 'I began to wonder if you were coming. Where do you want the mics?'

'I'd forgotten you were trying out a sound system. Put them where you like,' Bobby replied with atypical disinterest, waving his hand dismissively over the equipment.

'Hanging from the ceiling?' Jerry asked, as he slung his afghan coat over the back of a chair and sat down.

'Yeah, hang me with them.'

Jerry raised his eyebrows. 'Woah man! What's up? Have you been arguing with the old man again?' he asked through the fog he'd created with the cigarette which hung precariously from his lips, as he unscrewed the back of a plug.

Bobby merely nodded.

Jerry put the plug down and pulled out a chair, motioning to Bobby to sit.

Bobby tried to steady his shaking hands as he picked up the cigarette that Jerry placed in front of him.

'What were you arguing about?' Jerry asked.

'Working for him at Christmas.'

Jerry choked on the smoke. 'But you knew he'd insist.'

'That's not the point.'

Jerry shrugged. 'So just do the work and keep your mouth shut.'

Bobby replied through tight lips. 'But then he's won.'

Jerry hunched over the plug as he tightened a screw. 'It isn't a war.'

Bobby clenched his fists. 'I'm not working for him when I finish college and he's determined to make me, it's about winning. So it's war.'

Students began to drift into the club and hang around the bar and Dave, the ex-president arrived, interrupting Bobby's conversation.

'Thanks Bobby, every Friday night got too much. I knew you were the right guy to run the club.'

Bobby screwed up his face in concern. 'You don't mind if I make changes though, do you?'

Dave's reply was tinged with relief. 'Not at all, I love the music but I'm no organiser.'

'It's safe with Bobby,' Jerry laughed. 'He'll give it one hundred percent and expect the same from everyone else.'

Bobby's eyes were animated. 'I want to give the club the same structure as other folk clubs. We'll get guest singers once a month and organise raffles to raise money. On guest nights my band will warm up the audience as usual, and then we'll have the experienced floor singers, followed by half an hour of the guest singer ... and repeat the pattern after the interval.'

He was oblivious to the fact that Jerry and Dave were laughing at him.

'By the way, I'm looking for a good violinist.'

Jerry continued his conversation with Dave. 'He's only been interested in folk music for about eighteen months. A girlfriend took him to a folk festival. The girlfriend was fleeting like all the rest, but his love for the music remained.'

Bobby looked up as Jerry's girlfriend, Kate, entered the club with her flatmate, Jodie. There was something captivating about Jodie, a mystery, sadness maybe behind her smiling, sea green eyes, but she was never more than polite with him. He watched her as she took off her black coat and royal blue beret and twirled a strand of hair round her fingers. His eyes followed her until she passed out of sight in the bar. Kate walked across to where they were sitting and kissed Jerry on the top of his head.

'Hi, baby,' Jerry muttered without moving the cigarette.

She took it from his mouth and laid it on the edge of the ashtray in front of him before answering.

'Hi, did you finish that assignment?'

'Well ...'

Kate raised her eyebrows, waiting for a reply.

'I almost did,' Jerry grinned, 'that is, I almost did start it.'

Bobby's smirk mocked her.

'It has to be in tomorrow,' she continued, with an anxious air.

With a sideways glance, Bobby looked her up and down. 'Don't fuss. It won't take long.'

'Well we're not all geniuses like you are we?' she snapped.

Bobby nodded slowly. 'True.'

Kate muttered loudly as she walked away, 'Arrogant bastard.'

'Bloody bad-tempered redhead,' he retorted.

'Thank you Bobby,' Jerry said quietly, 'she'll be unbearable now.'

Bobby shrugged. In his view Kate was always unbearable. Dave grinned as he got up to go, and Bobby turned his attention back to Jerry.

'As long as there's some improvement by the end of term, I'll carry on running the club.'

Jerry looked at him with an expression of exasperation. 'That's only a few weeks away.'

Bobby shrugged. 'I'm the kind of guy who needs

encouragement.'

'More like the kind of guy who needs miracles.'

Bobby glanced at his watch and leapt to his feet, stubbing out the cigarette with force in the ashtray. 'Oh hell, the kind of guy who needs microphones. Put the mics at the front,' he ordered, gesticulating like a stage manager as he flung his leather jacket over the back of a chair and undid the top button of his psychedelic shirt. 'Arrange the tables in an informal fashion.'

He was shouting in order to be heard above the gradually increasing noise. Students were milling around under his feet and he was jostled as he attempted to put out tables and chairs. Some of them helped, and by ten to eight the room was ready. The room gradually filled with students and smoke, and at eight o'clock on the dot, he jumped up on the stage, leant into the microphone and began his performance.

'I'll begin tonight with a song that was especially popular in the West Country,' he announced with a smile. He took the microphone in his hand and casually sat on a stool, grinning out from under his blond mop. Jerry handed him a pint of Newcastle Brown and he took a slurp and put the glass on the floor beside him before he began. 'It is generally thought that *The Jolly Waggoner* dates back to the early nineteenth century, when most people didn't travel far from home. The waggoner looks back on his life without regret, despite the fact that his parents disapproved of his choice of career.' He laughed, 'I empathise with that.'

He leant down and had another slurp of his beer. As he tuned up, a hush fell over the audience. The group joined him and broke into *The Jolly Waggoner* as Bobby struck up in the chord of D, with a regular rhythm like the walking pace of a wagon. As he sang, his body rocked, as if jostled by the movements of the wagon. His folk band, The Cobwebs, sang a protest song next and their final song was one of Bobby's own compositions. After a slight bow, which brought whistles and applause, he announced the next performers. He walked briskly to the door and drew up a rough order for the evening.

'Kate hasn't signed up yet,' he said to Jerry, 'Ask her if The Corn Dollies are going to sing will you, and if so put them down to sing in between Barley Mow and Duncan Waite. We don't want too many long ballads in a row and if any new singers sign up, make sure they are later in the evening.'

Jerry caught hold of Bobby's shirtsleeve as he began to strut away. 'She's cross with you. She's refusing to sing.'

Bobby tutted impatiently and pushed his way through sweaty bodies to where Kate was sitting with Jodie. He stood beside Kate and said quietly, 'Don't punish the club just because you don't like me,' and then simply walked away. Kate looked wide eyed with surprise.

During the interval, he announced his intentions for the club, finishing with yet another request for a fiddle player. He smiled as Kate took the floor to sing in the second half of the evening, with her all-female group The Corn Dollies. She was pretty, he had to admit that. She floated across the floor in her full length Laura Ashley skirt with its tiny, red flowers, just enough to set off her auburn hair without making it garish. Her make-up, unlike the heavy black make-up that was popular, was light and subtle. The end of her first song was met with cries of 'encore' and with wolf whistles from Jerry. She stifled a grin and shot him a haughty stare, before putting down the guitar and taking the microphone in her hand for her second song. Bobby had respect for her playing, and her voice was as strong and penetrating as her sarcastic tongue. If it were not for his fear of the latter, he would have attempted to recruit her for The Cobwebs.

As the evening's music came to an end, the students drifted away.

'I think that went okay,' Bobby said as they cleared up and tidied the bar. He wedged the doors open to clear the air of the dense smoke and the odour of stale beer. As he mopped the sticky floor, he talked enthusiastically about his plans for the club. Jerry listened as he swept up the glass behind the bar.

They raced each other home on the pitch-black country roads as they always did. The village of Dernham would be dead by now; even during the day it was semi-comatose. He hooted his horn as he waved farewell to Jerry. *Idiot, you should have kept quiet,* he thought. He closed the wrought iron gates behind him, pushed the bike past the fountain and into the garage, and walked back towards the house, slowing his pace as he approached the front steps. The curtain at the front bay window moved, he was certain of it; his father had waited up. Bobby held back for only a second before gathering his courage. 'Ah well,' he said to himself, 'I can't stand out here all night.' He took a deep breath and leaped up the porch steps in one bound.

Colin Barron sat at the oak writing bureau in the corner of the elegant lounge, doing the monthly accounts as he waited for his son to return home.

'Success,' he said aloud as the figures finally balanced. He loosened the tie around his neck, put the lid on his fountain pen, and closed the bureau. Then he got up and paced the floor, glancing at his watch every now and again as if that would somehow accelerate time. The longer he paced, the more he stirred up the anger which had pre-occupied his thoughts since the boy had walked out at dinner time.

'I won't allow him to waste his talent,' he said to himself. Leaning on the grand piano in front of the bay window, he picked up a photograph of Bobby as a child, reflecting on the times when the boy had seemed to enjoy learning new skills in the studio. He felt a surge of pride. His son had artistic flair, and one day he would be able to take over the running of the business, Colin was sure of that.

He took a deep breath, crossed the room and sat down, resting his head wearily against the side of the platinum grey settee. He was just drifting off to sleep when he was awoken by the roar of the motorbike, and the blast of the horn as Bobby arrived home. Suddenly he was awake; he needed to be sharp to outwit the boy. The brakes screeched as the motorbike came to a halt. Colin heard the gate shutting as he got up from the chair and headed for the window. Slowly, ever so slightly, he pulled back the dusky pink, velvet curtain just as Bobby approached the house.

Colin positioned himself at the foot of the sweeping stairs. His heart beat faster as he heard the garage door shut. He quietly waited for the key in the lock.

'Good evening,' Bobby said without looking up, as he hung his leather jacket on the coat stand in the hall. *Insolent brat! How dare he act as if nothing had happened?* The smirk on his face made Colin seethe.

'I want to talk to you in the lounge. Now!'

Bobby attempted to brush past his father and up the stairs, almost dislodging a photograph from the wall.

'I'm tired, it will have to wait until the morning.'

Colin grabbed him by the back of the collar, choking him. 'It was a command, not a request,' he said as he swung his son round and pushed him into the lounge.

'Sit,' he barked.

Bobby moved his head from side to side and loosened the collar of his psychedelic shirt with his finger as he sat down on the settee. Colin paced the lounge.

'If,' he said through clenched teeth as he caught Bobby's eye, 'you ever walk out of the house when I am talking to you again, I will knock you from here to next week ... do you understand?

He could see that Bobby was in a defiant mood; *no doubt exacerbated by alcohol*, he thought. The boy leant back, clasping his hands confidently behind his neck.

'No, could you explain?'

Colin gritted his teeth and turned away, struggling to remain calm, but as he looked up he caught sight of Bobby's head cocked on one side. In two strides he was in front of the boy, lifting him from the chair by the collars. Bobby's expression changed in an instant. Colin dropped him and stepped back, almost knocking over the French vase on the glass-topped coffee table; he put out a hand to steady it. Bobby was furious now and started to get up. Hearing him move, Colin turned around and pushed him back into the chair.

'I said,' he sneered, up close to Bobby's face, 'that I want to talk to you.'

Bobby flinched.

'As I was saying before you so rudely stormed off after dinner. You will work in the studio during the Christmas holidays or you will not get another penny out of me.'

Colin smiled to himself. Removing Bobby's allowance was a good idea, but there was no sign of him giving up; indeed the boy adopted an expression of mock servitude, leant forward in the chair and bowed his head slightly, rubbing his hands together as he spoke.

'Please Mr Scrooge, would it be possible to have Christmas day off?' he taunted.

Colin took hold of him once more and Bobby finally put up his hand in surrender, muttering, 'Joke.'

'You are an insolent brat,' Colin spat, so close to Bobby that he could smell the alcohol on the boy's breath. He let go of him.

'Secondly,' he continued, as he tucked in his shirt, 'you can give up your notions about studying fine art. There's no future in it, and I'm not wasting my money helping you to study something useless.'

Bobby jumped to his feet. 'Just because you were an abject failure as an artist doesn't mean that I will be.'

Bobby looked over his shoulder, but he'd backed himself against the wall. Colin could sense fear in his eyes; he would use that to his advantage. He pulled himself up to his full six feet and closed in on him, very slowly.

'Don't you dare talk to me like that,' he said, his face taut with anger. 'Becoming a fine artist is pure fantasy, castles in the air. I taught you all I know about the graphic design business so that you wouldn't have to struggle.'

Colin held Bobby's face upwards as he spoke, with one index finger under the boy's chin poking into his throat as he continued. 'You will work at Christmas. Do you understand?'

This time there was no witty remark and no defiance; he had subdued him. Colin let go and walked away, determined to have the last word. As he closed the lounge door behind him he didn't hear his son's reply.

'I hate you, you bastard. You won't win.'

3

Jerry had lost track of the conversation between Jodie and his girlfriend, Kate, as they chatted at the flat the girls shared in Brockton. Something they said about Bobby triggered the memories, and he smiled to himself. He was brought back to consciousness as Kate slandered Bobby to Jodie. He got up and stood beside the window, mindlessly watching the worn out curtains waft in the draught from the sash windows. Jerry pulled back the net curtain hoping that Jodie's granddad would arrive to rescue her from this tirade, but he wasn't in sight and Jerry could no longer bear to listen to it.

'I've got more respect for Bobby than for anyone I know.' He spoke softly, raising dust from the old sagging chair as he sat down.

'For Bobby? Respect?' Kate replied.

'Aw come on Jerry,' Jodie added, putting her feet up on the coffee table and ignoring the appalled look on Kate's face, 'I know he's your friend, but you must admit he is ever so slightly arrogant.'

Jerry shuffled in his chair uncomfortably; they didn't know Bobby as he did.

'We'd all be a little insecure if we'd survived what he has,' he said, shying away from the gaze of either of them.

'He's an arrogant womaniser. He uses his blond good looks to bed any girl he fancies,' Kate said as she painted her nails.

Jerry stubbed out his cigarette in the ashtray. 'I know that's his reputation, but he's not like that now. The girls were as bad, they used him as a fashion accessory.'

The doorbell saved them and Jodie ran downstairs to let her granddad in, gathered a few things together, took her granddad's arm, and left.

Jerry was miles away. *Jodie would be good for him,* he thought.

She has quiet strength, maybe she could even give him the stability he lacks.

'She'd be good for Bobby,' he remarked. The moment the words had crossed his lips he silently cursed his indiscretion.

'She doesn't deserve to be hurt by a rogue like him,' Kate said with a finality that told Jerry that the subject was closed.

'His bravado is only a cover,' Jerry said.

Kate bristled. 'He gets what he deserves. He always has to have the last word.'

He resolved to say no more. Jerry replied in not much more than a whisper. 'There's a lot of stuff you don't know about him.'

Kate sat beside him and he put his arm around her, letting her wavy hair tumble over his sallow arm as he drew her closer. It was Kate who reopened the subject. 'He's a good artist though.'

'A perfectionist,' Jerry said. 'He's the same with music. He's constantly trying to get his dad's approval.'

Kate got up. At five feet, eight inches, wearing high heels and with her auburn hair, she cut a fiery image as she stood over Jerry.

'Oh come on,' she snapped. 'His dad is a respectable businessman. The problem has to be Bobby.'

'You haven't met his dad,' he replied with a sardonic laugh. The violin resting in its case on the sideboard caught his eye and he stood up and walked towards it. How come he'd only just noticed it? Was this the first time it had been here?

'Whose is the violin?' he enquired, stroking it.

'Jodie's,' Kate replied inattentively as she tidied the magazines on the shelf under the coffee table. And then, as if she suddenly realised the implication of the question added, 'No, don't tell Bobby.' She shook her head violently. 'She knows he wants a violinist. If she wants to volunteer that's up to her.'

He stared into space, struck by a thought that he wasn't sharing. He could feel Kate's eyes following him. Wait until

Bobby heard this. He would tell him tonight at the concert. Kate looked uncomfortable but said no more about it until Jerry left for the charity concert.

'It might be better if you don't tell Bobby about the violin,' she said as he approached the front door.

'Maybe,' he said.

Kate sighed.

Jerry arrived at Dernham Church at nearly four o'clock. It was dark inside and the lingering smell of incense hit Jerry as he pushed open the heavy oak door. Bobby arrived soon after.

'The acoustics are terrible,' Jerry said as he started unloading the sound equipment.

'We'll just do the best we can,' Bobby replied as they set up the system. By the time they finished it was six o'clock and they were exhausted.

'I'm going home to have a quick shower and something to eat then I'll pick up a bottle for tonight.'

'You might offend the Rev,' Jerry suggested.

'Okay,' Bobby said with hands held up in surrender.

Jerry watched him disappear from view. He was concerned at Bobby's alcohol consumption and suspected that he wasn't coping with the pressures of study, the folk club, and his home life. He could understand it; even the world of drunken mists and shadows must be less disorientating than reality.

Jerry returned to the church half an hour early and Bobby arrived soon afterwards opening his jacket like a dirty old man in a raincoat.

'Look, no booze.'

The smell of alcohol was on his breath but Jerry said nothing.

By the time people began to arrive everything was set up. The evening was likely to attract most of the village; not much else happened here.

'Pity you can't turn my old man down, or better still off,'

Bobby said as his father began a rousing organ recital.

'We could unplug the pump,' Jerry suggested nonchalantly.

Bobby laughed too loudly and two old ladies turned around and stared. He slumped down in his chair as if he was hiding from them.

'When are you playing?' Jerry asked casually.

'Just before the interval.'

'Good, I don't dig all this classical stuff.'

Bobby looked shocked.

'What some of these musicians were trying to do was quite radical in their day,' Bobby suggested, but stopped when Jerry raised his eyebrows.

Bobby had carefully chosen his songs. He lulled them into a false sense of security with *The Bell Ringing,* a traditional folk song based on the sound of church bells and went straight into a song entitled, *The Clergyman's Daughter.* The end of the song was met with silence until the Rev, (as the vicar was irreverently known to the local youth), got up and applauded and the flock followed the shepherd. The Rev announced the interval and Bobby joined Jerry again at the back until the vicar called him over. He was sitting half way down the church in one of the pews. Bobby perched on the back of a pew with his feet up on the pew beside the vicar.

'Interesting,' the vicar said nodding pensively, 'did you ever meet my daughter?' The Rev kept a straight face.

'I don't think so,' Bobby replied with a mischievous grin.

'I'm glad about that,' the vicar replied.

Bobby laughed. 'Oh I'm sure your daughter is more honourable than the one in the song.'

'I wouldn't like to think what my daughter gets up to ...'

The vicar hadn't completed the sentence when Colin came by.

'Get your feet off the pew, this is a church,' he said roughly.

'I'm sorry,' Bobby replied with wide eyes, looking around. 'I hadn't noticed.'

'How dare you sing something like that here? You really are a little bastard aren't you?' he said aggressively under his breath.

Bobby replied with hands raised in surrender. 'Well I can't argue with that, you were there after all.'

Colin clenched his fist at his side and shot Bobby a killing glare as he strutted away. The Rev looked uncomfortable.

'You shouldn't answer him like that. It only makes him worse,' the vicar said.

'He makes me angry. Why should he win just because he gets aggressive? Don't worry, he'll get his own back when I get home ... with interest probably.'

Bobby laughed and jumped down off the back of the pew, giving the Rev a friendly knock on the arm.

'That was a load of rubbish but at least it's made money for the youth club jukebox,' Jerry said at the end of the evening.

Bobby and Jerry packed the equipment into the car and set off for the pub. It was only as they sitting quietly that Jerry remembered the violin.

'Hey Bobby, I almost forgot,' Jerry said in great excitement, 'this afternoon when I was at Kate's, there was a violin sitting on the sideboard. I asked Kate whose it was, and guess who plays it?'

An arrow pierced Bobby's heart. He looked at Jerry with a mixture of surprise and dismay, before replying

'Not Jodie? She knew I wanted a violinist.'

Jerry nodded.

Bobby shook his head in disbelief. 'Are you certain?'

'Absolutely,' he winked.

4

Bobby couldn't expel thoughts of Jodie and the violin for the rest of the weekend. His emotions wavered between ecstatic delight, and hurt that she hadn't told him. By Monday morning he was emotionally exhausted.

Jodie was late as usual, and he watched out of the window as she wandered casually up the drive to the college, with her hands in her pockets and her scarf wrapped tightly round her neck, kicking the leaves. Her simplicity enchanted him.

As she drew close to the building, her eye caught his through the window but he looked away, rejecting her before she had the opportunity to reject him. When she walked in through the door he glanced up from his work, but she ignored him. 'Sorry I'm late,' she said to the lecturer.

Bobby ignored her for the rest of the lesson, but at lunchtime he plucked up courage to sit next to her in the canteen. She was involved in a discussion with other students about socialism and Bobby just listened.

'It seems to me that most council house dwellers create their own poverty,' Kate said.

'If you had grown up in poverty you wouldn't think that,' Jodie retorted.

Bobby smiled. She always seemed to stay cool; he admired that. He waited for the discussion to end before venturing a question. 'Jodie, is it true that you play the violin?'

She looked up accusingly at Kate, who raised her hands as a barrier, answering Jodie's look of annoyance abruptly and loudly. 'Nothing to do with me, Jerry must have told him.'

Jodie turned back to Bobby, but held his gaze for only a second. 'I do play but not very well.'

Bobby caught the expression on Kate's face which gave away the truth. He plucked up courage a second time. 'Well will you play in the band anyway?'

'I can't,' she replied.

He nodded gently as he spoke, trying not to show his disappointment.

'Okay,' he replied, but he left soon after.

Jerry jumped up and called after him, catching up just as he reached the canteen doors. 'Don't give up,' he said.

Bobby looked forlorn, but suddenly broke into a grin.

'I won't. She will play for me, damn it.'

Jerry nodded and gave him a friendly punch on the arm as he walked away, but the smile left Bobby's face as he pushed open the swing door. In the afternoon he applied himself to his project in total silence. In order to avoid Jodie, he waited until the class had cleared before he began to pack away, but Jerry wasn't easily fooled.

'Hey man, I have never seen you so cut-up over a girl.'

The reply was terse. 'I'm fine.'

'Do you want a lift into the college bar tonight?'

Bobby's reply was unenthusiastic. 'I guess so,' he sighed.

'Okay, I'll pick you up at eight.'

Bobby nodded and heaved the rucksack onto his back, muttering under his breath as he left, 'Maybe she isn't worth the effort.'

By the evening he had found a new determination. As he had a lift he could dress up, and before Jerry knocked at the door, Bobby had tried on just about every combination of the clothes in his wardrobe and finally settled on navy, flared cord trousers, a cornflower blue shirt, and silk, navy waistcoat, finishing the look off with Hush Puppy shoes and a splash of Brut aftershave.

'You've forgotten your handbag,' his father mocked as Bobby hurried into the lounge to pick up his leather wallet that he'd left on the top of the piano. Bobby muttered a curse under his breath and left.

Jerry grinned as Bobby opened the door. 'Dressed to impress?' he asked.

'It just makes a change not to have to wear leathers.'

'Of course,' Jerry replied, sporting an inane grin.

Bobby thumped him on the shoulder and got into the old Morris Minor.

'Aren't you picking Kate up?' Bobby asked as they passed the end of her road.

'No,' Jerry replied with a laugh, 'she says she'll cycle there because I drink too much.'

At Jerry's speed, it didn't take long to get to the college and, as Bobby followed Jerry into the student bar, he caught sight of Jodie sitting at the bar talking to the barman.

'I'll get the drinks,' he said to Jerry, ignoring the smirk on his friend's face. As he approached the bar, Bobby noticed that Jodie's glass was almost empty, so he seized his opportunity. Leaning on the bar, he allowed his arm to touch hers.

'Can I get you another drink?' he asked.

Her reply was curt as she moved her arm slightly. 'I can get my own thanks.'

He looked at her with a mischievous smile.

'Oh go on, humour me, I have more money than sense.'

She eyed him suspiciously. 'And what would you expect in return Barron?'

Bobby looked at her for a moment. *Why does she always choose to think the worst of me?* he thought. He replied out of his own hurt as he leant over and whispered, 'If all I wanted was sex I wouldn't try to buy it.'

He regretted saying it the instant the words crossed his lips. She turned on him so fast that he had no means of escape as she tipped the remains of her drink over his head and walked away, with him in hot pursuit. The bar fell silent. He pushed his damp hair back from his face with one hand and caught hold of her arm.

'I'm sorry,' he said quietly without looking at her, 'I shouldn't have said that.'

She tried to pull her arm away and he let go, but in two strides he was in front of her, blocking her advance.

'I just wanted to buy you a drink,' he said softly as he walked backwards in front of her, 'and,' he smirked, 'your glass is empty now.'

She laughed and flicked back her long dark mane, revealing smiling eyes. They seemed even larger this close, less shrouded by the thick, black, eye make-up.

'Okay,' she said, still grinning. 'Do you think you can trust me with a full glass?'

Bobby grinned now. 'Seems stupid to buy the ammunition for the enemy doesn't it?'

He bought her the drink, put it down in front of her and stepped back, guarding his face with his hand.

She didn't smile, simply whispered, 'I'm sorry.'

Bobby shook his head lightly. 'No need to be,' he replied, feeling magnanimous now that she was more kindly disposed towards him. 'It was offensive.'

She nodded acknowledgement of his remorse and he winked at her and walked away; but his heart was heavy. He longed to get close to her, longed for her affections, and yet he always managed to say the wrong thing.

'Whatever did you say?' Jerry enquired when he returned.

Bobby sighed. 'You don't want to know.'

Jerry raised his eyebrows as he offered Bobby a cigarette. 'If it's any consolation, that was an extraordinarily inordinate response and quite out of character.'

'Meaning?' Bobby shrugged as he took the cigarette.

Jerry paused as he lit the cigarette.

'Meaning,' he repeated, 'that if she didn't care about you then maybe her response would have been more indifferent.'

Once Kate had joined Jerry, Jodie came over to the table but sat beside Kate, as far from Bobby as possible.

'You're quiet tonight, Barron,' Kate said, sporting a smirk.

The tone of his response was contemptuous. 'I'm thinking.'

'I guess there's a first time for everything,' she laughed, although the others looked anxious rather than amused.

Bobby caught the look of anxiety on Jodie's face as she looked between him and Kate. He said nothing, which had more effect than speaking. Kate's normally pale, freckly face blushed.

Bobby glanced across at Jodie again and looked away. *Maybe Jerry's right,* he thought. *Maybe she likes me more than she wants me to know.*

5

Bobby looked at his watch. It was 4pm and there was still no sign of Dale. Apart from a few dog-walkers, the towpath was deserted as dusk approached. It suited him to meet Dale away from prying eyes, but now he would have to call at the flat. He ran up the steps by the side of the bridge, popped into the corner shop for milk and coffee, then crossed over the canal and sprinted to Dale's mum's house. As he reached the bottom of the steps that led to the basement flat at the back of the house, he was surprised to find the door open. He stopped briefly; what would he find?

Cautiously pushing open the door, his eyes scanned the room before he slowly walked across to where Dale lay asleep, or at least Bobby hoped he was asleep, on the mattress in the corner of the room. He tried to wake him.

'Wake up, its four o'clock,' Bobby said, shaking him slightly; but he didn't stir. Bobby sighed as he began to tidy the room. He picked up a carrier bag from the rickety table and gathered up the rubbish, carefully picking up needles, syringes and beer bottles which were strewn around the flat. The flat was dismal but Bobby's artistic eye viewed it with potential.

He filled up the old whistling kettle and put it on the dirty, grey gas cooker in the curtained off kitchen area. The cupboards were devoid of crockery. Even the few mugs and plates that Dale had were dirty, so Bobby set about washing up. There was no washing up liquid, but at least the water was hot. Having seen the state of the tea towel, he let the crockery drain. The kettle boiled and he made two mugs of coffee.

'Dale,' he called again as he sat on the edge of the mattress. This time Dale stirred slightly, but he tugged at the covers and turned away. 'Dale,' Bobby said louder this time, as he shook him harder.

Dale groaned. 'Bobby,' he said suddenly, sitting up with a start. 'I was meant to meet you.' He glanced around. 'You cleared up.'

Bobby simply nodded. 'Do you want coffee?'

'I haven't got any milk.'

'I bought some.' Bobby smiled. He didn't mention that he'd bought the coffee too. He knew very well that every last penny was spent on alcohol or drugs.

Dale rubbed his eyes. 'What day is it?' he asked.

'It's Thursday, how long have you been lying there?'

'I was awake at midday for a fix.'

Bobby returned to the kitchen area while Dale got dressed, but he couldn't help noticing how emaciated his friend looked, and how scarred his arms were. It must have been at least three days since he had bothered to shave, not quite long enough to grow a respectable beard. Bobby pushed back the filthy curtain partition and carried in the coffee, laying the mugs on a small space on the rickety table, the only surface that Dale hadn't sold. Dale was now dressed in scruffy jeans and a t-shirt which looked unwashed and definitely not ironed.

He lit up a joint and offered it to Bobby, who took it, had a few drags, and handed it back.

'Thanks,' he said quietly, but he was worried. He hadn't seen Dale for three weeks and the deterioration was marked. His face was pale and gaunt, and the unwashed, mid-brown hair which was hanging lifelessly around his face made it worse. Although only twenty-one, he looked as if he was in his thirty's or maybe more. His contemplation was interrupted by loud shouting and banging from the room above. Bobby looked alarmed.

'Is that Carl?' he asked Dale.

'Yes,' Dale replied. 'He's hit my mother a few times recently. I wish you could stop your sister seeing him.'

Bobby raised his eyebrows. The shouting didn't stop and

Dale put on socks and shoes and an old beige jumper with frayed sleeves.

'I'll check mum's okay.'

Bobby put down the coffee. 'I'll come with you.'

As they walked up the steps to the back yard of the house, Dale stopped and turned to face Bobby. 'I'm not joking. Your sister might be a manipulative spoilt cow, but my half-brother is as evil as his father.'

Bobby shrugged. 'She doesn't listen to me.'

A plate hit the far wall as Dale opened the door into his mother's lounge. Bobby spotted his sister, Elaine, standing in the doorway.

'What a nasty accident,' Dale said in a sarcastic tone that Bobby had only ever heard him use on his half-brother. 'You'd better sweep it up.'

Dale's half-brother, Carl, eyed him with contempt and turned back to his mother.

'I want ten pounds.'

His mother was shaking. 'I can't keep giving you money.'

Bobby moved across the room to face Dale's mother.

'We wondered if you'd like to join us for tea and cake in town. We can walk over the bridge to that little café.'

Dale looked surprised but quickly concealed it with a smile.

'Thank you, I'd like that,' Dale's mother replied, moving briskly towards the door into the hallway, 'I'll get my coat.'

Dale walked to the hallway, followed by Bobby. Just as Bobby reached the door, Elaine spoke to him under her breath.

'I'll get you back for this, we wanted to go out.'

Bobby replied in a sarcastic tone, 'You could try earning money like other people.'

But he knew it was true; Elaine *would* get her own back.

6

The old man lifted the gin bottle to his mouth and drained it to the last drop. He squinted through the blur to check that it was empty, before dropping it over the side of the settee onto the threadbare Persian carpet, which at one time must have had exquisite colours.

He peered through the half drunken mists. The once white ceiling was now discoloured and the flowery pattern on the wallpaper had faded; not from the sunlight, which barely got a look in through the narrow sash window with its nets and thick brown curtains, but simply from the passage of time.

Time had stood still for Joe since Ellen had died thirty years ago. A smile crossed his face as he remembered his childhood sweetheart once more, wincing at the memory of how his heart had been ripped to shreds the day that she had died in childbirth.

'Ten years and never apart,' he said aloud, as if it was the first time he'd had the thought. 'You were my only solace,' he said to the next bottle of gin.

'And you my son,' he said to a grainy photograph of his eldest son. 'What did I ever do to you?' He ran his index finger over the surface of the photograph. He had seen the look of resentment in his son's face. Many times recently he had caught Colin gazing at the portrait that he had painted to celebrate his marriage to Ellen.

He gazed into nothingness. 'My baby girl, where are you now?'

As waves of emotion overwhelmed him, he leant forwards, took hold of the bottle on the table, and was just about to sink further into oblivion when he heard the back door open and a cheery voice called out, 'Hello Dad.'

It was his youngest son, Max. Joe smiled; they understood each other. Max was lucky; he had a good wife in Grace, even if she detested Joe. She was like his wife, Ellen; she could manage anything.

'Come in, Max. Have you got my gin?' he asked.

Max sat down next to Joe on the ancient uncomfortable settee and produced the bottle. He placed it on the coffee table in front of his father.

'Would I forget?' he laughed. 'One for you and one for me.'

Joe sat forward in his chair, took hold of the bottle and stuffed it in the corner of the settee beside him. 'You're an angel,' he said, leaning over to take money from the drawer in the bureau beside the settee.

'I nearly forgot,' Max said, throwing a packet to his father, 'cigarettes.'

Max got up quickly when he heard the horn of Grace's car.

'Thanks son,' Joe said to him.

'Sorry I couldn't clear up,' Max said as he put his coat on. 'Grace is in a hurry.'

Old Joe forced himself out of the chair and gave his son a hug. 'Don't worry, Hannah will be in later, and Colin will be here tomorrow. He always comes on a Wednesday.'

Max nodded. Joe staggered to the front door and watched as Max got into his wife's car. As the car pulled out of sight Joe went back to his chair and returned to his musings.

They had never had much money when the boys were little, but they were happy. He smiled as he remembered the picnic by the river, one of his last happy memories. Ellen was supposed to be resting, or so the doctors had said, but then she had always been her own person. 'Pregnancy is not a sickness,' she would say, so she packed up a picnic and the whole family walked down to the river. Roughly every two years she had given birth to a son, and she was desperately hoping for a daughter this time. He recalled how they had taken the bus out to the country and the boys had played in the shallow water as he had sat leaning against the old oak tree. Ellen had been lying on the warm grass resting her head in his lap as he ran his fingers through her fair wavy hair, and he hoped for her sake that this time she was carrying a daughter. His fingers moved involuntarily as if he was stroking her hair, but he wouldn't allow himself to remember any more. He reached out and picked up the open bottle of gin and drank himself into oblivion once more.

7

Jodie shook back her long dark hair as she pushed open the door into the folk club.

Bobby was already at the microphone, reading through the words of a chorus, '*Plough and sow, reap and mow.*' He sang the chorus through twice and then began the verse. '*Here's a health to the farmer ...*'

Jodie wandered to the bar. By the time she had returned and sat by Kate, Bobby had begun to introduce his next song. 'We're going to sing *The Seeds of Love*, it was collected by Cecil Sharp himself. It was the first folk song he collected, but first, I have a story for you.'

Jodie watched as he began, he always knew the history of a song, or had a story to tell. He took the microphone in his hand and casually sat on a stool, grinning out from under his blond mop.

'It's a local story,' he said as he adjusted his position on the stool.

'There was a farmer, who lived on a remote farm with his three virgin daughters,' he began.

'What's a virgin?' a student shouted from the back of the room.

Bobby grinned. 'It's a girl who hasn't met you yet Tom,' he replied.

Jodie's mind drifted away and she didn't hear the rest of the story. As he finished, and the group broke into song, Jodie smiled to herself. He captivated the audience with a raw, natural style. At the end of the song he spoke again.

'On the subject of symbolism and flowers, I'm going to sing you a composition of my own entitled, *The White Carnation,*' he said as he adjusted the strings of his guitar slightly.

'One by one I had plucked up the Daisies I'd found
and made a small chain, but it withered and died.
So I sought a Carnation, a pure white Carnation,
a perennial flower, my joy and my pride.

I wandered each day where the Marguerites lay
and Convolvulus grew in the hedges and fields.
But I sought a Carnation, a pure white Carnation
of unparalleled beauty in all that it yields.

Well, I went and I sat at the foot of a Willow
remembering the scent of the Lilac I'd passed.
But I seek a Carnation, a pure white Carnation
None other will do 'til I find it at last.'

As Jodie looked up, he caught her eye. Kate nudged her.
'I bet he wrote that for you.'
Jodie sighed. Despite what she tried to tell herself, she had
a soft spot for him. She didn't know whether she was
flattered or frightened by his advances, but either way, she
didn't want Kate to get any hint that Bobby interested her.
Her heart was in enough turmoil without Kate's judgement
ringing in her ears. Hearing the conversation, Rosa, a second
year student, leant across.
'It's Victorian flower language,' she said.
'What does it mean?' Jodie asked, not sure that she really
wanted to know.
'I only understood the first verse. The daisy symbolises
*innocen*ce,' she said with a wink, causing Kate to raise her eyes
heavenward. 'But the carnation I know 'cos my dad grows
them. It's the symbol of *affection*.'
Jodie looked relieved until Rosa smiled. 'But ...' she
continued with a smirk, 'the white carnation is very
specifically *a woman's love*.'
Jodie felt her cheeks flush and was grateful for the dimmed
lights

'Oh,' Rosa leant across again, placing her hand over her heart as she spoke, 'And of course, the Willow is melancholy.'

Bobby's band, The Cobwebs, began every folk evening with two or three songs which brought the club alive. Jodie watched his fingers move deftly over the strings of the guitar, betraying his classical training. He pushed his thick, blond hair back from his face, exposing his haunted, pale blue eyes and fair, freckly skin and she felt her heart rate rise. She looked away before her mind got further out of control. She sat back and crossed her arms. Was she really afraid of Bobby or was she afraid of being rejected again? Her mind felt full of cotton wool, and she was only vaguely aware of Kate speaking to her at the end of the evening.

'Are you all right?'

'Yes thanks,' she replied dreamily.

Do you want Jerry to give you a lift home?'

'No, I'll walk,' she replied. She needed to clear her head.

'As long as you're sure,' Kate replied. 'We're leaving now.'

'Yeah I'm fine,' Jodie said as she picked up her coat from the back of a chair and walked up the steps behind them. As she wandered home, she tried to concentrate on the portrait she was meant to be planning for the next lesson, but the only face that came into her mind was Bobby's.

She was part way home when she heard the roar of the motorbike in the distance. As she glanced over her shoulder she knew it was him. He pulled up beside her and switched off the ignition.

'Want a lift?' he offered, his speech slightly slurred.

'I'm okay thanks,' she replied as she repositioned her bag on her shoulder.

'You shouldn't be walking alone so late,' he said.

She assumed the pose of a monster. 'Do you think the big, bad bogeyman is waiting behind some hedge to pounce?'

'Of course not,' he grinned, 'he'll be at home waiting for me.'

He looked embarrassed but she didn't even flinch.

'Then I'm safe aren't I?' she retorted.

He dismounted and kicked the motorbike stand into place. He took off his crash helmet and handed it to her.

'I'd feel happier if you'd accept,' he replied as he flipped up the stand and got back on the bike.

She hesitated, aware that he had been drinking heavily. Eventually she took the helmet, which was much too big, and climbed on as he started the engine and revved lightly.

'It's safer if you hold on round the waist. I promise I won't get the wrong idea,' he shouted above the roar of the bike. Then he turned his head round and winked at her, 'Unless you want me to of course.'

She ignored his last remark as the bike pulled away. As she put her arms around him, she could feel the rise and fall of his chest as she leant in against his back to shelter from the wind. It felt natural, and when the bike came to an abrupt halt outside the flat, she didn't want to move.

She briefly caught his eye as he steadied her with his hand. In her haste, she struggled to undo the helmet. Bobby took off his gauntlets and undid it for her. She held his gaze for a second, his pale blue eyes seemed uncertain what to do and neither of them moved for what seemed like forever. Would he attempt to kiss her? She stepped back, embarrassed now as she handed him the crash helmet and thanked him for the lift. She didn't know whether she was relieved or disappointed that he made no further approach.

Every step to the door was painful. *Is he watching me? I need to look nonchalant.* Her legs felt like lead, her heart was pounding fast and her breathing was quick and shallow. *He's the most interesting person I have ever met ... so why am I afraid of him?*

He didn't see her to the door, merely got back on the bike and rode off. Her hand was shaking as she turned the key in the lock and opened the door, hardly moving for a moment as she glanced down the street. She despised much of what he stood for and yet she was strangely drawn to him.

'I want him,' she told herself aloud. She took a deep breath. She couldn't afford to let herself be beguiled by his charms. She closed the door and shut him out of her mind.

8

The country roads were clear tonight and the moon lit the road ahead, so Bobby was soon home. He put the motorbike in the garage and walked briskly up the steps to the front door. As he let himself in he could hear movement in the kitchen.

'Hello,' he grunted as he realised that it was his sister, Elaine.

She peered out at him through her lank, mid-brown curtain of hair. 'You were at Dale's yesterday,' she said.

Bobby's response was curt. 'Yes.'

'He's a junkie,' she snapped.

'He's my friend.'

'What does he sell you?' she taunted.

'I go to visit my friend,' he replied, but he'd been drinking and was tired. He knew she was winding him up and he knew that he shouldn't respond. The taunting continued.

'I'm sure dad wouldn't see it like that.'

Bobby turned on her aggressively.

'Neither would he be pleased to hear that the "concert in London" he's paid for is a Stones' concert. Just because *he's* too ignorant to know doesn't mean that *I* can't work it out.'

Elaine stood with her hands on her hips, 'He'd believe me rather than you.' She walked towards the door into the kitchen and opened it.

'I ought to tell Dad,' she said loudly.

Bobby was tired, irritable, and fed up with being threatened by his seventeen year old sister. In a fit of temper he took hold of her by the collar of her dress and pushed her against the doorway.

'You had better keep your bloody mouth shut.'

He couldn't believe that she could just stand there smiling, until he let go, turned around, and came face to face with his father. He could recognise a hint of anger in his father's eyes and there was more than a hint tonight. He took a step back, but there was no way of escape and he knew instantly that she had set him up; pure, sweet, revenge.

As his father closed in, Elaine slunk away to a vantage point in the doorway, sporting a smug grin. Bobby was frozen to the spot. Every muscle tensed and his eyes darted to and fro as he sought to conceal his fear. Any chink in his armour would be rapidly detected and mercilessly penetrated. He could feel his heart pounding in his chest and silently reminded himself that it wasn't audible.

'Just what,' his father demanded, 'must she keep her mouth shut about?'

Elaine was right, he would never be believed, so he didn't answer.

Colin didn't even raise his voice. 'What?' he repeated so close to Bobby's face that he felt his father's hot breath. Bobby turned his head to avoid his father's angry glare as he maintained his silence.

Colin slapped the cheek that faced him but still Bobby didn't reply, finding a perverse power in his silence. He put his hand to his stinging cheek, but smiled at the notion of power in saying nothing.

'You find it amusing do you?' his father asked as he slapped the other cheek with the back of his hand so hard that Bobby lost his balance and hit his head on the kitchen cupboard, before falling to the floor. Finally he spoke, in a condescending, emotionless tone as he got up from the floor.

'Does that make you feel better?'

He had barely finished the sentence when his father took hold of him by the collar and slammed him up against the wall.

'I will find out you bastard, and when I do you will pay for whatever you are hiding from me.'

Colin let go of him.

Bobby moved towards the door where Elaine stood

sporting a victorious grin. 'Bitch!' he spat under his breath as he pushed past her and went to his room. He locked himself in his bedroom and propped himself up in the corner of his bed, desperately trying to stop his hands from shaking as he attempted to light a cigarette.

Getting up made him feel dizzy, but he staggered to the record player and put on a Fairport album, with the volume down low. As he stumbled to the bed he felt drowsy, so he stubbed out the cigarette which he had barely begun, lay down on the bed, and fell asleep.

An hour later he woke up with the light on and his head throbbing to the rhythm of the click, click of the record that still spun round and round. Briefly disorientated, he looked around and heaved himself off the bed. As he walked across the room to switch off the record player, he caught sight of his face in the mirror. With prominent bruises on the cheekbone and the temple on one side of his face, there was no way that he could be seen in college for a day or two, and he didn't want Jodie to see him like this.

The house was quiet now and he could think, but all he could think of was Jodie, so he picked up a pencil and sketched her. What should be his next move? How could he convince her to play the violin for him?

Feeling restless, he ventured quietly downstairs and made a cup of hot chocolate. He sat down at the kitchen table pondering the state of his life; not something he did often. He stopped his philosophical musings. It was far more important to think about how he could win Jodie's affections. She was his heart's desire, and there was nothing his father could do to get in the way of that, he just had to captivate her heart.

9

Bobby's absence from college all week fuelled the rumours surrounding his relationship with his father.

'Don't shoot the messenger,' Jerry said at the end of the week as his comments met with Bobby's anger. 'I just wanted you to be aware. People are genuinely concerned.'

'Can't they find something interesting to gossip about?' Bobby snapped.

'Chill out,' Jerry said, offering him a cigarette.

He took one, lit up, and then added more calmly, 'Does Jodie know?'

'She knows the same as everyone else.'

Bobby sighed. He couldn't afford any more time off college, but he dreaded returning.

'I have to go,' Jerry said. 'Kate's running the club tonight and I promised to be there early.'

After Jerry left, Bobby sat on his bed leaning on the wall with a sketchpad on his knee, roughly outlining a picture of Jodie again. He tossed the pencil across the room and laid the sketchpad down. *What's the point?* he thought. *She'll never bother with someone like me.* Hammering on his door interrupted his thoughts. He sighed deeply as the voice bellowed.

'I want to talk to you downstairs in five minutes.'

Bobby didn't reply. 'Evil bastard,' he muttered under his breath, careful to wait until he had heard his dad's footsteps retreating. He thumped his fist on the edge of the desk angrily, picked up the guitar and plucked at the strings quietly for five minutes, then went downstairs.

'He's waiting in the dining room,' his mother said as he put his head round the kitchen door.

'Great,' he replied, tight-lipped.

'Don't rise to the bait,' she called after him.

He nodded acknowledgement of her wisdom before

crossing the hall to the dining room, where his father was sitting at the table.

'Sit down,' his dad ordered.

'I'm fine standing,' Bobby answered.

'Sit,' his father repeated harshly.

Bobby shrugged, 'Okay,' he said raising his eyebrows disrespectfully and reminding himself to stay calm.

'Right,' his father said as Bobby sat down, 'I have heard rumours about you and drugs.'

He spoke sternly as if he were concerned, though Bobby's instinct told him that it was a ploy to pick another fight.

'Really?' Bobby replied as he nodded his head slowly.

Colin thumped his fist on the table. 'Don't take that tone with me.'

Bobby looked up with his well-practiced silent insolence as his father continued. 'Is it true?'

'Yes, painkillers,' Bobby retorted.

Colin thumped the table, 'Is it true?'

'Strange,' Bobby said with his finger to his lips in a look of mock puzzlement. 'Why anyone would spread such rumours unless ...' he paused for effect, interrupting himself. 'Did you ask where she heard this rumour?' he asked with as much insincerity as he could muster.

Colin thumped the table again as he spoke. 'I don't give a damn who told her. Is it true?'

Colin stared at Bobby who was grinning to himself now; *so it was Elaine.* Colin's eyes demanded a reply, he didn't even blink. Bobby's resolve dissipated and he lost his temper. He got up and thrust the chair under the table.

'Yes it is. What does it matter to you if I kill myself?' He backed towards the door as he spoke. 'I sometimes take amphetamine to keep awake for concerts. I know what I'm doing, okay?'

'No it's not okay,' Colin replied as he stood up and moved towards Bobby. 'I have my reputation to think of.'

Bobby spat his reply. 'Ah so you don't care whether I live

or die, provided I don't ruin your impeccable reputation.' He bowed in mockery. 'I'll try not to die on your premises,' he said, adding just as he reached the door, 'I've been smoking pot under your roof for years, how else could I relax in this lunatic asylum?'

He backed quickly out of the dining room, throwing a chair into his father's path to slow his advance. Then he shut the door behind him, before picking up his coat and keys from the hallway, and storming out of the front door. By the time his father got to the front steps, Bobby was on the motorbike.

'Don't you dare talk to me like ...' the revving of the motorbike drowned out his voice.

'Calm down,' Bobby instructed himself aloud as he raced out of the drive. 'The bastard isn't worth it.' He slowed his pace as he got closer to Brockton, stopping the bike by the river on the outskirts of town. It was a clear night and he sat for a while to regain his composure.

The gentle rippling of the water over the stones calmed him. He stayed a while, leaning against a tree and watching the moon play on the moving water. Driven by a longing to see Jodie, he set off for the campus and slipped in at the back of the folk club, grateful that Kate had agreed to run it for the night. As he pushed open the inner door to the folk club, he was momentarily taken aback. Jodie was singing. He was not only hurt, but also deeply mystified. *Why would she choose to sing when she wouldn't expect me to be here?* He knew she played the violin but this was a surprise. He felt the sting of her rejection.

She caught his eye but looked away. He was transfixed. Tonight she was dressed in a long flowery skirt and a white smock which made her look innocent; but she hadn't dressed for him.

He pushed himself away from the wall and went over to Jerry. 'I must have her.'

'What?' Jerry replied, only half listening.

'Forget the sound, if I can get her to sing for me she'll sound heaps better.' Bobby waved a dismissive hand over Jerry's equipment.

'I'd put bass on it,' his eyes lit up in typical animated fashion, 'in fact bass runs, and pick out a guitar harmony over the top. Just listen to that lilting voice, she could sing beautifully à càpella, just think how wonderful I could make that sound.'

'You're an egotistical, arrogant rat,' Jerry said calmly.

'One day I'll get her, you'll see,' Bobby replied, not really listening.

For a moment Bobby just listened, her voice was clear and strong. He moved a chair and sat beside Jerry.

'She sings so naturally, almost apologetically, if I had a voice like that ...'

'You'd need hormone treatment, now shut up.'

The finality in Jerry's interruption silenced Bobby. When she had finished her second song, he followed her with his eyes as she sat down by Kate. He saw her get up and move towards the bar and he squeezed through the crowd and smoke to follow her, catching her up as she was about to leave the bar.

'Jodie, don't go,' he said, touching her arm.

'Careful, I'll spill the drinks,' she replied impatiently without looking up.

'I want to talk,' he persisted.

'Okay,' she shrugged, 'talk'.

The pose she adopted was hostile and her tone was condescending. At least they could hear each other talk in there, which would be great if only he knew what to say.

'Why have you never sung here before?' he asked.

'I'm not comfortable singing to an audience, Kate talked me into it. I said I couldn't sing Irish folk songs in an English folk club but she disagreed.'

'For once I agree with her,' he grinned. 'You sing with a strong Irish lilt, where did you learn?'

'My granddad used to sing to me and he taught me Irish songs. I lost most of the Irish accent after we moved here, but a hint of it comes through when I sing.'

'Does your granddad have a collection of Irish songs?' Bobby asked enthusiastically.

'He doesn't have a *collection* of anything,' she snapped with disdain. 'He just sings.'

He winced slightly as he straightened his pale blue shirt, but quickly regained his composure.

'I didn't mean to offend you. I just ...' he paused as he reflected on what he should say. No, he couldn't trust her with his feelings.

'I hope you'll sing again.'

He walked towards the bar without looking back, as if he had never intended saying more, bought two pints of Watney's and strode back to Jerry.

'That was quick,' Jerry smirked, 'did she give you the brush-off?'

Bobby put the beer down on the table in front of Jerry.

'I don't care,' he answered nonchalantly.

'Liar,' Jerry laughed.

Bobby grinned. 'She won't be able to resist me forever,' he insisted as he patted his pockets, looking for his lighter. Jerry offered him a match. Bobby wandered off to talk to club members, who were mostly enquiring after his health. He deliberately flirted with other girls in front of Jodie.

Jerry called to him across the noise, 'Bobby, are you going to sing?'

'If there's time,' he replied, encouraged by those around him, 'but I'll have to borrow a guitar.' He returned to his seat.

'That was extremely childish,' Jerry said in a schoolmasterly tone.

'Maybe, but it made me feel better,' he smirked. 'I'll get her, you'll see.'

10

'Karen,' the art teacher said on Monday morning, picking on a student at the back of the room as she held up Bobby's painting, 'what do you think of Bobby's painting?'

'I like it. It makes her look confident.'

Jodie watched Bobby's response. From the first day of college his understanding of art had impressed her. He questioned everything. He would never agree simply to keep the peace, she respected him for that; indeed his ideas inspired her to think more deeply. He didn't use his father's reputation as she had seen others do; he was talented in his own right.

As she looked across at him, she noted his pained expression. *Why is he so critical of his own work?* she thought. Sometimes it irritated her. He had such sensitivity with brush and pencil and yet it was never good enough, which didn't fit his arrogant reputation. His criticism of his portrait of Anne, today's guest model, was typical.

'It doesn't capture personality,' he commented dismissively. 'In fact I wonder if it's possible with a stranger.'

'I can't see why not, other artists have achieved it,' Jodie contradicted.

'I suppose so,' he mused. 'But how can you be sure whether what you have captured is a dominant feature, a flicker of something deeper, or just an image they are trying to create? Maybe it doesn't matter,' he shrugged. 'I remember seeing a painting that Rubens did of his son and it appeared real, he clearly knew him. It captured strength and weakness in one frame,' he rambled on.

'What about Michelangelo's *Statue of David?*' another student volunteered. 'That has personality.'

'Yeah, right,' Jodie said taking up the offensive as she turned to face Bobby, 'and God creating Adam in the Sistine chapel.'

'Did God create Adam in the Sistine Chapel?' he smirked. 'I thought that was in the Garden of Eden'.

Jodie took up the nearest book and hurled it at him. He ducked and it landed a short distance from his feet. After a few moments of chaos the discussion resumed.

'To be honest,' Bobby continued unabashed, 'I don't like the statue of David. Its emotions seem a bit excessive.'

'Pity you weren't around to advise Michelangelo,' Jodie retorted as she turned her back on him. He replied calmly as if unhurt.

'That's life,' he shrugged, 'we all have to make it alone, but I agree, that Sistine Chapel picture puzzles me. Somehow it has hope, as if Michelangelo knew God, though the philosophy that suggests gives me problems.'

'Let's get back to Bobby's painting,' the teacher said, in an attempt to regain control. 'What are its strengths and weaknesses?'

The remainder of the lesson continued uninterrupted through to lunchtime.

'I didn't intend to cause World War III,' Bobby said despondently to Jerry in the canteen. 'She always disagrees with me.'

Jerry shrugged. 'There's plenty more fish in the sea. Why go angling after one fish when you could have netted a shoal?'

'If you had seen a mermaid, would you bother with the minnow?' Bobby replied morosely.

Jerry laughed. 'Maybe not, but I wouldn't attempt to catch it with a harpoon either. Why do you have to rile her?'

'It's not intentional,' he grinned, 'she's just easily provoked.'

'If you cared about her you wouldn't do it.'

Bobby was mindlessly stirring sugar into his coffee. 'I suppose you're right. Do you think she'll accept an apology?

I've got her book here.'

'Public humiliation demands a public apology,' Jerry laughed, shaking his head in disbelief.'

Bobby could see Jodie ranting at Kate in the far corner of the canteen. She steadfastly ignored him as he approached. 'Your book,' he said unflinchingly, despite the lack of response. She looked up at him with a quizzical gaze.

'The one you threw at me,' he elucidated.

Kate laughed and Jodie instantly averted her gaze.

'I wish I hadn't been at the dentist's, I'm sorry I missed it,' Kate chuckled

Bobby shot her an evil glare before looking Jodie in the eye. He gave a slight bow as he spoke.

'Humble apologies.'

'I'm surprised the word *humble* appears in your vocabulary,' she snapped, snatching the book from his hand.

'Which proves you can't tell a book by its cover,' he said.

'You can get a bloody good idea,' she retorted.

Bobby grinned, hiding his hurt. 'Perhaps you're right. How foolish of me.'

'On that point I'm prepared to agree,' she snapped.

'How magnanimous,' he replied.

She dunked her biscuit in her coffee and ignored him again. This time, unable to conceal his hurt, he walked away.

'You're cruel to him,' he heard Kate say, almost as if she felt sorry for him.

He didn't hear Jodie's reply, but she got up and left the canteen. Bobby sighed deeply as he sat down again with Jerry.

'Do I take it your apology wasn't accepted?'

'She's furious with me,' he said.

Jerry let out a deep sigh and shook his head as he replied. 'You're both so damned obstinate that I don't have much hope for you.'

'Okay,' Bobby said impatiently as they got up to leave. 'I'll apologise properly this afternoon.'

On the way over to the art room Bobby ran to catch her

up. 'I am sorry … really …' he panted, out of breath and walking backwards in order to face her.

She looked at the ground. 'I was none too gracious myself.'

'I deserved it. I open my mouth before I think. It wasn't meant to be unkind, well, not much anyway,' he said with a mischievous smirk. 'Just that in my overactive imagination I could see God …'

'Creating Adam in the Sistine Chapel.' She broke into laughter as she finished the sentence, nervously twirling her hair around her finger and adjusting her brown suede bag on her shoulder.

'It's such a beautiful image. I could have stayed there for hours if they'd let me,' he remarked wistfully. 'Have you seen it?'

She stared at him open-mouthed.

'I'm sorry,' he said in answer to her look of astonishment, 'I guess most people haven't.' He looked away in obvious embarrassment.

'So,' she laughed, 'the spoilt rich kid knows so much about the history of art because he's seen it all.'

She clapped her hand over her mouth as if to stem the flow but it was too late. He walked ahead of her into the classroom, sat down heavily, and let his bag fall to the floor. She moved towards him cautiously but he didn't look up, so she crouched down beside him, resting a hand on his arm. He tried to ignore her as she spoke.

'I'm sorry,' she said softly. As he lifted his head and looked up at her, there was fondness in her eyes. She shook her head gently as she spoke to him, her hair flicking softly from side to side. 'I had no right to say that.'

He smiled contentedly. 'It's a free country,' he said and then paused a moment before continuing. 'I'd like it if we could be friends.'

'Me too,' she said.

11

Jodie picked up the photograph on her bedside cabinet and clutched it to her heart. Her lips brushed it softly and she started to put it back down, but she couldn't bring herself to let go of it. The vision that stared back at her had thick, dark hair like hers and beautiful, green eyes. *It's like looking into a mirror that reveals your future*, she thought. 'I wish you were here, Mum,' she said aloud. 'Just a hug from you on days like today would help.'

She stood the photograph back on her bedside cabinet, then went to the kitchen and poured herself a glass of cheap, white wine from the opened bottle in the fridge.

Kate appeared. 'You'll never get up in the morning if you drink too much,' she said.

'Maybe not,' Jodie replied, not wishing to discuss it further. She took the glass into her bedroom and closed the door.

'Yes, I know,' she said to her mother's photograph as she put the glass down next to it. 'Granddad's father was an alcoholic.' She sat up on the bed, leaning against the wall behind her and took a sip of wine. *That's not the answer*, she said to herself as she pushed the glass away.

Leaning forward, she took a small photograph album out of the drawer in the bedside cabinet. *It's a long while since I've looked at this*, she thought as she opened it slowly with a kind of reverence. As she turned the first page she smiled to herself; she had been just a baby in that first picture. It was so simple, so rural, so Ireland. It was a picture of her mother in a field beside a river, holding Jodie in her arms.

Jodie thumbed the pages slowly, purposefully, until she came to a photo of Kieron, her childhood sweetheart. But she couldn't stop there, she flicked past others of him, and of her family's move to England, until she reached the newspaper cutting; folded up and tucked into a photograph pocket. She unfolded it slowly. *How will it feel after all this time?* she wondered. Nothing had changed. It still shocked her when she saw the state of the car. Her parents and her brother never stood a chance. 'How could you have left me,' she said aloud to her mother. 'I was only thirteen.' She folded it up, put it back in its slot in the album, and turned over to the final pictures.

'I'll never forget you,' she said quietly, as she fingered the picture of the gravestones of her father, her mother, and her brother, before tucking the album back in the drawer.

She got ready for bed, laid down and switched out the light, but sleep eluded her. Her mind was in turmoil. Eventually, the sounds of the street outside the window began to fade and she drifted off.

She heard the screech of brakes; her father's panicked expression came into sharp focus; she saw the lorry veering towards her and heard her mother's piercing scream which became hers as she cried out, waking herself up.

There was a gentle knocking at the door. Kate didn't wait for an answer, just pushed the door open slightly.

'Are you okay?' Kate asked, not much above a whisper. 'I heard you scream.'

'Just a nightmare,' Jodie replied. 'I'm okay.'

The room filled with light from the hallway as Kate opened the door fully.

'Do you want to talk?' she asked, sitting down on the edge of the bed.

Jodie sat up and switched on the bedside light. *Maybe I should have told Kate the truth last time it happened,* she thought.

'It's my own fault,' she began. 'I was looking at photos.'

'Of your family?' Kate asked.

'Well yes, and of the accident,' Jodie replied.

Kate furrowed her brow. 'You have photos? Of the accident?'

Jodie leant over and took the album out of the drawer and took out the newspaper cutting. She handed it to Kate.

'Oh, newspaper cuttings,' Kate said, changing positions to look Jodie in the eye. 'What happened?'

Jodie waited for Kate to read the article. 'I should have been there. My brother was going back to university in Cardiff but my Father insisted I had to go to school.'

'But if you'd gone, you would have died too,' Kate said.

'And many times I wished I had.'

'But you don't wish that now?' Kate asked.

Jodie shook her head. 'No, but I still feel lonely. I only have my granddad.'

'But your granddad is brilliant.'

'But he could have gone back to Ireland if I had died too. At least then he would have family around him.'

Kate looked shocked. 'That's ridiculous. At least you gave him a reason to pick himself up and carry on. I'm sure he doesn't regret staying here for you. He has friends.' She handed the newspaper article back to Jodie, who took it and put it back in its place and laid the album on the top of the bedside cabinet.

'After the first few weeks when even cooking a meal was a major effort, he asked me if I wanted to stay here or go back to Ireland. I couldn't bear the thought of losing my friends as well as my family, but maybe I should have thought of him. He only came to England to be near my mum when my dad got a job here.'

'He didn't have to ask you what you wanted. My guess is that he really wanted to do what was absolutely right for you, that's love.'

Jodie wiped away tears. 'But I didn't think about the best thing for him.'

Kate looked exasperated. 'Why are you doing this to yourself? You were a child. What is this really about? Is it about Kieron?'

It was about Kieron, she couldn't deny it. Childhood promises meant nothing; she knew that, but he had always been a link to Ireland and he was secure and predictable. She wasn't even aware that he had a girlfriend, so the engagement announcement card had come as a shock.

'I know it's stupid,' she said, looking Kate in the eye now, 'but I guess I was clinging onto the idea of Kieron because he was a part of my childhood.'

'And holding onto a part of your childhood kept your parents alive, so to speak,' Kate added.

Jodie nodded.

'And,' Kate continued, 'presumably it kept you from having to consider getting close to anyone, and so prevented you getting hurt.'

Jodie winced.

'We all do it,' Kate said. 'Pain avoidance.'

Jodie smiled. There was so much more to Kate than she'd ever given her credit for.

'So is this about Bobby?' Kate asked. 'Because you know it's none of my business, even if I do seem to interfere.' She looked away as she continued this time. 'I can see the attraction, but he's just ...' she thought for a moment, 'complex,' she said eventually. Jodie simply laughed, which made Kate laugh too.

'That's pretty tactful for you,' Jodie said.

'Okay, bloody screwed up,' Kate said when she'd stopped laughing, 'but I can't stop you going out with him if that's what you want.'

Jodie looked pensive. 'I really don't know if it is. I'm not sure I'm brave enough.'

12

As she approached the folk club, Jodie recognised the song's introduction as one of Bobby's and almost turned and ran, but she wouldn't allow herself the luxury of walking away. She needed to see him as just a friend. Now she'd faced up to the truth, she didn't need a man in her life. She saw Bobby look towards the door as she entered, almost as if he had been expecting her, so she averted her gaze and sat down next to Kate. Leaning on the table, she closed her eyes to escape his gaze, but his voice still penetrated her heart. She felt vulnerable, transparent even. Kate was pre-occupied and Jodie considered leaving. *If I really want only his friendship, then why does it hurt like this?* she thought. She stood up and turned to Kate. 'Do you want a drink?' she asked in order to escape to the bar.

'Yeah, half a cider please,' Kate replied without looking up. Jodie ambled to the bar; she didn't really want a drink but ordered one anyway. She could still see him from the bar though he wasn't watching her now, yet still his voice pursued her. He had been singing *The Rosebuds in June* when she arrived and she had to admit he was good, he really sounded like a country shepherd. Indeed he could act any part, and she wondered who he really was.

As he began to play again, she recognised the introduction this time as one of Donovan's and she was suddenly aware that the song was for her. He was saying, 'I really want to get close to you, but I might as well attempt to catch the wind'.

She blushed, grateful for the darkness as she desperately tried to keep from looking in his direction as she left the bar, but she couldn't help herself. She handed Kate the drink. Fortunately for Jodie, Kate's mind was elsewhere or she might have picked up on Jodie's distress.

'I should never have come,' Jodie whispered to herself.

Quickly looking around, she grabbed her coat and bag and left before anyone saw her go.

Close to tears, she leant on the wall of the building just at the top of the steps and eventually put on her black maxi-coat. As she struggled with the right sleeve she was suddenly aware that she was being assisted.

'Allow me,' he offered.

'Bobby … er … thank you.'

She caught her breath, not daring to turn round; she didn't want him to see her tear-stained face and desperately hoped that her tear-stained voice wouldn't betray her.

'Are you all right?' he asked, concern evident in his voice.

She dabbed her eyes lightly, hoping that her mascara hadn't run. Whatever she said in reply would be futile; it must be plainly obvious that she was not okay. She didn't reply as she began to walk slowly away, she needed to put distance between them; to hide from him, although she was painfully aware that she couldn't hide from herself. She heard him following softly behind and with one quick stride he was in front of her, an annoying way he had of getting her attention. She stopped.

He stared at the ground. 'I don't really know what to say,' he shrugged.

'That must be a novel experience,' she quipped and instantly wished that she hadn't.

'I'm serious,' he said softly, 'this is hard to say, I was fond of you from the first time we met and nothing has changed. I meant the words of Donovan's song.'

'You sounded just like him,' she smiled, in an attempt to alleviate the tension.

'That's just acting,' he replied gesturing dismissively with his hand, 'but the words weren't an act.' His confidence grew as he continued. 'Go out with me Jodie? Give me a chance?'

'I'd rather we were just friends.'

Her tone was apologetic but too frantic and her eyes darted around as if looking for a means of escape.

'When you sang that song last week, was it about anyone in particular?'

It was as if he could read her mind. Her reply was confused.

'Yes ... no, well ... not really,' she eventually replied as she pondered the truth. Finally she spoke honestly, looking directly at the ground. 'Not anymore.'

She could see him mulling over her reply and she tried to walk on. He barred the way again.

'Hold on,' he said as he raised his hand in front of her. 'If you are so sure of your feelings, then why are you running away from me?'

She couldn't handle this tonight, she felt too vulnerable. She was brought back to reality by his voice, which sounded like a distant echo.

'Why, Jodie?'

It wasn't angry or harsh, just questioning. He put his hand gently on her arm as he asked a second time and she could feel tears welling up. His touch was gentle and caring and she pulled away from him this time as she voiced the truth.

'I have doubts. I can't risk ...'

She felt her voice break and fade away, so she stepped up her pace. He didn't follow her this time but called after her. 'Our doubts are traitors and make us lose the good we oft might win, by fearing to attempt.'

She wiped the tears away as she increased her pace still further. Maybe she should ignore the rumours and gossip. She needed to know, needed to put her mind at rest. However hard she tried to expel thoughts of him they wouldn't be evicted. She'd hurt him tonight, she was sure of that; he had bared his soul and she had trampled on it.

Once home, she sat alone with her thoughts until Jerry and Kate arrived much later. When Kate left the room to make coffee, Jodie seized her opportunity.

'Jerry?' she said.

'Uh huh,' he replied absently with a cigarette still in his mouth.

She sat on the edge of the chair and gazed at him intently. 'Are the rumours about Bobby true?'

He took the cigarette out of his mouth and jumped up, choking on the smoke as he spoke, 'I can't betray his confidence; you'll have to ask him yourself.'

Jodie was angry; she just wanted to know the truth, to be reassured that she wouldn't get hurt if she got involved with him. She got up and left the room.

That night she fell asleep with it unresolved. She woke often and every time she woke she saw his face, longing and pleading. She was glad when morning arrived; torture seemed less painful in daylight. She needed to see him. She wanted to know the truth, however bad it was.

13

Bobby surfaced at half past eight on Saturday morning, and had a slice of toast. Attired in full football kit, he wandered across to the green to meet Jerry.

'I feel lucky today,' Jerry declared.

'Oh we don't need to try then,' Bobby replied sarcastically.

Jerry spoke behind one hand, gesturing towards a group of lads in their early thirties.

'We'll need more than good luck with this bunch of geriatrics.'

Bobby stared at him in alarm. 'Do we have to push the one in the wheelchair?'

'No,' Jerry replied, shaking his head vigorously, 'he's brought his walking frame.'

Bobby fanned his face in obvious relief. 'I'm only here because I couldn't say no to the Rev,' Bobby said with a sigh.

'Same goes for us all,' Jerry laughed.

The opposition won the toss and had scored the first goal before Jerry had even finished lacing his boots. The Rev shoved him onto the pitch. 'The game's already started Jerry, get out there!'

Jerry had barely got his balance when the ball landed close to his feet.

'Pass it. Pass it.' Bobby said as he found a space, right in front of the goal.

Jerry passed it to Bobby, who missed the ball and collided with the goalkeeper. Jerry roared with laughter, leaving it to the geriatric members of the team to race to the other side of the pitch in pursuit of the ball, which the opposition had rescued. The first half never got beyond a joke for Bobby and Jerry and at half-time the frustrated vicar lectured his team. Bobby lit up a cigarette and promised to do better. To his surprise, Kate and Jodie arrived. He didn't know where to look. *Whatever do I say to her after last night?* he thought.

'Did you tell them we were playing?' Bobby asked.

'Oh yes,' Jerry replied with an innocent smirk, 'didn't I tell you?'

Jerry rummaged in his kit bag and took out a camera. 'Kate?' he said casually, snapping a picture of her as she turned around, then he threw her the camera.

'Take some photos of the game,' he said.

Kate pouted. 'Only if you don't criticize my photography,' she replied.

Even in the second half, Jerry only began to take it seriously after Kate shouted at him, and soon after, he equalised. Not long after that, a cross from Bobby to Jerry on the left wing resulted in the second goal, leaving the opposition goalkeeper leaning on the goalpost in frustration.

'Eat your heart out Georgie Best,' Jerry shouted, punching the air.

Jerry laughed but Bobby didn't look up for fear of distraction. Jerry scored the final goal of the match too.

'Well done,' Kate said to him after the final whistle.

'Actually,' Jerry declared, 'they ran out of energy in the second half. All we had going for us was the advantage of youth.'

'Not forgetting talent, genius and fitness,' Bobby added, flexing his muscles.

Kate raised her eyebrows in irritation behind Bobby's back as he walked away. 'He's joking,' Jerry said, putting a calming hand on her arm.

'He really believes it,' she replied.

'No, he's always admitted that I'm a better footballer than he is,' Jerry insisted.

'You were good,' Kate said.

Jerry gave a slight bow. 'Thank you.'

After Bobby and Jerry had changed, they all wandered to Jerry's house. Sarah ran down the path to meet Bobby, almost tripping him up until he picked her up and plonked her on his shoulders as he jogged to the house ahead of the others. She led him into the warm kitchen and begged him to play dominoes. Anything was better than trying to make polite conversation with Jodie.

The dominoes were already scattered on the kitchen floor.

'You knew I was coming,' Bobby said to Sarah.

She nodded and shared them out.

'I start,' he announced as they squatted on the kitchen floor, 'I've got the double six.'

He didn't notice when the others entered, but they talked quietly as he gave his undivided attention to Sarah.

'Okay, okay,' he confessed. 'You win.'

'Will you sing me a song?' she asked.

Bobby was about to reply when Jerry answered for him.

'That's enough, you're never satisfied are you?'

Bobby shot Jerry a look of bewilderment as Sarah ran off.

'There's no need for that,' he reprimanded, before running into the hallway after her. He took her hand and led her into the lounge, where the baby grand sat resplendent. 'You and I will play the piano,' he said, sitting her beside him in front of the magnificent piano.

She looked at him with big, brown eyes. 'Nobody plays the piano here,' she said.

'Then why,' he asked, pausing for effect, 'don't *you* learn it?'

He reached in front of her to play her the Beatles song, *Yesterday.* Suddenly she jumped off the stool and stood beside him with her hands on her hips.

'I *will* learn it,' she declared.

He moved up for her to sit where she could reach to play.

'Okay. This note here is middle "C" right in the centre by the metal tag. Put your thumb on there, and let your fingers go up and down the white keys like this.' He showed her how. 'Practice that lots of times every day until I come again,' he said, getting up to join the others in the kitchen.

'Oh and one other thing,' he said as they left the room,

'don't take any notice if anyone complains.'

Her big eyes smiled and Bobby joined the others as Sarah ran off down the corridor.

'You play like a classical pianist,' Jodie said as they drank coffee around the large old table.

'He *is* a classical pianist,' Jerry declared.

'Play us something classical then,' Jodie asked.

Bobby was embarrassed. 'I don't normally play classical music in company,' he protested.

'Only on the pipe organ at the village church,' Jerry retorted.

Kate raised her eyebrows. 'You play a pipe organ?' she asked.

'Not well,' he replied, hiding his embarrassment behind his almost shoulder length hair. As he looked up, he caught Jerry nodding at Kate.

'Come on then, let's hear you play,' Jodie said.

He relented and played part of Chopin's *Nocturne in D flat Major*.

They sat in silence for a while until eventually Jodie spoke. 'Don't you ever play?' she asked.

'I sometimes play when I'm alone,' he said, looking at the floor.

'What a waste,' she said as she walked away from the piano.

He didn't want to explain to her the memories that it brought back; the images that flashed through his mind of his father teaching him. He had played today simply because she had asked him to. He smiled at the thought, wondering what else he would have done if she'd asked.

'So,' she asked him, 'were you the school genius?'

'Not exactly,' Bobby said.

Jerry and Bobby exchanged grins while Jodie looked from one to the other, awaiting a more complete explanation. 'I was good at Art, Music and English, but I was a scientific dunce, and I wasn't perfectly behaved either,' he said, looking directly at her. He continued. 'In a Grammar school that doesn't endear you to the staff.'

'Or to your father,' Jerry added.

Bobby's response was curt. 'Nothing endears me to my father,' he snapped, with a sideways glance at Jerry.

The conversation evaporated. Jerry broke the awkward silence.

'Let's go to the pub.'

As they left the house, Bobby spoke quietly to Jodie.

'There's your school genius,' he said, nodding in the direction of Jerry. 'Not that you'd ever guess. They begged him to apply to Oxbridge, but he refused. He comes from a clever family.'

Jodie smiled as she stared after Jerry. 'You're right, I wouldn't have guessed.'

'So what about your academic achievements?' he asked.

Jodie grinned. 'I did pretty well in most things,' she replied, but it was so casual that he guessed that she was hiding something.

'But?' he asked intently with a smile.

'I never got Maths O'level. I got a worse grade each time I sat it, and I finally gave up. I failed French and Chemistry too.'

Bobby was relieved. It made him feel less stupid.

They passed the village shop on the way to the pub, where Bobby stopped to juggle with the tomatoes outside, until Ernie, the greengrocer, appeared. 'You should have been a clown, Master Barron,' he said, using the name he had always called him since he was a little boy. Shaking his bald head, Ernie carefully took the tomatoes from Bobby's hands. As they were walking away, Bobby realised that Jerry was eating an apple. He laughed.

'Jerry,' Kate exclaimed, shocked.

Bobby laughed. 'You don't know how many times he's done that while I distracted Ernie.'

Jodie merely smiled.

Arriving at the pub, Bobby took orders for drinks and they sat down to talk. The conversation ambled from Vietnam to Czechoslovakia.

'Czechoslovakia isn't our responsibility,' Jerry said, with a shrug.

Bobby looked at him with wide-eyed anger, 'How can you say that? Martin Luther King once said, "Injustice anywhere is a threat to justice everywhere." Hitler would have taken over the world if people like you had been politicians,' he ranted, until he suddenly caught the glint in his friend's eye. He laughed, 'I hate you.'

Jerry grinned. 'And he forgot to tell you,' he said, addressing Jodie, 'he was president of the debating society.'

'I'll get you back for this,' Bobby promised.

Jodie smiled at him, and he sensed a fondness that gave him hope.

14

After leaving work early on Wednesday, Colin drove his Mercedes onto the downtown estate in the city. There was no joy in visiting his father; only duty. The car attracted attention from the local children as it always did and he slipped a coin to the oldest.

'Keep an eye on it,' he winked. 'I'll give you another when I come back.'

Colin glanced over his shoulder as he approached the front door and smiled to himself. The youth stood with arms folded, resting one foot on the nearside wheel. He remembered the days when he would do anything to escape poverty.

He turned the key in the lock and pushed the door open. The dark brown paintwork and the narrow hallway closed in on him as he entered and the smell of alcohol and smoke hung in the air. He shut the door behind him and picked up the post from the doormat as his father called out.

'Is that you Ellen?'

Colin sighed as he took off his coat and hung it on the peg in the hall. His father was clearly drunk; his mother had been dead for decades.

'No dad, it's me, Colin.'

'Why haven't you been to see me?' His father stumbled over the words as he spoke.

Colin said nothing in his defence. Sometimes his father was reasonable but on other occasions he turned violent, so Colin stayed quiet and kept his distance.

'Do you want a drink?' his father offered as he attempted to get up. He fell back into the chair laughing.

Colin didn't laugh.

'No thank you,' he replied.

'Sanctimonious bastard,' his father said.

Colin cringed at the venom in his father's voice.

'I think I deserve a drink after bringing you all up alone ... and you give me nothing in return.'

The next time his father tried to stand he succeeded but then lurched forwards, almost falling on Colin as he spoke. Colin pushed him slightly in the opposite direction, enough to move his centre of gravity, but he was angry with his father now.

'I've paid your bills for years,' he said, holding out the bills that he had just picked up off the sideboard. 'If I hadn't paid them then you would have no gas, electricity or water by now.'

His father fell back down in the armchair.

'But you never give me anything to spend on myself,' he said.

'I'm not giving you money for drink,' Colin said, raising dust as he slammed his fist on the side of the dirty, stained settee.

'Don't you tell me what to do,' his father replied, raising his voice.

Colin winced. He collected up the dirty crockery, glasses and ashtrays from the coffee table and took them into the kitchen but his father's accusations followed him. He looked around; it never got any better. He called in here every week, and he knew that Hannah came in every other day, but that was all the time that it took his father to make the place filthy again.

He cleared a broken bottle from the sink and wrapped it carefully before putting it in the bin. He took washing up liquid from the cupboard beside the old white sink, turned the tap on the little gas water heater that he'd had installed for his father last year, and filled the sink with hot water. As he washed up, he caught sight of the portrait of his mother which hung above the sink. It tortured him with memories, triggering his anger once more. He looked up again and touched the portrait gently with his soapy hand; life had been so different before she died. In that moment he felt sympathy for his father.

When he returned to the lounge his father was asleep. Colin tidied up and put away the food he'd brought with him, then he picked up the bills from the coffee table and gently kissed his father on the top of his balding head. Colin sighed at the memory of his once proud father. He shut the lounge door behind him, took his coat off the peg and put it on. Looking back briefly over his shoulder towards the stairs, he dismissed the idea of checking the upstairs. As he opened the front door to leave, he heard the key in the back door.

'Hannah,' he said as he walked back into the kitchen and embraced her.

'Is he asleep?' she asked quietly.

'Drunk,' Colin replied.

'Do you want to come for coffee?' Hannah said with a smile. 'I'm sure your minder will keep an eye on the car a bit longer, at a price.'

Colin laughed. He thought for a moment before replying.

'Okay.'

He smiled as he saw the youth patrolling beside the car and handed him another coin, with the promise of another. They crossed the street to Hannah's bright, terraced house which had been like a second home to him when he was growing up. For the first time that afternoon, Colin felt as if he had returned to the home of his childhood. He studied her as she put on the kettle. Her dress sense matched her personality; practical and elegant.

'I talked him into a bath yesterday and his whole body looks yellow,' Hannah said with concern.

'All I noticed was his mood, that was black.'

Hannah laughed. 'Miserable old thing isn't he?'

Colin smiled. She was still able to lift his spirits after all these years. He didn't stay long, and as he drove away his spirit sank again. He had hoped for change for too long; all he had now was despair.

15

'Please Jodie,' Bobby begged in the canteen on Monday morning. 'What harm could it do to practice with us? Why didn't you tell me that you played the violin?' he asked her.

'Because I assumed you'd pester me until I played. I don't play without music the way you do.'

She sensed a hint of irritation in his tone.

'The more you practice without the music the easier it gets,' he said.

She was purposely deceiving him. She had played folk fiddle long before she had learned classical violin.

'Please Jodie,' he begged again.

'Can't you take no for an answer?'

'No,' he replied, laughing.

She got up to leave but he took her arm quickly. 'I'm sorry. I shouldn't have laughed. When can I meet your granddad?'

She sat down again, wishing that she hadn't mentioned him. 'Oh all right,' she sighed with exasperation, 'but remember he's a person, not some useful resource you've dragged out of the archives.'

He looked hurt. 'Do you really think that I'm like that?'

'I don't know or care,' she replied with greater conviction than there was in her heart. She didn't intend hurting him, but her feelings troubled her. Even as a little girl she had dreamed of romance, love and dashing white knights on steeds. Once upon a time she would have ridden off with Bobby into the sunset.

Bobby rested his chin on his hands, watching her. Suddenly she saw him gazing at her and looked away, embarrassed. 'When do you want to see him?'

He sat up and his eyes opened wide with enthusiasm. 'Tonight?'

'Why not yesterday?' she snapped.

He reached his hand across the table and gripped her arm. Looking right into her eyes he spoke to her impatiently. 'Why do you treat me with such contempt? What are you so afraid of?'

Her breathing was fast and shallow; it was the first time she had seen anger in his eyes. In that moment she was frightened, not of his anger, but of her own emotions. She experienced both fear and love in overwhelming tides, and the strength of the emotions frightened her, but the thought of him as her enemy was unbearable. All she could manage was a mild apology, which he accepted. He released his grip on her arm. *Is that regret I can see in his eyes?* she thought. 'Okay, tonight's fine. What time?' she asked handing him a peace offering.

'Whenever suits your granddad,' he said. 'Maybe after lectures, Jerry might give us a lift. That way I can leave the bike here and get a lift into college with him in the morning.'

Jerry obliged. Bobby seemed apprehensive.

'Where shall I drop you off, Jodie?' Jerry asked.

'At the end of Horseshoe Lane will do,' she replied.

Bobby's nervous chatter stopped abruptly as they alighted from the car. Sensing his discomfort, Jodie spoke first.

'It's at the other end of the lane, quiet isn't it?'

'Yes, even our sleepy village isn't this quiet,' he replied.

'Sleepy. I can't imagine the residents of your village being allowed to doze never mind sleep, with your inability to remain silent for more than thirty seconds,' she remarked.

'You broke the silence,' he snapped.

The lengthy silence that followed unnerved her and she was aware that she had wounded him again. He had always seemed invincible.

'The lane comes out by the side of Granddad's cottage,' she stated, providing neither apology nor comfort.

She pushed open the door and walked in, watching him with fascination as his eyes darted around the room, gazing at pictures and trinkets. *What is he thinking?* she thought.

'Hello Jodie, I didn't expect to see you today. This is a friend of yours, I assume?' her granddad said, shaking Bobby's hand.

'No, this is Bobby,' she replied curtly.

'Thanks,' Bobby muttered.

'Have a seat,' her granddad said. 'Just push the papers on the floor. What brings you here?'

Bobby explained his interest in folk music and in collecting old English folk songs. 'Jodie told me that you used to sing,' he smiled.

'All the songs I know are Irish,' her granddad lamented.

'Oh, I'm interested in all folk music,' Bobby replied quickly. 'It's just that I'm particularly interested in the English ones. I'm after all sorts of new material, or rather, new, old material if you get my meaning. Because we play every week we have to keep coming up with something different.'

'Hmm,' Granddad said pensively as Jodie watched the way he studied Bobby. 'I don't think I have anything written down.'

Bobby became animated. 'All you'd have to do is sing, I can write them down.'

'I haven't sung much in recent years,' Granddad replied.

'You're as bad as Jodie,' he laughed, 'she won't even practice the violin with us, she says she isn't good enough.' He smiled at her but she looked away.

'Well I think she's good but I'm biased,' her granddad laughed.

Jodie wasn't laughing. 'I wish you'd stop talking about me as if I wasn't here. I'll make the coffee.' She slammed the kitchen door behind her which made Bobby jump.

'I'm sorry, she isn't usually so easily offended,' her granddad said.

Bobby answered dolefully, staring at the floor. 'She is with me.'

'Oh, I see,' Granddad said slowly, as he cocked his head on one side and looked directly into Bobby's eyes.

'Are you fond of Jodie?'

Bobby blushed and looked away. 'Yes, but the feelings aren't reciprocated.'

A wide smile beamed at him as Bobby looked up. 'Well I shouldn't quit if I were you.'

Bobby replied with a wry grin. 'I'm not a quitter.'

'Good,' Granddad said, 'so Jodie told you about me, did she?'

Bobby laughed this time. 'Yes. She sang on Friday at the folk club. I'd never heard her sing before and she sang with a hint of an Irish accent.' Granddad nodded as Bobby continued. 'If she had only sung the *Curragh of Kildare,* I'd have probably paid little attention, but then I heard a hint of an Irish accent when she sang an English folk song. She tells me that you taught her to sing and to play the violin too.'

The second he heard the kitchen door opening, Bobby stopped talking. Jodie pushed it with her foot and set the tray down on the table in the corner.

'So do you come from a folk background?' Granddad asked, shrewdly changing the subject. Bobby looked taken aback.

'Goodness no,' he replied, 'only classical music, piano, pipe organ, that sort of thing.'

Jodie watched him studying Bobby's moves. He wouldn't have missed the speed of that response. As if on cue, he asked, 'Do I detect that your folk music is not entirely approved of at home?'

Bobby answered with a shrug of the shoulders, fixing his eyes on the floor.

'My dad doesn't approve of anything I do, but he thinks my musical talent is wasted on folk music.'

Jodie recognised a hint of resentment in his tone. Her granddad leant his head slightly to one side, but he looked away when she caught his eye. She gave Bobby the coffee, and sat down on the settee.

'I'll tell you what,' her granddad said, continuing his

conversation with Bobby whilst putting his arm protectively around Jodie, 'I'll write down the words of some of the songs I know, and tell Jodie when I've finished. Then if you come again I'll sing them to you, and you can write down the music.'

'That's fabulous, thank you,' Bobby replied with his usual excitement. Once the conversation became small talk, Bobby finished his coffee and made his departure. Jodie saw him out.

She leant against the doorpost as she watched him walk away. He glanced round before he disappeared from view. She sat down in the front garden, on the old wooden bench in front of the bay window, wishing that she could retract her hurtful words. Eventually dark clouds approached, and it was too cool to sit comfortably outside. Weary of her inner strife, she returned to the cottage. She sat beside her granddad and after a while he spoke.

'You hurt him,' he said softly.

'I didn't mean to,' she answered morosely.

'He doesn't know what you're feeling.'

'And you do?' she snapped angrily.

'Maybe. Bobby isn't like Kieron.'

That was partly what frightened her. Kieron had been predictable; that gave her a sense of security but it certainly wasn't a word she would ever use of Bobby. He was clearly more sensitive than she had imagined at first, but the rumours troubled her. She wanted to share her feelings with her granddad, but was afraid that he would give her an answer that she didn't want to hear. She was flattered by Bobby's attentions, but perplexed by her own responses. In her vain attempt to protect her own heart she had wounded his.

'He always seemed arrogant and self-assured. I never imagined it was possible to hurt him that deeply.'

Granddad nodded before replying. 'Those who appear invincible are frequently the most wounded.'

Jodie sighed deeply. 'Then he gives you the impression of one deeply wounded?'

He raised his eyebrows. 'I could be wrong.'

Jodie looked away and responded sarcastically, 'There's a remote chance.' She paced the floor.

Eventually he spoke. 'I see an insecure, young man, fearful even. The image we portray is often a mask to hide our true feelings … isn't it?'

She half-smiled as she recognised his challenge. 'His intensity frightens me.'

'So he's not worth the risk?' he asked.

'I don't know,' she replied, exasperated with herself, 'I'd better go, I've got a project to finish.'

'I'll give you a lift back to town.'

Few words passed between them on the way home.

'Thanks, Granddad,' she said as he left her outside her flat.

He wound down the window and called after her. 'Ask Bobby to come and see me. I've got something that might interest him.'

Jodie frowned. 'What?'

'It's a surprise,' he replied with a wink.

She wasn't happy to leave without sorting out her own heart, but she couldn't face discussing it either. She knew for certain that until she resolved it, her mind would be in turmoil.

16

Jodie began her request as she sat down next to him in the student bar. 'Bobby?'

He eyed her suspiciously. 'Why do I get the impression that there's a favour about to be asked?' he said looking her directly in the eye.

'I have a problem,' she said, uncertain how to ask him. She sensed he was enjoying this. He leant his head on one side, raised his eyebrows and urged her to continue.

'Go on,' he said. She wanted to get up and walk away, but she needed his help so she continued.

'When I was in sixth form I began a successful string quartet. We used to play all over the area.' She couldn't look him in the face as she spoke now; his eyes pierced her every time she looked up. 'Before I left, my headmaster asked me if we would return to play at this year's school charity concert to encourage others.'

'And ...' Bobby said, still in that condescending tone.

'Well,' she continued tentatively, 'it's going ahead and the quartet is playing *The Lark*.'

'But,' he added with a grin before she had a chance to say it.

'But,' she echoed with a smile, 'I intended playing Fauré's *Sonata No.1* as well and I've only ever been accompanied by the school music teacher. She's not great on the piano. So when I heard you the other day, I wondered ...' her voice trailed off, too embarrassed to ask him; after all, she had turned down his request for her to play in his band.

'You want to know if I'll play for you.' He finished the sentence for her and she merely nodded. 'If I don't have a folk club booking then I don't see why not,' he shrugged.

The words assented but the body language didn't match it. He looked hurt and she had no idea why.

'What's the matter?' she asked him anxiously.

'You told me you didn't play well.' He didn't look at her as he answered. 'If that were true then you wouldn't be playing for your old school's concert.'

He slowly took out a cigarette and lit it. She shot him a look of defiance now.

'I told you I didn't play very well without music. Anyway, you said you didn't play the pipe organ well, and Jerry says that's not true?'

She averted her eyes and his expression changed from hurt to laughter. 'Modest aren't we?' he said with a smile.

Jodie looked up and smirked.

'Would you like another drink?' he asked softly.

The softness of his tone, and the look in his eye would have melted her if she hadn't steadfastly resisted it.

'Jodie?' he repeated. 'Would you?'

'Sorry I was miles away. Yes please, half a cider.'

As he got up and went to the bar she wondered about the wisdom of asking him. By the time he returned with the drinks Kate and Jerry had arrived.

'I suppose you want me to go back to the bar again?' he said with mock irritation.

'Could you?' Jerry replied. 'I'm skint.'

Bobby shook his head. 'I don't know how this bar would manage without my dad's support.'

Jodie watched the interplay between Bobby and Jerry. There had to be more to Bobby than she had seen or Jerry wouldn't be so fiercely faithful. As Bobby got up to leave he turned to Jodie. 'Let me know the date and I'll let you know if I'm free. Then we'll fix a date for a practice.'

'Sure,' she replied.

Jerry looked at her in surprise. 'You haven't asked him to play for your school concert have you?'

'Yes,' she replied with a slightly anxious look.

'Fool,' he proclaimed with a grin. 'Playing with him in a folk band would be child's play compared to the perfection he'll expect for a classical concert.'

Bobby's expression betrayed nothing as he turned to leave. None of them stayed long after Bobby left.

'Do you want a lift back to the flat,' Jerry asked Jodie as he and Kate got up, 'or are you staying a bit longer?'

She shook her head. 'I'm leaving now. I'm getting the last bus to my granddad's. I'm staying overnight because I've left some of my work there and I'm borrowing his car tomorrow,' she said.

'I'm going back home now to do some work so I'll give you a lift if you like,' he offered.

Jodie accepted. Kate and Jerry chatted in the front of the car until they got to the flat and then Jerry dropped Jodie off.

Her granddad opened the front door as she got her key out. Once they were sat down she ventured a question.

'I asked Bobby to play and he will as long as he's free,' she began.

'That's good,' he replied.

'Well yes, but it's not nice being in his debt. I wondered if I should pay him.' She turned a serious gaze on him. He looked taken aback for a moment before replying.

'You're not seriously suggesting that are you?' he asked. 'Put yourself in his position. I imagine he would be both hurt and offended.'

She sulked. 'I wish I'd never asked him.'

'What do you honestly feel for him?' he asked cautiously as he put his glass of red wine down on the coffee table and looked her straight in the eye.

She frowned; she had been expecting the question sooner or later.

'I don't know, at first I had no time for him although I respected his artistic ability. Now I'm not sure. I don't think I know who the real Bobby is. I'm intrigued by him, but I'm frightened by him too.'

Her thoughts were safe with her granddad; experience had taught her that.

He got up and put another log on the fire before he spoke. 'I believe the first impression he gives is an act. I think he's afraid to expose the real person. Maybe you should be flattered that he's allowed you to see a hint of the real person.'

If it was intended to bring comfort it failed, indeed it made her more uncomfortable than ever. Sleep didn't come easily that night. She couldn't stop thinking about her granddad's words. It was true; somehow Bobby did seem to be able to be honest with her. She finally fell asleep without having decided what she really felt.

17

Hannah knocked on Colin's office door and pushed it open gently.

'It's Max on the 'phone.'

'Put him through,' he replied.

'Max, what do you want? I'm trying to run a business,' he said to his brother as he picked up the phone.

'I can't come running every time you have a problem ... oh all right,' he snapped. 'I'll call in after work ... no I can't get there any sooner.'

He slammed down the receiver and took a deep breath before he entered the studio. He walked across to Hannah's desk and sat opposite her. There was caution in Hannah's voice as she flicked back her wavy blond hair nervously.

'I should have told you,' she said quietly, but loud enough to be heard above the noise of the printing machines. Colin didn't answer but his facial expression said, "Go on".

'Grace is moving in with me for a while,' Hannah said. 'We arranged it last night when she told me she was leaving Max.'

'It would have been easier if you'd warned me,' he snapped. Once he'd regained his composure he sighed, 'I don't blame her, but Max will be a nuisance to me now.'

Hannah retied her pale blue chiffon scarf, still unable to look at him. She picked up on his anger. 'You're still angry with your father aren't you?' she asked without judgement.

'It's his fault,' Colin snapped.

The discussion ended abruptly when Colin heard the bell ring as the main door was opened. He crossed the studio to Simon. 'I think that's the delivery arriving, would you check it please?'

He knew he could depend on Simon.

'Yes sir,' Simon said as he rose to his feet and went to the door.

The telephone rang and Hannah answered it. Colin stared briefly out of the window beside Hannah's desk, and then returned to his office. He tried to concentrate on the cover design of a college prospectus, but his mind kept wandering back to his brother. In the end he spoke firmly to himself. 'Keep your private life out of your business life. Think what you're doing.'

Once he had completed the day's tasks he set off to see Max.

Colin rang the bell of the detached bungalow and Grace came to the door. She opened it but walked away quickly. He eased his way past boxes and cases piled in the hall and went into the lounge. Even now he could smell alcohol on his brother's breath.

'I've told her I'll give up drinking, but she won't listen,' Max slurred.

Colin grabbed hold of him by the collar, pushing him up against the wall with his clenched fist. 'Just look at you, you useless drunk,' he said through taut lips, thrusting his reddened face into his brother's. 'What's the bloody use of telling her you'll give up when you never do?' He dropped Max and stepped out into the hall.

'I'm sorry,' Grace said.

Colin shook his head, his breathing still fast and shallow, 'You've put up with it long enough. I shouldn't have bailed him out so often.'

Grace shrugged as she continued to pack. 'If it's anyone's fault it's your father's. I only hope that by having no contact with him the others have done better.'

Colin nodded.

'If I stay any longer I'll have a breakdown. I earn the money and do everything else as well. I just have to get away.'

Colin understood. He'd felt like that for years. When they were just four young boys, he had carried the burdens of looking after his brothers and of dealing with his father's drunken outbursts, without ever having opportunity to grieve for his mother himself. His mother had been barely in the grave before his father had disappeared into the bottle.

'I'll help you carry these to the car,' Colin said to Grace as he emerged from his memories. 'Do you need help unpacking at Hannah's?'

She shook her head. 'I'll be fine thanks, Hannah will give me a hand,' she said with tears in her eyes.

It hurt her to do this, he knew that. After helping her pack the car, he returned to his brother in the lounge.

'You're a bloody fool,' Colin said, raising his voice in anger once more, 'you'll end up just like Dad.'

Colin said goodbye to Grace before getting into his own car and driving home. He was angry with his brother. *Surely he can see what the alcohol did to dad. Surely he can see how it had destroyed the family.* His mind went over and over the past, stuck in a loop. He got caught up in the rush hour traffic in the centre of Brockton and grew increasingly impatient. By the time he got home he was agitated. As he drove into the driveway he could hear Bobby's group practising in the partially converted barn, and as he got out of the car, the laughter grated on his frazzled nerves. He strode over to the barn, flinging the door open angrily. 'Keep that noise down. Whatever will the neighbours think?' he railed.

Bobby came to the barn door. 'The neighbours can't hear at this distance,' he replied, rolling his eyes.

Why does this child always have to have the last word? Colin pointed a finger in the boy's face. 'Just do as I say,' he ordered, as Bobby walked away. Colin slammed the door behind him.

He took out his keys as he plodded wearily up the steps to the front door. He hadn't even taken his coat off when Mary came out into the hall; a drab, slow, forlorn looking apparition.

'I'm glad you're home,' she said.

He knew that meant that she wanted something. 'For goodness sakes,' he yelled, thumping his fist down on the hall table. 'I've just this second walked in. You could at least get me a cup of tea before you start whining.'

She didn't look at him, just turned away and went into the kitchen to make the tea. He went into the lounge and sat alone in silence. After a few minutes she brought in the cup of tea, setting it down on the coffee table in front of him without a word, before leaving.

Colin rested his head against the wing of the chair. He knew it was selfish, but now that Grace had left Max, he would lean heavily on him again. He had enough problems coping with a moaning wife, a rebellious son and an alcoholic father. Sometimes he wished that his privileged children could see the things that he had kept hidden from them, then they would know what he had overcome to get where he was today. He preferred not to expose them to that environment, fearful that they would have no respect for him at all if they knew his roots.

18

Bobby didn't go straight home on Friday night after the folk club; he wasn't sleepy. Even when he slept these days it was fitful and he never woke up refreshed. He noted the concern in Jerry's eyes when he said that he planned to ride out and find somewhere quiet; it wasn't a normal thing to do after midnight. Jerry left him with a reminder.

'Don't forget the mini-festival at the town hall tomorrow. I'll pick you up at half past one.'

'I'll be ready,' Bobby replied with a smirk. 'It's no big deal.'

Jerry lifted his eyes heavenward and got into the car as Bobby disappeared into a cloud of dust. It was a clear night and he loved the feel of the wind against his face.

No matter how hard he tried, Bobby couldn't rid himself of thoughts of Jodie. He longed to be near her and yet when he was, he felt unsure of himself, overawed. It was only by acting that he could appear to be at ease in her presence.

He rode to open fields not far from home, where he could wander undisturbed. He contemplated every aspect of his life in those hours as he strolled in the full bright moonlight. Being alone out there gave him a sense of freedom.

At half past two, he walked briskly back to the bike, rode home and went to bed. It was past 3 a.m. when his head hit the pillow but he had no cause to get up early. He felt peaceful and fell asleep easily.

He was unprepared for the abrupt awakening as his father pounded on his bedroom door. He crawled out of bed and flung on a dressing gown, rubbing his eyes gently between his thumb and forefinger as he unbolted the door. Colin stormed in, grabbed him by the collar and pushed him towards the side wall. Bobby was too disorientated to respond.

'Move your bike out of my way,' his father yelled.

Bobby felt limp and weak as his father let go of him and

powerless; most of all he felt powerless. He put on slippers and meekly followed his father downstairs and moved the motorbike, although his father could easily have manoeuvred the car around it.

'Happy now?' Bobby muttered under his breath as he raised his eyes heavenward.

It must have been louder than he intended, and he saw too late that the car window was open. The speed with which his father opened the car door and grabbed hold of him took Bobby unawares. He felt the slap on the left cheek with the back of his father's hand and, as he lost his balance, he knew that he would hit the garage wall side-on. He instinctively put out his hand to save himself but the side of his head hit the wall just the same.

He heard the car door slam and the sound of his dad driving off, though it all seemed a bit distant. Eventually he managed to sit upright and lean against the wall, clutching his throbbing head. He forced himself to get up and go back to bed but sleep eluded him, all he could feel was a surging anger. He was terrified of the rage inside him and even more terrified that he might become like his father, and in that moment he knew that he could.

Thoughts of vengeance filled his mind as he tossed and turned in bed, and he struggled to expel them. His head throbbed and he had no idea whether it was physical pain or pure anger. He lay there sleepless for hours, finally surfacing around midday.

'What do you want to eat?' his mother asked, ignoring the state he was in.

'Nothing,' he replied curtly.

'You didn't eat anything last night love,' she persisted.

'I'm okay,' he said, raising his voice, but that only made his head pound louder. He sat on the doorstep and leant against the wall. *However can I sing this afternoon feeling like this?* He was glad Jerry was collecting him; he wouldn't feel safe on the motorbike. He was still sitting on the doorstep when Jerry arrived.

'Surprise, surprise,' Jerry called buoyantly as he jumped out of the car. 'I've brought two guests to hear ...' He stopped in his tracks. 'God, what happened to you?'

Bobby looked up, hiding his face and wishing that Kate and Jodie weren't there.

'Just an accident with the bike,' he replied, but he sensed that Jerry knew the truth.

'Hey man, let's get the guitar,' Jerry announced striding off inside the house. As soon as they were alone he took Bobby by the arm. 'The bastard hit you didn't he?'

'How did you guess?' Bobby said sarcastically.

Bobby looked Jerry in the face for the first time since he'd arrived. 'I feel sick and I've got a raging headache, I don't know if I can sing.'

'I should take you to the hospital?' Jerry suggested, putting a hand on his friend's shoulder.

Bobby replied swiftly. 'I'll be alright.'

He got into the car and greeted Kate and Jodie with all the jollity he could muster, which wasn't much. Nobody asked any questions and Bobby imagined that they guessed. For the rest of the journey conversation was unusually strained but once they arrived Bobby cheered up and went off alone for a while. 'I won't be long,' he said as he walked away and Jerry shot him a knowing look.

It took him less than five minutes to walk to Dale's flat. For once, Dale was awake when Bobby arrived.

'Come in. Have you met Alice?' he asked.

Bobby had recollections of meeting her, but they were distant. 'I think so,' he replied looking at her tentatively.

She appeared to Bobby to be only half resident on the planet, like most of Dale's friends. Dale suddenly put a hand on Bobby's shoulder.

'Are you okay?' he asked.

Bobby shook his head lightly but he was too embarrassed to reply in front of a stranger.

'Your dad?' Dale asked, obviously sensing Bobby's embarrassment.

Bobby whispered his reply. 'Yes.'

Dale embraced Bobby.

'I'm jittery,' Bobby said as Dale released him.

'Bobby is my longest-standing friend,' Dale explained to Alice before turning back to Bobby. 'So you need something to calm your nerves?' he asked with a smile.

Bobby nodded again. 'Can you roll me a joint here? I'm playing at the Town Hall.'

Dale reached under the mattress and had rolled the joint almost before he had finished the sentence. Alice heaved herself off the floor and, still with the glazed look, offered Bobby coffee.

'No thank you,' he replied softly.

She went into the kitchen area of the bedsit and as Bobby lit up, Dale questioned him further.

'What did he do?'

'Oh just the usual,' Bobby sighed, 'but it was in the garage and I hit my head on the wall. I'm not sleeping well either.'

It was more than a statement and Dale recognised it.

'I can give you something,' Dale offered, sounding like a doctor offering a prescription. Bobby nodded.

'Just a couple; don't overdo it,' Dale recommended as he threw him a small packet. 'You don't want to end up like me. Anyway,' Dale continued, clearly about to change the subject. 'How's Jodie? Are you getting anywhere?'

Bobby shrugged. 'Not really. But I'm hoping to talk her into singing today and if I succeed then I'll trick her into playing the violin.' He took another drag of the joint and handed it to Dale.

Dale laughed. 'Barron you never give up, do you?'

Bobby glanced at his watch. 'I'd better go or I won't have time to sweet talk her.' Bobby rose to his feet. 'Thanks,' he said, discreetly paying him.

'Glad to be of service,' Dale replied as Bobby set off for

the Town Hall once more.

The headache still plagued him but as he arrived back he felt more relaxed.

'Jodie?' he said tentatively, with the expression of a little boy asking for a bag of sweets.

She eyed him suspiciously. 'That sounds ominous.'

'No, no,' he answered before adding, 'well maybe, yes,' he smiled. 'If I sing two songs that you know would you harmonise for me ... please?' he begged on bended knee.

Jodie laughed and Kate stared at her indignantly.

'I'll think about it,' she replied as she walked away.

He followed her, excited now. 'I've got a better idea, sing the song that you sang the other day about the labouring boy and *I'll* accompany *you*.'

As he spoke he walked backwards in front of her. Jodie looked at him, puzzled. 'Half an hour ago you looked like death warmed up. How did you make such a miraculous recovery?'

He winked at her. 'I have secret methods,' he said, quickly changing the subject back. 'What's your answer?'

She thought for a moment. 'I'll do it. Just this once,' she said which brought an instant response as he jumped in the air in delight.

'Hold on,' she said grabbing hold of his arm, 'I haven't finished yet. I'll do it on one condition,' she continued, as she let go of his arm and focused steadfastly on the ground.

'What?' he replied, a bit sceptical, his brow furrowed in anticipation of her response.

'Tell me the truth about your dad.'

Bobby looked both surprised and subdued. He was terrified of telling her the truth, afraid that she would judge him adversely or maybe even reject him. Postponement was his answer. 'Okay, but not until after the festival,' he replied without their eyes meeting.

Jodie's singing of *The Bonny Labouring Boy* was a resounding success. The combination of her lilting voice and his playing and harmony was electric and prompted enthusiastic applause. Once it began to fade, Tony, the big, bearded banjo player, broke into a lively version of *The Jolly Waggoner* and Bobby kept his eyes on Jodie as she sang. He had felt depressed and ill earlier, but despite the pounding head, he felt much better now.

At the audience's demand for another song, he spoke to Tony, jumped down off the stage and borrowed a violin which he thrust into Jodie's hands, whispering instructions to her.

She tried to say, 'no,' and mouthed, 'I hate you,' as he walked back across the stage, but he blew her a kiss, counted them in and they broke into a jig to the delight of the now animated audience. Despite her reluctance, Jodie rose to the occasion.

Finally Bobby took her hand and, together with the rest of the band, they took a bow to rapturous applause. He was exhausted and despite cries for more he refused, collected the violin and returned it to its owner before going back for the guitar. He stumbled a little as he walked off stage and he handed the guitar to Jerry before going outside for fresh air.

As he sat outside on the pavement leaning his head heavily against the wall, the pounding grew louder and the distant music sounded like a dream. After a few minutes Jodie appeared and crouched beside him on the path. It would have been easy to play for sympathy with her eyes so full of compassion.

'You'll freeze out here, come back inside,' she pleaded.

'I can't, my head's pounding and I feel sick. Get Jerry for me will you, I have to go home.'

She stroked his blond hair gently back from his face and looked into his eyes, forcing him to look at her. 'Tell me the truth Bobby.'

There was kindness in her beautiful green eyes that pleaded with him with such longing. It was obvious that she cared deeply. He wanted to tell her, but he barely had enough

energy to speak above a whisper. 'I will tell you. I'll come round in the morning, my head should be better then. But I need to rest.' His breathing was laboured and Jodie looked worried.

She went to find Jerry, returning with him quickly.

'You look dreadful,' Jerry said, 'I'll fetch Kate. Wait with him Jodie I won't be a minute.'

He ran to fetch Kate and they returned quickly with the instruments.

'Let me take you to the hospital,' Jerry pleaded.

'No,' Bobby said emphatically. 'I can't go to hospital, just take me home.'

'Jerry's right,' Kate said, but he ignored her.

He rose to his feet very, very carefully, clutching his head in his hand as he trudged unsteadily to the car. Jerry dropped Kate and Jodie off en-route and drove quickly to Bobby's house. Bobby didn't say a word all the way home. Jerry jumped out, unlocked the boot and carried the guitar into the house, gently putting a hand on Bobby's shoulder as he turned to leave.

'Are you sure you're going to be okay?'

'Sure, I just need to sleep.'

Bobby moved to his room as swiftly as his body would allow and locked the door behind him. As he lay down, his head began to spin; it felt as if it would explode. He slowly drifted away, sinking deeper and deeper into the mattress until everything faded.

19

Bobby sat up with a start, then lay back with a thud and a deep sigh when he realised what had woken him. The shouting and door slamming continued unabated. The noise merged somewhere in his head with the rhythmic throbbing, which seemed to almost vibrate his body. 'Oh God I can't stand any more of this,' he said aloud to himself. He felt slightly dizzy as he stood up and waited a moment to get his balance before moving slowly towards the window. At least he didn't feel sick this morning. As he pulled the curtains open the Autumn sun shone through the window, bringing tranquillity and hope to an otherwise gloomy start to the day. The hammering in his head reminded him of yesterday's battle and the memory of Jodie's gentleness toward him.

As the banging and slamming came closer, Bobby withdrew under the covers and lay low, waiting for the storm to pass. He had no intention of letting his father ruin what he hoped would be a good day. There seemed little point in trying to go back to sleep now; he could take his time showering and getting dressed before riding over to Jodie's place. His Dad would be gone soon; he always went early to church on a Sunday to practice the organ. His Mum would walk down later, alone.

Once he was sure his dad had gone, he got up and went downstairs, made a cup of coffee and lit a cigarette.

'Not in here,' his mother whined as she looked up from her book, so he went out into the back garden. He watched the wind dancing in the trees as he wandered down the garden path towards the stream. A light, low mist covered it this morning as it often did at this time of the year.

Leaning over the gate, he remembered the times he had watched the carpet of dead leaves, as gusts of wind lifted them into the air. He thought of how they floated back down to earth, drifting back and forth. He remembered the first time he had seen a kingfisher here, and how he had run excitedly to tell his mother. He remembered making boats and rafts with his friends, and how they had made stepping-stones across the stream and had fallen in. He remembered that once they had tried to dam it up altogether; they failed but it had been fun trying. Suddenly he remembered that he was supposed to be seeing Jodie.

He wandered over towards the back door and stubbed the cigarette out on the step with his heel.

'You should try smoking, it might help your nerves,' he said to his mother as he opened the kitchen door.

She screwed up her face in disgust. 'Ugh, I couldn't, it's a nasty habit. Do you want egg and bacon?'

'Ugh I couldn't,' he grinned mischievously, 'it's a nasty habit.'

She made toast which he ate mindlessly. He looked up at his mother and fixed her with a penetrating gaze. 'Why do you put up with it? Why don't you leave him?'

His mother let out a deep, weary sigh. 'I promised "for better, for worse",' she lamented.

Bobby was angry. 'Yes,' he retorted, 'and no doubt he promised to "Love, honour and cherish," too.'

As he gazed at her sorrowful face he felt compassion for her. She was an intelligent woman, an avid reader and yet her life was shrouded in sorrow. She wasn't beautiful, but she could make much more of her appearance if she tried.

'I have to do what's right,' she replied.

She walked behind him as she spoke, resting her hand on his shoulder. 'Arguing with him only makes things worse.'

'But Mum,' he insisted with increased fervour as he turned around to look her in the eye, 'that means that he can ride roughshod over us, that our lives don't matter.'

His mum let out a deep sigh, 'I guess you have to do it your way and I have to do it mine, anyway I must get ready.'

'But,' he remarked casually, 'we all have to live with the

consequences of the other's responses.'

'We certainly do,' she nodded.

As he got up to leave, he felt a twinge of guilt. He had always despised her for her weakness but today he felt sorry for her, there must have been life in her once. He glanced back briefly at the lifeless apparition that stood in the kitchen doorway, but he couldn't let it concern him right now.

He put it out of his head; today was his day for Jodie. Not that he was expecting it to be easy. He was half expecting her to grill him like the Spanish Inquisition. He was nervous; unsure that he wanted to share the details of his life with anyone, let alone someone he knew so little about. Added to that, he felt physically vulnerable. He put a hand to his head.

'Are you alright?' his mother asked, with genuine concern.

'I've taken painkillers, I'll be okay,' he replied.

He picked up his jacket from the hall, putting it on as he walked out of the back door and rode off at top speed on the road to Brockton, only to be stopped at the top of the hill by Hugh Williams, the local policeman. Bobby sat astride the bike and removed his crash helmet.

'I didn't know you were around on a Sunday,' Bobby volunteered with a grin.

The local policeman replied abruptly without looking up from his notebook.

'That's obvious.'

'Have you got girls' telephone numbers in there?' Bobby teased him, pretending to look over his shoulder.

Hugh replied in an indignant gruff voice as he put away his notebook and looked up at Bobby.

'I stopped you on account of a matter of speeding.'

'I was in a hurry,' Bobby said.

'In a hurry to get where, hell?'

Bobby smiled. Though he respected him, Bobby had known P.C. Williams too long to be afraid of him, or of the authority he represented. 'Actually,' he remarked, hand over heart, 'I'm hoping to be transported to heaven today.'

Hugh tutted. 'Whatever is the world coming to? Don't tell me Bobby Barron's in love now?'

Bobby laughed aloud and put his hand on the old policeman's shoulder. 'How did you know what I was talking about?'

'I may be old, but I'm not stupid,' Hugh replied with a superior look and cleared his throat. 'Anyway you've changed the subject. If you don't ride that thing with more care you most certainly will end up in heaven or hell or wherever, sooner than you ought.'

'Oh, I've no illusions, the old man's always telling me to go to hell,' Bobby smirked.

'And what do you reply?' Hugh grinned with his hands on his hips, which Bobby thought looked rather camp for a policeman.

Bobby laughed, mimicking his stance. 'Last time, I told him that I thought I was already there.'

Hugh broke into raucous laughter, and asked, 'And what did he reply?'

Bobby looked at him condescendingly. 'I'm not stupid either, I didn't wait around for a response. Aw come on, are you booking me or can I go?' he continued impatiently.

Hugh took a deep breath. 'Well, I think you could at least show a little respect for the law.'

'Sorry sir,' Bobby replied as he saluted.

'That's better. I'm not booking you, but take it easy on that thing,' he said earnestly.

He had barely finished the sentence before Bobby had the helmet back on and had started the engine. He shouted his thanks, opened the throttle, and pulled away slowly until he was out of view.

Bobby laughed to himself. Hugh was a bit of a walkover. He'd always been a little bit soft, and Bobby wasn't averse to taking advantage of his kindness.

Bobby's thoughts drifted back to Jodie. His mind was spinning now, *how much should I tell her? Will she see through it if I play down my feelings? What will I say if she doesn't understand? Will she be afraid that underneath I must be like my father? What if really, underneath it all I am the same? Ah well, I'm almost there now,* 'Nothing ventured, nothing gained,' he said aloud as he arrived at the entrance to the flat. He was excited about seeing her, but terrified of losing her friendship.

20

Arriving at the flat, Bobby dismounted and suddenly slowed down. He was afraid of being rejected, and he knew it was a real possibility, but he'd promised. Mustering all the expertise of the actor within, he strode to the door. Kate answered it, still in her dressing gown.

'Did you want something?' she asked in an off-hand manner.

'No, I just like ringing doorbells.'

He leant on his elbow on the wall and as she tried to close the door, he stopped it with his foot. 'I came to see Jodie,' he said, pushing open the door with his arm.

Kate opened the door fully, and since Bobby had his weight against it, he almost fell inside.

'Jodie's still in bed.' The tone of her voice was still not welcoming. 'We never get up this early on a Sunday.'

Bobby was inside now and had shut the door behind him. His tone was one of mock surprise. 'But you just did.'

Kate raised her eyebrows in a haughty manner without saying a word. He rapidly changed the subject. He'd never have admitted it to Kate, but in the verbal frolicking with her, he had lost his nervousness. 'Can I wake her?'

Kate looked horrified, 'No, leave her until she wakes.'

His tone was impatient now. 'I can't wait that long.'

She furrowed her brow and answered him crossly.

'Why, where are you going?'

His patience dissolved. 'I'm impatient to see her. By the way, do visitors make their own coffee here?' He was now displaying the arrogance for which he was renowned. No matter how well he treated her she was still obnoxious to him, so there was no point being kind. He had no idea at all what a nice guy like Jerry saw in her.

Kate shot him a look of disbelief. 'Her original instincts

were right, you are arrogant. Make your own coffee, and make me one while you're at it. I'm going to get dressed.' Then she strutted off.

Bobby hunted in cupboards until he found all he needed, put on the kettle, made the coffee and returned to the lounge. He saw a guitar propped up in the corner, so he picked it up and strummed quietly. Kate returned in jeans and a t-shirt.

Bobby spoke quietly, still strumming. 'Can I just peep in?'

'I'll see if she's awake,' Kate said, getting up.

Bobby followed her. 'I'll come with you.'

Kate bustled to the door and Bobby pushed past her and knelt on the floor beside Jodie's bed. Kate shouted at him, 'Don't wake her!' which caused Jodie to stir slightly.

Bobby put out his hand to touch her face and began to sing to her.

Kate shouted at him and Jodie half-opened her eyes. 'You've woken her now,' she scolded and left, slamming the door behind her. Bobby looked back towards the door and gave a heavy exasperated sigh.

'Is this a private nightmare or can anybody join?' Jodie's speech was still slightly slurred. Her eyes struggled to adjust to the light but met his as he turned his head back towards her. His face broke into a wide smile as he leant on the edge of her bed and looked her in the eye.

'Not just anyone, but *you* can.' *It must be strange for her to wake up and find me sitting here,* he thought. He jumped up quickly. 'I'm sorry, I shouldn't have intruded.' He looked around at the chaos and forgot himself for a moment. 'Do you live in this mess?'

Jodie feigned offence. 'I think it's time you left. I'll get dressed.'

He made for the door and turned back briefly. 'Shall I make you coffee? Black isn't it?'

She opened her eyes wide with astonishment, 'You've got a nerve,' she replied, but she smiled and nodded.

Kate ignored Bobby as he entered the kitchen. After a long

pause she spoke. 'There was no need to wake her.'

Bobby was not about to let her get the better of him. 'I think you'll find,' he replied confidently, 'that you woke her'. Then he used the old tactic of changing the subject. 'Is Jerry coming round today?'

'Yes, at a reasonable hour,' she snapped through gritted teeth.

'Nay, come Kate come you must not look so sour,' he quoted and then added 'Okay, I shouldn't have woken her. Forgive me.' At which he got on bended knee with hands clenched together in front of him.

Kate visibly relaxed and laughed at last. 'Oh all right, get up you idiot.'

Just then, Bobby caught sight of Jodie, leaning on the wall in the doorway; he had no idea how long she had been listening. He gave a slight bow as he greeted her. 'Good morning.'

'You are rude,' she replied and hit him as he pretended to cower.

'What, me?' he feigned innocence.

'Yes,' she continued. 'You quoted from *The Taming of the Shrew*. The implications are obvious.'

Kate left the kitchen and Bobby instantly became serious. He spoke to her softly. 'Are you busy today? I made you a promise yesterday which I intend to keep.'

'I'm not busy until later; I go to Granddad's most Sunday evenings and he drives me back later.' She looked at him earnestly.

'Then how about taking a walk over Morley Hill? There's a quaint pub over the other side which has a restaurant at the back, we could eat there,' he suggested.

'I know it, The Windmill Inn, good idea.'

'Okay, hurry up unless you're coming barefoot,' he said just as Kate entered the room.

Kate looked up at him. 'Why are you always in such a hurry?'

He answered her with yet another quote.

'Gather ye rosebuds while you may
old time is still a flying,
and that same flower that smiles today
tomorrow will be dying.'

'Now what are you talking about?' Kate replied.

'Make the most of time,' Jodie said.

Kate slumped into a chair. 'Why couldn't he say that then? I thought you were going out picking rosebuds in case they were all dead by tomorrow.'

It was Bobby's turn to give a patronising look now. 'Winter rosebuds! Not even you are that lacking in imagination.'

His tone held scorn and she got up and left the room.

Jodie looked troubled. 'Don't do that to her Bobby.'

Jerry arrived just as they were leaving and spread-eagled himself against the wall to let them by in their haste. He looked at Kate in surprise. 'Are they going out?' he asked, still in earshot of Bobby and Jodie.

Kate's reply was both abrupt and loud, and Bobby was in no doubt that he was intended to hear it. 'I sincerely hope not.'

Bobby let it go, but it hurt nonetheless. *Why does Kate hate me?* he thought, but was determined to put it out of his mind. All that mattered was that he finally had Jodie to himself.

21

'You planned that yesterday, didn't you?' Jodie turned to face Bobby.

He stared at her in surprise. 'What?'

'You forced me into a position where I had no choice but to play the violin.'

'That's quite an accusation you know.' He smiled as he backed away from her. 'Anyway, you were good and I knew you would be.'

'That's not the point,' she sulked.

'Well,' she said after a few minutes silence. 'It's too late now. So you keep your part of the agreement.' She could see it was hard for him; she had given him no lead in to the conversation.

'I don't know where to begin. What do you want to know?' he asked.

She felt uncomfortable now, half wishing that she hadn't asked him but at the same time wanting to know the truth. He sat down on a felled log and she sat beside him peeling the bark from a small twig, which she had picked up along the way. *How can I answer that? How can I tell him about my fears?* Eventually she made an attempt, she owed him that much.

'I'm fond of you, Bobby,' she said, fixing her eyes on the twig she was nervously playing with, 'but I'm a little afraid of you too.' She shook her dark hair out of her face and turned to look at him fleetingly.

'Because of the rumours?' he asked, and she heard his voice quaver slightly.

She didn't reply but in her embarrassment she turned her head still further away. She was close to tears, though she hid it from Bobby. At least she hoped she did. *How can I be so untrusting? Aren't I only adding insult to injury?*

'Jodie,' he spoke her name in a way that nobody else ever

did. 'I don't mind you asking. I'd rather you shared your fears with me than spread more rumours like others do. I understand the fear, families are meant to be safe places.'

He laughed at himself before he continued. 'Before I met Jerry I didn't realise there was anything wrong with my family.'

She paused and swallowed hard before she spoke. She had expected it to be hard for him to say, but she never realised it would be so difficult to hear, and he'd hardly begun yet. 'Was he really violent to you, even when you were little?'

He looked into her wide anguished eyes. 'He was especially violent towards me when I was little. I couldn't fight back then, though eventually I tried.' He laughed and shook his head gently. 'Even now it's hard because he's so much bigger than me. He'd keep me off school until the bruises had gone.' He paused momentarily. 'How much do you really want to know? You see, with the benefit of hindsight I think there is something quite sadistic about him. There was always a hint of enjoyment in his eyes and a look of satisfaction when he'd had enough.'

Jodie recoiled, *how has he endured the pain and terror?* A magpie took off from the hawthorn bush behind them and Jodie startled. He briefly put a hand on her arm to calm her.

'Why do you hide it? All the time you laugh when really on the inside you must want to cry.'

He even laughed this off. 'There was a French dramatist who said, "I force myself to laugh at everything for fear of being compelled to weep."'

'But that means that you never truly live in reality. How did you survive?' she whispered.

'Well, like I said, I didn't know it wasn't normal.' He let out a thoughtful sigh. 'I guess survival is instinctive. I learned not to let him know I was afraid because he seemed to get satisfaction from my fear. I would compose songs in my head, detaching myself from it. If he was holding me by the collar and banging my head on the wall I would use the rhythm to create a song. It seems bizarre now.'

Jodie was unusually quiet, she smiled but inside she felt sick. *How could he speak of it so indifferently, almost as if he was describing someone else's experience?* He leant back casually onto the tree as he continued.

'The worst times were when he used a leather belt on bare flesh. It was hard not to look afraid then.'

She jumped up and walked away feeling sick. 'You're joking now, tell me you are.' Getting no reply she turned back to look at him. He wasn't smiling. 'Aren't you?' Her question was more searching now, and her face was contorted with anguish. He looked embarrassed and shook his head.

'I'm sorry. I thought you wanted to ...'

She interrupted, 'I did, I just never realised that the rumours barely touched the truth.'

There was anger in her voice as she moved back towards him, and she fell accidentally into his arms as he got up. She brushed herself down as she extricated herself. She was embarrassed for a moment, but quickly recovered. 'So what's he like now?'

He loosened his grip to let her go and they strolled on as he replied, 'In some ways it's harder now. I was terrified as a child but it seemed normal.' She looked at him with a puzzled expression.

'I never knew life any other way,' he explained and she nodded. 'He seemed okay for a while but now he's twice the bastard he ever was.' She could hear the hatred in his voice. 'He punches me or slaps me so hard I fall to the ground, that's what he did yesterday. I lost my balance and hit the garage wall. Do you wish I hadn't told you?' he asked, pausing before slowly continuing. 'Are you afraid that I could be the same?'

She couldn't respond for what seemed like an eternity. He said no more, just waited. She had to answer him, but what could she say, what would she tell him? He was still looking at her, his face still enquiring. She was shaking nervously. 'I can't tell you the truth, because I don't know what the truth is.' She let out an exasperated sigh. 'All right, I'll try.'

Whatever she said to him she wanted to be as sensitive as she could, she had lost the desire to mock him now. Today she had seen a totally different side to him. The courage she saw was not the image he presented to the world. She plucked up her own courage just to speak. 'I'm glad you told me, because not knowing is somehow worse.' She hesitated, uncertain whether to say more, her eyes flitting uncomfortably between him and the ground.

'Tell me what you're really thinking,' he said.

'I think it's the strength of the emotions you evoke in me that makes me so afraid.' She stopped, she'd said too much already; *maybe I'm giving away too much of my heart?*

'Go on,' he urged again.

'Okay, like when you made a fool of me over Adam and Eve in the Sistine Chapel ... '

'Yes, I'm sorry about ... '

She broke in again. 'It's okay, that's in the past, but I hadn't really felt anger like that for a long while. It only mattered because it was you. Then yesterday, I was so angry at what your father had done to you, and at the same time I felt such tenderness for you. I wanted to hold you in my arms and take away the pain.'

He looked at her with mischievous eyes. 'I wouldn't have complained.'

She ignored him and continued. 'I'm afraid of what I would feel if you ever hurt me, and of what I would feel if I hurt you, or anyone else hurt you for that matter, but I'd be a liar to say I'm not afraid that you could become violent like him.'

He drew closer to her, speaking in a near whisper. 'I live in abject terror that I might turn out like him. If I ever thought that I was becoming like him I would commit suicide.'

He changed the subject and she asked no more questions.

As they walked on he took her hand again, and this time she didn't resist. When they reached the pub, he bought lunch, despite her protestations.

'Give me a chance,' he pleaded across the table.

She sighed. He'd won. She gazed across the table at him without a word ... inside she had already melted. He must have read the signs because he instantly reached across, took her head in his hands and kissed her. Nothing in her could resist, and when they got up to leave, she took *his* hand.

22

'Okay, okay,' Bobby said to Jodie, coming to an abrupt halt in the middle of the sonata as they practised the piece they were due to play the next evening. 'We need to be more concise in that third movement in order to highlight the amazing rhythms.'

Jodie removed the violin from under her chin and placed it on top of the piano in front of him. He looked up at her.

'*You* are the one who wanted to do this.'

She snatched the violin back off the top of the piano, tight lipped. 'I asked you to accompany me not to criticise me,' she replied.

He got up from the piano stool, closed the sheet music and threw it onto the coffee table. 'If you had wanted shoddy playing you could have settled for your teacher,' he said as he began to walk away.

She wanted to appease him, to say something to pacify him, but she couldn't.

'You really are arrogant aren't you?' she said.

Hardness crept across his face as he replied this time. He turned around and looked her straight in the eye. 'I did you a favour, invited you into my house to practice, and you think it's okay to treat me with contempt because I have the audacity to want to play the piece as Fauré wrote it.'

She recognised the voice of rejection. She needed him to play and she didn't want to hurt him, so she had to act instantly. 'I'm sorry,' she said, holding his gaze, 'I'm probably not enough of a perfectionist for classical music.'

His demeanour softened. 'Then play folk for me!' he winked mischievously. She couldn't help but smile but she followed it with a haughty stare which still said "no".

'Will you give me a second chance?' she asked, picking up the music from the coffee table and handing it to him. He said nothing, merely took the music from her and sat down at the piano. Suddenly he stood up. 'Would you like coffee?' he asked.

'Thank you,' she sighed, glad of the break.

She followed him into the kitchen and sat down at the old oak table letting her eyes wander around the room. It had clearly been extended into the scullery at one time.

'Why did you choose Fauré?' he asked casually as he filled the kettle.

She took a deep breath. 'I don't know really. We always played Haydn or Mozart or Beethoven. I wanted something different.'

He looked up at her as he stooped to get the milk from the fridge. 'It's an interesting choice, it has flexibility within a formal setting ...' He interrupted his own flow briefly, holding up the bottle to her, 'You don't take milk do you?'

She shook her head as she replied, 'The style is quite like Debussy, but less fluid.'

He continued making the coffee as he spoke, 'But Fauré pre-dates Debussy doesn't he?'

She was momentarily taken aback. Eventually she answered him. 'You're probably right,' she remarked with a look of exasperation which he didn't see. Part of what frightened her was his intense interest in whatever he was doing. She knew she'd offended him by singing at the folk club when she hadn't expected him to be there, but she could never have admitted her fear of his criticism. He turned around and placed the coffee on a coaster in front of her before sitting opposite her.

'How old were you when you started to play?' She looked up at him awaiting an answer and was surprised at the expression on his face, anxiety mixed with pain.

'I don't know,' he replied, visibly regaining his composure.

She heard a key in the lock and studied him with interest as the front door slammed. He jumped and she saw the faintest, half-hidden sigh of relief as his mother entered the kitchen.

He got up from the chair.

'Er ... Mum this is Jodie, Jodie this is my mum ... do you want coffee, Mum? The kettle's just boiled.'

'Hello Jodie,' his mother said without emotion but her answer to Bobby was flustered. 'I don't have time to sit around drinking coffee. Your father will be home soon.'

Bobby looked across at Jodie, an expression of either nervousness or embarrassment on his face; she couldn't tell which. Sensing his discomfort she got up.

'Let's try that piece once more,' she suggested, and he winked as if to say, "thanks". As they played this time she made a conscious effort to improve the third movement and, judging by his comments, she succeeded.

'That's much better,' he beamed at the end of the piece.

Jodie laughed. His praise wasn't an easy thing to earn but it felt worth the effort. He looked up at her, worried. 'I'm sorry, am I patronising you?' he asked and she shook her head lightly as she replied.

'It's okay. Thanks for doing this. I'd better go,' she said, 'I'm on my way to see Granddad.'

She began to pack the violin into its case and didn't notice as he disappeared. Suddenly he reappeared with her coat and held it for her like a gentleman. As she entered the hallway she could smell burning. 'What's burning?' she asked him anxiously.

Bobby laughed. 'Dinner I expect,' he replied. 'As the saying goes, "If you can't smell burning, mum's not in the kitchen". I'll give her a hand in a minute.'

'Thank you,' she said with an embarrassed smile. 'I'll see you in college tomorrow.'

He nodded gently then suddenly called her back. 'Jodie,' he said, causing her to turn around. 'Do you really think I'm arrogant?'

'I shouldn't have said that,' she said with an awkward smile.

'That's not an answer,' he replied stepping outside.

'Maybe a little,' she said, 'but not as arrogant as you pretend.'

He nodded thoughtfully. She could see that it troubled him so she blew him a kiss, which he pretended to catch before jumping down the steps after her, putting his arms around her and kissing her. Her heart was beating faster and she felt like a traitor to herself. She had wanted to take it slowly but a part of her was racing ahead, longing to let go and love him with abandon ... but she wouldn't; not yet.

23

After work the same day, Colin drove from Brockton to the city centre and parked at the front of the Hospital. *This place wouldn't improve your health,* he thought to himself as he walked up the crumbling steps, through the swing doors and past the reception at the front of the old Victorian building. He knew the ward well; it wasn't the first time his father had been admitted here. Too impatient to wait for a lift, he walked briskly up the stairs and along the corridor to Cranmer Ward. He knocked on the Ward Sister's door even though it was open.

'Excuse me,' he asked, 'could you tell me which bed Joe Barron is in?'

'Ah yes come in a moment. You're his son aren't you?' she asked, raising her eyebrows.

'Yes. Colin Barron,' he replied, extending a hand.

He was weary. He wished that his father would get on with it and die, but he was racked with guilt for feeling that way.

'Basically, Mr. Barron, your father is dying.'

The word shocked him when it came from the sister.

'His liver isn't functioning any more. We've removed some of the fluid from his abdomen which should make him more comfortable, and we're giving him blood transfusions but he's very sick. The treatment is purely to ease the symptoms. He's in heart failure as well.'

Colin didn't look up, simply nodded as one hundred and one things went through his head. The duty was almost over, but with his father's death, the possibility of acceptance would die too. His brothers should be told and he'd somehow have to keep it from his own children.

'Thank you Sister,' he said, 'let me know if he needs anything.'

The Sister smiled courteously as she got up. 'I'll do that,' she said as she led the way to his father. Colin pulled up a chair beside his father's bed.

'Hello Dad,' he said quietly, looking into his father's jaundiced eyes.

His father stared at him blankly. 'Where's Max?' he said eventually.

Colin cringed as he replied. 'I'll pop in on my way home. I'm sure he'll come in tonight.' *If he can stay sober long enough*, he thought.

'His nasty wife has left him,' Joe remarked.

This wasn't the time or the place to upset his father so he toned down what he was feeling. 'Grace can't cope with Max's behaviour anymore,' he replied.

Joe became aggressive, always a danger when he couldn't get the alcohol he craved; or when he could for that matter.

'Don't talk about Max like that,' his father said.

For a few uncomfortable moments neither of them spoke. Colin wasn't about to retract his comments and Joe was blind to any weakness in Max. Colin clicked his nails nervously.

'I want a cigarette,' Joe said.

'You're not allowed to smoke,' Colin replied, and another uneasy silence hung between them. The silences seemed more intense in hospital. There was nowhere to go.

'Do you need me to bring you anything?'

'I just want a cigarette and a drink.'

'Well you can't have either,' Colin said abruptly, getting up from his chair and putting it back against the wall, 'I'll see you tomorrow.' No matter how hard he tried, he always ended up angry.

He drove home quickly and as he turned the key in the front door he could smell the familiar family fragrance ... charcoal. He threw his briefcase to the ground and hung up his coat in the hall. There was laughter in the kitchen as he entered and it grated on his frazzled nerves. Pushing open the door he caught sight of Bobby juggling eggs.

'Put those down,' he shouted.

The laughter ceased and Bobby put the eggs back in the egg stand as Colin sat down.

'A kitchen's not for messing around in. Get out,' he ordered, motioning with his head towards the door, but the boy didn't leave. He took a bow.

'My apologies,' he said in a patronising tone, 'I didn't realise helping my mother with the cooking was against the rules of this bloody madhouse.'

Bobby's disrespect triggered Colin's anger. He rose to his feet quickly and grabbed Bobby by the collars, screwing them up in his fist as he forced the boy up against the wall. He held Bobby's gaze with squinted stare.

'Don't you dare talk to me like that,' he said, banging his son's head on the wall by the side of the door, desperately trying to gain control of his temper. He held him up with his right hand and attempted to punch the side of his face. Bobby blocked the punch with his arm and tried to push his father away. Colin held tight to the shirt collars and heard it rip as the boy pulled away.

'You're mad,' Bobby said with contempt as he pushed his father away, successfully now, and left the kitchen as Colin lost his balance. 'Totally mad.'

24

Jodie looked at her watch and quickened her pace as she walked through the door of the art studio at college; she was late again. She caught the tender look in Bobby's eye and her heart melted.

'Do you mind getting a move on?' the lecturer said.

Jodie looked around. All eyes were on her. She smiled awkwardly and tossed back her dark hair as she began to unpack her bag. Out of the corner of her eye she caught the look in Bobby's. He winked. As soon as the design lecturer had given instructions, Jodie got up and walked across to Kate.

'You should have woken me up.'

Kate looked her up and down. 'You've got an alarm clock,' she bristled, 'and you didn't have to stay so late at lover boy's.'

Bobby leant over Kate's shoulder and spoke to her in a patronising tone. 'Her granddad is lovely, but he's hardly a lover boy.'

Kate turned around with anger in her eye, but in his well practised manner, Bobby had fled.

'You asked for that,' Jodie said. 'I left Bobby's house before six to spend the evening with my granddad.'

'There's still no excuse for being late,' she muttered.

'Probably not,' Jodie admitted. 'Do you have a spare rubber?' she said, changing the subject.

'No I don't,' Kate snapped. 'You should check you've got what you need before you leave home.'

Bobby stifled a laugh as he looked up at Jodie and wagged his finger at her out of Kate's view. He threw her a rubber. At the end of the lesson she walked across the room to hand it back to him.

'I don't want it back,' he said shaking his head. 'I steal

them from my dad's studio ... pencils too. Do you need any?' he asked producing a handful from his bag.

'Rogue,' she replied.

'Are you coming to coffee?' Kate called impatiently to Jodie.

'Yes Ma'am,' Bobby whispered.

Jodie followed Kate, struggling to keep a straight face. It was lunchtime before Jerry arrived and he sat down next to Kate in the canteen.

'Mum's car wouldn't start.'

'You should allow for things like that,' Kate snapped.

'Yes,' Bobby remarked. 'You should leave time to get the bus instead and,' he continued, the weight of sarcasm increasing, 'allow time for the bus breaking down, and not forgetting allowing time for twisting your ankle in a hole in the pavement should you have to walk, and ...'

'Shut-up,' Kate snapped and got up and walked away. Jerry hit Bobby on the arm and went after her.

'Why do you do that?' Jodie asked him.

He shrugged. 'She's bossy.'

'But she was talking to Jerry, not you,' Jodie replied.

'He's my best mate.'

Jodie frowned. 'Jerry can look after himself.'

'Okay,' he said, lifting his hands in surrender, though she got the impression that he just didn't want to argue, 'You're right. What time do you want me there tonight?'

She grinned to herself at his swift change of subject. 'I'll collect you at quarter to seven. Jerry and Kate are coming so try to behave,' she begged.

To his surprise, she arrived at precisely quarter to seven.

'How did you do that?' he asked as he opened the door.

'Do what?' she replied with a quizzical expression.

'Get here on time.'

'Well ...' she replied quickly, with a smirk on her face, 'firstly I allowed time for the car not starting and having to get the bus, and then ... good grief Bobby, you make me look scruffy.'

He shook his head. 'I could never do that. You look stunning,' he whispered.

She felt her face flush and turned around.

'Come on then; it would be good to get a chance to practice,' she said.

On arrival at the school he jumped out and opened the door for her. She leant over to pick up the violin from the back seat and handed it to him before she got out. 'Take this for me would you?'

As she got out of the car she noticed that he was about to light-up. 'Bobby we're in a school.'

'I'm nervous,' he said as he put it back in the packet.

She smiled. 'It's just a school concert.'

He didn't reply, but she sensed his anxiety and held out her hand. He gripped it as they walked towards the school building. Jodie stopped in the entrance hall to introduce Bobby to her old headmaster. 'This is my pianist for the evening, Bobby Barron.'

The headmaster shook him formally by the hand. 'Are you related to Barrons ...?'

'The graphic designer, yes,' Bobby interrupted.

'Ah,' Mr Myers continued, 'so I guess you are at art college with Jodie.'

'Yes sir,' Bobby replied with a slight bow. She smiled to herself as she led the way across the hall to the piano. The headmaster followed.

'Try it,' she suggested.

Bobby sat down and played a piece which seemed to cover just about every note on the piano. He nodded softly as he finished.

'Is it satisfactory?' the headmaster asked.

'It's in very good condition. Most school pianos aren't well looked after.'

'It was bought by a parent and we try to keep it tuned.'

'It shows,' Bobby replied and Jodie noted the pleasure on Mr. Myers' face.

'Well?' Bobby said to Jodie, slightly abruptly.

'Oh yes,' she exclaimed, jumping up to get the violin. 'I hope I brought rosin.'

'You should check you've got everything you need before you leave home.'

She spoke sternly to him as she found the rosin. 'Please don't upset Kate tonight,' she pleaded.

He promised.

The rest of Jodie's string quartet arrived as Jodie and Bobby practiced and she introduced him to them. Bobby escaped while the quartet practised. She could smell the cigarette when he returned, but she said nothing, simply took his hand.

They sat through countless recitals from gifted and not so gifted pupils, until eventually the headmaster introduced the string quartet, and Jodie and her friends made their way to the stage. She didn't dare look up at Bobby as they played the piece, for fear of his critical gaze. As they neared the end of the piece, he moved quietly to the piano and when she looked up he was ready.

She took a deep breath and counted him in with a slight movement of her right arm. It took all her concentration to play to the level he demanded of her and she let out a sigh of relief at the end. Bobby's approval was obvious. He left the piano and took her hand to take a bow in acknowledgement of the applause.

'Okay,' she said to him as they drank stewed tea with Kate and Jerry in the hall after the event. 'What did you think of my playing?' It was a brave question.

'I think,' he said pensively, 'that it would be better if ...'

'If you stopped being so critical,' Kate interjected.

Jodie hid her face behind her hair. She didn't want a scene here. For once it was Bobby who showed restraint. He turned towards Jodie. 'What I was saying was that I think it would be better if you played more often … like in the folk group with me.' He spoke softly and she sensed a little mischief. 'Although,' he continued with a grin, 'there may be a little self-interest involved in my assessment.'

'I'll think about it,' she replied with a smile.

She thought about it all night. It would be hard work playing for him, but playing with him tonight had challenged her to improve, so maybe he was right.

25

It was silent on Sunday morning when Jodie arrived in Dernham. She took her time walking across the fields, shading her eyes against the dazzling winter sun. She pulled her woollen hat tighter round her head and re-wrapped the matching cream scarf around her neck to keep out the bitter wind. Last time she had driven to the house it had been dark, but today she could see the canal from the bridge over the river that passed through Bobby's village; no wonder he adored it.

There wasn't a soul in sight as she arrived at his house. It was easily recognisable by its stone wall; all the other houses were bordered by hedges. She slung her bag over her shoulder, opened the gate quietly as if she was disturbing something sacred, and walked up the gravel drive, conscious of the crunch of every step. The garden was meticulous. She stood on the imposing doorstep and rang the bell, turning back briefly to survey the view, amazed at the statuette fountain to her right and the gnarled old tree to her left. She faced the door quickly when she heard footsteps approaching.

Bobby's sister came to the door. Jodie tried not to look surprised. Elaine looked nothing like Bobby; her mid-brown hair was long and straight and her face was more angular.

'Come in. Bobby's busy with a pressing matter.'

Jodie looked concerned. 'What's the matter?'

'See for yourself,' Elaine shrugged, 'he's in the kitchen.'

As she stepped inside the house she could hear shouting. The old portraits frowned at her from the sweeping staircase and she felt small and insignificant.

'Go through,' Elaine said, directing her past the study on the right. She cautiously pushed open the kitchen door. Blond hair and angry words flew in all directions as Bobby shouted at his father. None of his descriptions had prepared her for the reality. She spoke softly to him in a moment when he sought to catch his breath, aware that her tone must have betrayed her shock.

'Bobby,' she said, and he turned and looked at her.

Colin seized the advantage, pinning Bobby to the wall. Bobby attempted to push his father's arm away with his hand but the grip around his neck tightened, and Bobby stopped fighting as he struggled to breathe.

'You must be Jodie. Now you can see what he's really like,' Colin taunted, suddenly letting go and causing Bobby to fall over.

Bobby picked himself up, brushed down his trousers with his hand and answered the taunt himself as he led Jodie towards the door with anger seething just below the surface. 'Get stuffed.'

Colin stormed after him but Bobby shut the door quickly. Jodie was shaking. Home to her was a place of retreat from the evil of the world. *How can he cope when the evil world pervades his home?* she thought.

'Why do you talk to him like that?'

There was no accusation in her voice, only concern.

'He's an evil swine and I wish he was dead.'

She put her hand on his arm to quell his anger. 'But you sing love songs and hate your own father. How can you reconcile the two?'

He wrenched his arm away with more force than was necessary and snapped, 'Don't lecture me.'

She'd obviously got a bit close to the conflict in his heart. As she stood in the garden, leaning against a tree, she was desperately trying to keep a grip on her emotions. *What right have I to lecture him?* He longed for his father's acceptance; she knew that and she felt ashamed of adding to his torment. He looked away when she caught his eye. She pushed herself away from the tree and walked over to him.

'I'm sorry. It made me feel insecure, frightened even.'

He took her in his arms. 'I never wanted you to see that,' he motioned towards the house, 'but I could never hate *you*.'

Jodie spoke quietly. 'If you harbour hate in your heart you have the capacity to hate anyone.'

She watched him flinch as he loosened the embrace. He took her by the hand and his breathing slowed, but the pained expression remained and he didn't look up as he spoke.

'I know you're right,' he nodded. 'I'm terrified of becoming like him.'

That was Jodie's deepest fear too but she wasn't about to tell him. She put her arm around his waist and leant on him. 'It can't help to talk to him like that?' she ventured again.

She felt the question was safe now that his anger had subsided, although, like the retreating tide, it would inevitably return.

'How would you deal with it? I'm not allowed to disagree with him on anything. Mum and Elaine bow to his every whim. I'd rather be dead than live like that.' He paused for breath. 'In fact in my view they already are dead. If I challenge him, he attacks me. If I don't, he controls me. To give in is to sell my soul.'

Jodie heard what he said but it was beyond her experience. She looked up at him and he kissed her gently, took her hand and squeezed it, then he led her toward the gate as she changed the subject.

'That's a beautiful old tree.'

'It's a walnut tree, it's stunning but it's planted in hell.'

'Why do you stay?' she asked, genuinely puzzled.

She waited as he carefully considered his answer; maybe he didn't know why, or perhaps he had never given it thought. Whatever his reason, she couldn't understand. He remained quiet for a few moments and eventually they came to a bench overlooking the village green. He sat down and drew her next to him, holding her close.

'My mother,' he said, looking at the ground.

Jodie pulled away from him slightly. 'Does your father hit your mother?' She asked him, shocked.

'Not normally,' he replied.

Jodie sat up, looking right into his eyes. 'Bobby there is no "normally" about hitting a wife.'

She saw the embarrassment in his eyes and wished that she'd said nothing.

'I have seen him hit her,' he said softly, 'and I tried to stop him so he attacked me instead. I know she's quite dopey, but it's the anti-depressants that do that. I don't know what he'd do if I wasn't there.'

'But it's not your responsibility Bobby,' she said.

'I know, but I'd never forgive myself if ...' he didn't finish the sentence.

'Anyway,' he said eventually, filling the silence. 'I know it seems stupid, but I hope that by staying here my dad will eventually appreciate me for who I am.'

His dream seemed unrealistic to Jodie but right now he needed a friend and she didn't want to hurt him by telling him the truth. Maybe her granddad could do that.

Jodie jumped up. 'I've got an idea,' she said dragging him by the hand. We can walk through the village over the bridge and across that field that says, "Beware of the Bull".'

'Where there's never been a bull,' Bobby interrupted.

'Yeah, and up the hill to Overton Barrow and call in at Granddad's for lunch.'

Bobby looked anxious, 'But he's not expecting us.'

'He's my granddad,' she exclaimed.

An easy silence rested between them as they walked to the other side of the village. Apart from her granddad, Jodie had never felt at ease like this with anyone. It was a disturbing thought in some ways, one which made her feel vulnerable but excited. A voice called to them from the other side of the road and as she looked up she saw the local vicar.

'I guess we won't be seeing you this morning then?'

Bobby mocked, 'You just have.'

'I meant in church,' the reverend replied with raised eyebrows.

'I'm a bit busy this morning but don't worry, the demon organist will be there,' Bobby glanced at his watch, 'in fact he'll be there practising already.'

'Oh dear,' the vicar said, looking flustered, 'he always gets there before me and hints that I arrive a bit late.'

Bobby couldn't keep a straight face but teased him anyway. 'I've told you before, Rev, you should get a motorbike.'

'I'd get my cassock caught up in the wheels,' he laughed.

Jodie couldn't help laughing as she pictured the scene.

'You could tuck it up and sit on it,' Bobby replied with a dead-pan face. 'Anyhow Rev, Dad's in a really bad mood today so don't listen to the miserable old sod.'

Jodie and the vicar replied in unison. 'Bobby!'

With a quickened pace, the vicar headed towards the church as Bobby and Jodie continued on their way, and the church bells called the faithful to worship. They came to a stile that led to the field, and Bobby helped Jodie over, lingering as he caught her in his arms. She took no persuading to rest there and leant her head on his chest where she could hear his heart beating, pounding fast. She knew in that moment that she had fallen in love, and she guessed by the pace of his heartbeat that the feelings were reciprocated.

She knew she could get hurt again but it was too late. For a few short moments she felt secure, which would probably be a rare feeling with Bobby. *Who can tell what a future with Bobby will hold?* she thought.

26

Jodie had finally relented, although many times since she had regretted playing the violin for The Cobwebs. Bobby not only gave one hundred percent but he expected the same from everyone else. The band practised for two hours every Thursday in readiness for the folk club on Friday. Her laissez-faire attitude irritated him sometimes, she could sense that. The rest of the group tended to appease him rather than face his wrath. Nobody but Jodie would have dared to walk through the barn door nearly half an hour late without giving prior notice. He spoke to her with heavy sarcasm.

'You deigned to grace us with your presence, thank you.'

She sensed his restrained anger.

'It seems appropriate to visit one's subjects when one's schedule permits,' she replied smugly, waving a royal arm.

The smirks on the faces of the rest of the group were quickly replaced by broad grins. Jerry burst out laughing. He had always told Jodie that Bobby had met his match in her. She casually took off her jacket, got out her violin, walked over to where he stood sulking and kissed him on the cheek. 'Sorry,' she said softly.

She had him over a barrel and they both knew it. He sighed heavily. The practice had degenerated already as she sought to tune the violin, so he sat down.

'Sometimes I think you do it just to humiliate me,' he said morosely.

'Aw come on Bobby,' she said with feeling as she walked away, 'not even you can live up to your standards.'

He followed her and took hold of her arm to stop her walking away. 'Unless we practice we let the club down,' he snapped. He let go of her and walked away.

'Folk music isn't intended to be respectable, intellectual middle-class entertainment; if people want that they can attend an organ recital.'

Jerry held his breath awaiting the response, his eyes flitting from one to the other. Bobby grinned and Jerry breathed again.

She stared at the ground; she hadn't intended to humiliate or hurt him, though she was conscious that she had achieved both. Undermining his leadership wasn't fair. She crossed the room to him and broke the uncomfortable silence. 'I'm sorry ...' she said loud enough for everyone to hear, 'I shouldn't have spoken to you like that.'

'Perhaps I do drive everyone too hard,' he said with a sigh. 'I'll try to ease up a bit.'

He gave her time to tune the violin and then they began the practice in earnest.

'Okay,' he announced. 'We'll begin with something lively first, let's sing *Joe the Carrier's Lad*, that will get the club going. After that we'll sing *Pleasant and Delightful*, so they can join in the refrain, and we'll end with a quiet ballad.' They practised *Joe the Carrier's Lad* with Bobby playing the mandolin and Tony singing the verses in his strong bass voice and they all joined in the choruses. After that they began *Pleasant and Delightful* with no break. Every few phrases he stopped them to correct notation, harmonies or rhythm.

'We need to make that first phrase punchier.'

'The bass syncopation needs to be better pronounced.'

'The rhythm's not staying regular enough.'

Jodie looked across at Jerry who grinned. She looked away and smiled broadly. Bobby caught her eye. 'Now what's the matter?' he sighed, sporting an exasperated expression.

'I'm just glad you're easing up a bit.'

Bobby laughed. 'Okay, let's run through that one more time and then we'll have a break,' he said, looking more relaxed.

Jodie began the introduction on violin as instructed.

'Stop, stop,' Bobby cried at the end of verse two. 'Tony, you sing as if you're William starting from, *I'm bound far away*, and in verse three Jodie can sing the parts sung by Nancy.'

'Okay,' Jodie shrugged, 'but I can't play the violin at the same time.'

They started again. She played on the first two verses and choruses, and sang on the third verse and then played the violin for the rest of the song. 'Oh,' he added just as they were beginning again, 'and harmonise the chorus on the violin would you Jodie?'

She saluted him behind his back and he swung round and caught her, almost as if he had expected it. He smiled to himself but she felt guilty. Finally they had performed it to his satisfaction and they stopped for a rest.

Bobby sat alone strumming and plucking the guitar for a while before he tentatively approached Jodie as she sat leaning against the wall. She could see he was hesitant and reached out a welcoming hand.

'Are you still angry with me?' she asked anxiously.

He took her hand and sat down beside her on the old mattress on the floor. 'No, I just wanted to ask you something. Will you teach us that Irish song that you sang the first time you took the floor at the folk club?'

This time she spoke quietly, not wishing to hurt him or humiliate him. 'I'd rather not,' she said without looking him in the eye.

'Why?' he asked. He didn't sound angry at her, just mystified.

'It meant something to me then,' she said, looking up at him.

He stroked the back of her hand with his thumb. 'That's okay. It doesn't matter.' He leant his head on her shoulder with his eyes shut for a moment.

'*Fotheringay,*' he suddenly said out loud.

Jodie looked bemused. 'What about it?'

'Would you sing it?' he pressed further, his eyes holding hers intently.

She was a bit taken aback.

'I'm not sure I could remember it all. It's such a beautiful song and Sandy Denny's voice is so penetrating. I'm not sure I could do it justice,' she concluded, shutting her eyes and leaning back on the wall again.

Bobby rose to his feet and began to play the introduction. He nodded to Tony who came in with an improvised bass rhythm and Jodie began to sing. At first she merely sang from her slouched position on the floor, but after a couple of lines she got up and began to sing with feeling. Not once did she falter over words and Bobby didn't stop her to correct timing or notation. Nobody spoke for a moment or two and it was Bobby who finally broke the silence with a confession that tonight he had learned a lesson.

'You were right. It doesn't necessarily make things better to practice them again and again, that was brilliant.'

Jerry took a pen from his top pocket. 'Get it in writing Jodie.'

Bobby walked towards him as if to threaten him and Jerry puffed out his chest and clenched his fists as though he would stand his ground. Jodie gave him half a smile and went back and sat down. She'd felt the pain in that song: the emptiness, the loneliness and all the memories came flooding back as she sang; memories of how life had felt, alone.

'Will you sing it tomorrow?' he asked.

She looked right through him, barely registering that he was there. 'Okay,' she said.

'Let's finish there,' Bobby suggested. 'First round's on me.'

27

The next afternoon, Bobby sat alone in the bar strumming his guitar. Going home between college and the folk club maximised his chances of incurring his dad's wrath, so he stayed in the bar, alone. Anyway he'd been writing this song for three weeks and it still didn't sound right.

'Damn it,' he exploded, throwing the plectrum across the room in frustration.

He didn't see Jodie watching him from a distance. She tiptoed to where the plectrum lay but he heard her footsteps on the red-tiled floor and turned and looked over his shoulder.

'I didn't mean to disturb you,' she said as she walked towards him holding out the plectrum. He took it and she sat beside him.

'How did you know I was here?' he asked.

She stroked the side of his face as she spoke to him patronisingly.

'I hate to deflate your ego but I didn't, I was looking for somewhere quiet.'

He said nothing, but smiled as he dropped the plectrum into his shirt pocket. Leaning over the guitar, he reached out his hand and drew her closer to him until he could kiss her gently on the forehead. Then he let her go.

'So,' she began, 'why was the temperamental artiste so vexed?'

He looked frustrated again. 'I wrote a song three weeks ago but there's something missing.'

At her request, he played it again. She sat back in the chair with her legs stretched and her feet crossed as she listened, and by the time he'd played it through three times, she was singing along with the chorus and began to tap the side of the chair with her granddad's car keys. Suddenly Bobby stopped playing. 'That's it!' he exclaimed.

Jodie looked puzzled. 'What is?'

'It was missing a beat. It needs a drum or a tambourine or something,' he declared, speaking fast and excitedly. 'Tap that rhythm out as I play it through and see if it works, then I'll sing it at folk club while you play the tambourine.'

She leant across and whispered in his ear. 'It would be more polite to ask me first?'

He put the guitar down and leant close to her.

'I am *so* sorry,' he said with a wink. 'Please would you play the tambourine for me?'

She laughed and kissed him. 'Okay … when?'

'Tonight,' he replied abruptly. 'Just play it really gently. Okay let's run through it once more.' He picked up the guitar and appeared more relaxed as he played this time, nodding to himself as she beat out the rhythm with the keys. As they finished the song she jumped up.

'Let's go somewhere quiet for something to eat,' she suggested. Bobby longed to say "yes" but she had wanted to be alone and he didn't want to intrude, especially as something had obviously been stirred in her last night.

'No,' he said softly as he returned the guitar to its case and carefully closed the lid, 'you came here to be alone, I'll go.'

'I've changed my mind, I want to be with you now.'

She was quite emphatic and it wasn't worth arguing about, but he felt awkward, as if he was in the way.

'Let's just walk to Princes Café,' she suggested, returning the keys to her coat pocket.

They huddled together to keep warm. Despite the cold wind, he had never felt warmer.

'Do you mind if we pop in and see Dale? He was acting strangely when I last saw him,' Bobby asked Jodie.

Jodie shrugged. 'No. That's okay.'

It was just beginning to get dark as they arrived on Dale's doorstep. Bobby knocked on the door.

'Who is it?' Dale called, which was always an ominous sign.

'Bobby,' he shouted.

'Come in,' Dale replied and Bobby could hear the relief in his tone.

As he opened the door, cries of pain pierced the air, and Bobby could see Dale leaning over an indiscernible form on the mattress. He caught sight of the syringe in Dale's hand and instinctively stood in front of Jodie to shield her from it. As he stepped inside, Bobby recognized the person as Alice, the girl he had met here the other day. Dale injected her and the cries soon ceased as she lay flat-out on the mattress.

'She'll be all right,' Dale said, but Bobby noticed Jodie's troubled expression and he wished he hadn't brought her there. She gripped his hand tightly as if she was afraid.

'What can I get you … black coffee or er, black coffee?' he asked clearly a little embarrassed.

'Nothing thanks,' Jodie replied, still half hiding behind Bobby.

'We're on our way to get something to eat,' Bobby added.

'I'm sorry,' Bobby said in his usual exuberant manner. 'I haven't introduced you two have I? Jodie, this is Dale. Dale, this is Jodie.'

'I kind of gathered that,' Dale said. 'I recognised you from his description. He never stops talking about you.'

Jodie looked embarrassed and Bobby rested his arm on her shoulder protectively.

'So,' Dale said, addressing Bobby, 'To what do I owe this honour?'

'Just checking up on you,' Bobby replied as he let go of Jodie and sat on the floor, reaching for her hand and pulling her down beside him.

Dale sat cross-legged in front of them.

'Is she all right?' Jodie asked looking in the direction of Alice.

'Yeah fine, well as fine as any addict is,' he replied. 'I've known her for years, she'll probably be gone again tomorrow.'

Jodie looked a little coy as she asked her next question. 'What about you?'

This time it was Bobby's turn to look embarrassed.

'My life isn't worth worrying about,' Dale replied.

Bobby tensed, awaiting the lecture that he knew would follow.

'Every life is precious,' Jodie said with force, 'and you have as much to offer as anyone else.'

'It's too late,' Dale declared.

Jodie reached out and touched his hand. 'It's not too late until you've breathed your last breath.'

Bobby watched her, intrigued. He was sure from her reaction when they arrived that she had never met an addict before, but she was gentle and compassionate.

'Well,' Dale replied as he moved his hand and held hers, 'that might not be so very far away.'

'But you don't know,' she replied.

Jodie and Dale talked for a little while. She chatted to him about his views on apartheid and other protests and eventually Bobby stood up.

'Time to go,' he said softly.

Jodie reached the concrete steps ahead of Bobby, and as he began to follow her, Dale called him back. 'You have impeccable taste,' he declared with a wink.

Bobby laughed, and caught up with Jodie at the top of the steps. He took her hand as they wandered on to the Princes Café two roads away.

They sat opposite each other in the table in the bay window and Jodie held her hands around the coffee cup to warm them. The café was plain with blue gingham tablecloths and cheap wooden chairs, but the coffee was good and they had homemade scones with jam and cream. As she stared out of the window into the distance Bobby watched her intently. There was something she wasn't telling him, something that had been triggered when she sang *Fotheringay* last night. He looked at her deep, green eyes and wondered, *why would you bother with me?* She looked up and he caught her eye.

'What is it?' he enquired softly. 'What did that song do to you?'

She waved a hand dismissively. 'It's something from a long time ago, when my parents and my brother died in a car crash.'

Bobby felt embarrassed and became agitated. 'I'm sorry, I'm so sorry. I shouldn't have pried. I didn't know. Is that why you came to live in England?'

'No, my family had already moved here because of my dad's job. My granddad came to be near my mum. I've lived with him since the accident.'

He wanted to ask more but he didn't want to appear morbid, and he certainly didn't want to open old sores unless she wanted to expose them. He began to apologise profusely. 'I shouldn't have asked you to sing that song. We can sing something else tonight ... I know ...'

She put her hand gently on his and interrupted his apologetic flow. 'It's okay, I'll sing it.'

That night they sang just as they had practised. They performed as if they had been practising for weeks. The general chatter slowly died away as Jodie began *Fotheringay*, until everything except her lilting voice stood still. There could hardly have been a soul in the place who didn't feel the despair and loneliness, and Bobby felt a mixture of pride and intrigue as she sang.

As he sat down by Jerry he was showered with praise. 'I would use her every time for a ballad, that was haunting and you two work together really well.'

'Thank you,' Bobby replied with a sigh. 'I only wish I played well enough to do her justice.'

Jerry looked heavenward, shook his head but said nothing.

A little later Bobby played his new song and Jodie gently beat out a rhythm on the tambourine. After he had played he disappeared to the bar and Jodie moved up a chair to sit next to Kate and Jerry.

'You performed together as if you've done it all your lives,' Kate remarked.

Jodie raised her eyebrows, questioning Kate's comment.

'It would take me a lifetime's practice to match his guitar skills.'

Jerry laughed aloud and Jodie looked offended. He put his hand over his mouth as if to stop the laughing but she had turned away. Kate shot him a look of disdain and Jerry reached across her to touch Jodie on the arm.

'A few minutes ago, Bobby said that he wished that his playing could do justice to your voice.'

She smiled now, and her sulky expression lifted as Bobby appeared. As folk club president, he took his responsibilities seriously, and strode off to mingle with the members. He took Jodie by the hand and led her away to help him.

At the end of the evening she left before him. He walked her to her car before returning to clear away.

'See you soon,' she called out of the window as she drove away.

'Sooner than you think,' he replied after she was out of sight.

28

'Surprise, surprise!'

Bobby turned up uninvited at Jodie's house the next morning and burst through her bedroom door. Kate had tried to bar the way as she opened the front door but Bobby was undeterred. He didn't care if it *was* Saturday or that Kate thought it was too early. The noise he made could have woken the neighbours, or according to Kate, the dead. Jodie sat up with a start but quickly began to laugh. She put her finger to her lips to tell him to be quiet, but nothing would quell his enthusiasm this morning.

'Come on,' he urged loudly. 'Get out of bed.'

He turned up the radio until the volume was intrusively loud and shouted, 'Wakey wakey!' at the top of his voice.

Jodie looked at him seriously now. 'Turn it down, the neighbours will complain.'

He swung around to see Jerry leaning on the doorpost in his dressing gown.

'I didn't know you were here,' he said, startled. He looked at Jerry and wagged his finger as he spoke. 'And don't tell me that you came around here this morning, not dressed like that you didn't.'

Jerry just smiled patronisingly.

'Come on, come on,' he said enthusiastically as he turned back to Jodie. 'Get dressed, we're going out.'

He marched out of the room and waited in the lounge with Jerry. Kate put a mug of coffee down on the table in front of him.

'Thank you,' he replied graciously, 'I'm glad to see that women still know their place.'

She threw a cushion at him with great force so he picked up the coffee and hid behind it.

Jodie came in dressed but still looking a little sleepy. Bobby jumped up and bent down on one knee at her feet, clutching her hand and began to quote, "Take me to you, imprison me for I, except you enthral me, never shall be free."

Jodie raised her eyes heavenward and smiled. 'Get up fool,' she said.

'I'm glad you're taking the court jester out for the day,' Kate said.

Bobby mimicked her and she turned slightly and whacked him around the head with her arm, much harder than she had intended. He put his hand to his head and she quickly apologised.

'I'm sorry, I didn't mean to hurt you.'

He fell to the ground clutching his head and gasped as he hit the floor. Kate looked frightened and stooped down beside him. Suddenly he sat up.

'Aha,' he said, 'you can't get rid of me that easily.'

'Sorry,' he said looking ever so slightly sheepish as he got up.

'Are you ready?' he said to Jodie.

She led him to the settee and pushed him hard so that he sat down. 'Sit there and wait quietly,' she said as if scolding a naughty boy, 'I haven't finished my coffee yet or put my make-up on. If you'd tell me where we're going, I could get ready.'

He pulled her down onto his lap and whispered to her, 'I've borrowed Elaine's car and we're going to London to the National Art Gallery and then to a West End show.'

Jerry spoke to nobody in particular. 'Kipling once said that, "The silliest woman can manage a clever man but it needs a very clever woman to manage a fool,".'

Bobby looked at him as if he had been betrayed. 'Thank you Jerry,' he replied with a dead pan face.

Jodie kissed Bobby on the cheek and went off to change. Suddenly she turned around looking anxious. 'I've just realised ...'

He cocked his head on one side as he interrupted her, 'It's

124

okay. I've let Granddad know you won't see him today.'

She smiled, a genuinely loving smile. 'That's okay then. I didn't want him wondering why I hadn't turned up.'

'Go!' he said sharply clapping his hands, and she went.

Kate glanced over at him. 'You are an egotistical bully.'

He looked her square in the face. 'Excuse me, I may be egotistical but I am *not* a bully.'

She shrugged and left the room.

Bobby became serious. 'I really can't see what attracted you to Kate.'

'Maybe I just can't resist auburn hair,' Jerry grinned.

'Now that's a good basis for a relationship,' Bobby replied.

Jerry took a packet of cigarettes from the pocket of his flowery shirt and offered one to Bobby, who stared at them in disbelief, screwing up his face. 'What are these?'

'They're menthol. Kate bought them, she thought they were healthier.'

Bobby burst out laughing as he put the lid down on the packet. 'Have one of mine,' he offered, taking a packet from his jacket pocket.

Jerry looked at Bobby's mischievous smile and a broad grin slowly crossed his face as he took one and lit up.

'Thanks,' he said. 'Kate isn't all she seems to be on the surface. She just speaks her mind. You always know where you stand with her and she gets things done.'

'I always know where I stand with her, but she'd drive me mad,' he retorted.

'I think the feeling would be mutual,' Jerry replied as Kate returned.

Jodie appeared in a black mini-skirt, white ribbed polo-neck sweater and black velvet jacket with knee length black boots. Her black make-up and dark hair created a stunning effect.

'Wonderful,' Bobby remarked, taking her hand. 'Let's go.'

She was silent in the car while Bobby babbled incessantly. He suddenly realised he was performing a monologue and stopped himself mid-sentence.

'I'm sorry, I'm talking too much. What are you thinking?'

'I was just wondering,' she said, 'which person is the real you.'

Bobby laughed. 'Just a minute,' he said and stopped talking while he manoeuvred a major roundabout. Once he was sure he was on the right road he began again.

'We all act. I mean, I know Kate thinks I'm arrogant, but the truth is, I lack confidence so I act.'

He hoped she believed him. He was baring his soul and he had no way of knowing what she was thinking.

'That's exactly what Granddad said about you,' she said softly, 'but I told him he was wrong.'

Bobby kept his eyes steadfastly on the road as he spoke. 'That's quite unnerving. When I am with him I feel as if my thoughts are naked. It's as if he answers what I'm thinking.'

He parked the car on a side road behind Ealing Broadway station and walked the short distance to the underground station. They didn't have to wait long for a train to Oxford Circus and on arrival there, they got on a train to Victoria Station. The streets were busy and he took her hand as they wandered past Buckingham Palace. He lit up a cigarette as they started down The Mall.

'I haven't been here since I was a little girl,' she said.

He couldn't help wondering what life had been like for Jodie as she grew up. She never said much; one day he would find out.

29

As they approached Trafalgar Square it began to feel like Christmas to Bobby. The enormous Norwegian Christmas tree dominated the square. For Bobby it held a kind of splendour in its simplicity. He gradually slowed his pace until he stopped and when he looked up, Jodie was watching him. She laughed.

'What were you thinking?' she asked as they walked on.

He was embarrassed; afraid to share his thoughts for fear that she might mock them. He glanced up at her. 'There's something awe-inspiring about that scene,' he said stopping again as he looked up at Nelson's Column. 'The top seemed so far away when I was a child.'

They crossed the road towards the National Gallery, passed by the main entrance, closed for extensive building work, and queued by the West entrance. As they waited, he watched a child looking up at the four columns, and he flinched as a childhood memory flashed uninvited into his mind. He remembered looking up at those columns, and the jolt of his father's hand pulling him into line.

The harsh words resounded in his head. 'Walk properly.'

'Bobby?' Jodie jolted him back to reality.

'Sorry,' he replied absently, 'I was far away, or rather, long ago.' He had shared his anxiety with no-one. Over the last few weeks, snippets of memory had invaded his consciousness, which he found deeply disturbing. He evicted the thoughts, took Jodie's hand and proceeded through the corridors, past the noise of the building work, to a quiet place in the Central Hall.

'I'd really like to see the Christmas exhibition,' he announced.

'That's just here in the Board room,' she said as she scanned the plan in her hand. 'Let's go.'

'When I see a painting of the nativity I want to creep into it and kneel beside the manger,' he whispered.

Jodie raised her eyebrows, 'You're insane, Barron.'

He didn't look her in the eye; he was still staring at Giusto Menabuois' painting. He sighed. 'Christmas at home is soulless, sterile even. The nativity scene is wild and exciting, yet simple.'

They moved slowly on and as they stood in front of the next painting, Bobby quietly read the text aloud, "The growing love and veneration of Mary required that the scene of her motherhood should be as dignified as possible." He was excited and animated as he rambled on. 'Isn't it incredible that you can tell so much about the era of a painting by its style? It relates to so many aspects of society, culture, environment and the writings of the time.'

'Yes,' she replied but he wondered if she was listening. He took her hand as they wandered slowly through the rest of the exhibition.

'Now it feels like Christmas,' he said as they went downstairs to the canteen on the floor below.

'Do you like Christmas?' she asked him, wrapping her hands around the white canteen cup. He didn't know how to answer.

'Not in my house, but I like the idea of it,' he replied. 'What about you?' he asked, rather than risk further interrogation.

'Christmas,' she replied wistfully, 'is a mixture of memories good and bad, happy and sad.'

He laughed at her reply which was totally uninformative. Once they'd finished the coffee, they wandered back to the Central Hall as they discussed where to go next. Jodie ran her hand over the highly polished leather seats and looked up in awe at the high ceilings.

'This place is so ...'

'Majestic?' he offered, without looking up from the catalogue.

'Bobby, do you come here often?'

'Are you chatting me up?' he asked winking at her.

'It was a serious question,' she said, looking offended.

'Okay,' he said, resting his hand on her knee. 'Two or three times a year.' He pointed back to the catalogue. 'What did you want to see apart from the ceilings and marble door frames?'

'I'd like to see The Execution of Lady Jane Grey,' she said absent-mindedly.

He sported a wicked grin. 'What time do you think that's likely to take place?'

She looked up at him quizzically for a split second before she hit him. The look he shot her feigned remorse and she laughed.

'Anything else? We've come all the way to the National Gallery and you only want to see one painting,' he said.

'Van Gogh,' she said suddenly.

'Okay,' he said getting up. 'Let's go and see the nineteenth Century French School section first then.' He took her hand again and pulled her up off the seat.

'Rooms twenty-one, twenty-two and twenty-three,' she said looking at the plan. As they stood in front of the painting she had longed to see, he looked from her to the painting and back to her again. His father would admire this art.

'Why did you want to see it?' he whispered, as if he stood on holy ground. She didn't answer him for a long time and he wondered if his voice had reached her wherever she was.

'Well …' she said slowly. 'I've seen a picture of it and the story fascinates me.' She stopped.

'And?'

'The tragedy is striking. She looks young and vulnerable, a personification of innocence expressed so clearly by the light emanating from her white satin dress. It has so much energy, from the despair of the distraught courtiers to the indifference of the awaiting executioner.'

She stopped and he stood back to look at the painting. He could feel what Jodie described and it troubled him. *I wonder*, he thought, *if I have shut out any interest in this type of art, simply because my father enjoys it?* 'How old was Lady Jane when she died?' he asked, still speaking barely above a whisper.

She shrugged as she walked away from the painting. 'Seventeen?' she suggested.

He followed her around the room, more enchanted by her than by the art. When they passed through to the next room he took his time studying Van Gogh.

'What are you thinking?' she asked him.

'He broke free of boundaries, Delaroche worked brilliantly within them, but Van Gogh broke free.'

'And what does the picture make you think and feel?' she asked. Bobby stepped back as if to avoid the question.

'You probably don't want to know.' His reply was evasive for fear of exposing the extent of his inner turmoil.

'Try me,' she said.

'He broke free of the system but went mad in the process, which gives me no hope.'

He didn't see the concern etched on her face as they moved on towards Monet's paintings.

'What do you think about Monet's paintings then?' he asked her, deliberately changing the subject.

She tilted her head to one side as she studied *The Water Lily Pond*. 'I reckon,' she said mischievously, 'that Monet painted this in your back garden.'

He suppressed a grin as he replied. 'If he did, then I think he got the wrong impression.'

She laughed aloud and took his hand.

'Idiot,' she said softly.

They moved on slowly. Whenever he went there, Bobby had the desire to create something supremely beautiful. He picked out a painting here and there which captured his imagination and waited and watched as Jodie did the same.

It was dark when they left the gallery, precisely 5.35pm, he could read it on the illuminated face of Big Ben in the distance. 'We'll eat in an hour or so. We don't want to be late for the theatre,' he said casually.

He took her hand and crossed the Strand, strolling towards the river. A restful silence hung between them as they stood and gazed across the Thames. Bobby watched the reflection of the lights playing on the ripples of the water, while Jodie rested her head on his shoulder.

'What show are we going to see?' she asked.

'Surely you can guess,' he said. 'You mentioned it a couple of weeks ago.'

She looked puzzled for a moment before realisation dawned on her face.

'*Hair?*' she guessed with a laugh as she cuddled up closer to him.

They retraced their steps so that they wouldn't get lost in the side roads. Passing through Trafalgar Square again, they crossed over to St Martin's Place into St Martin's Lane, in full view of the beautiful church of St.Martin-in-the-Fields, conspicuous by the impressive spire with its silver clock on the blue background. Jodie stopped to examine a statue that Bobby had never noticed before, a memorial to Edith Cavell. She read the inscription aloud.

'Patriotism is not enough; I must have no hatred or bitterness for anyone.' Logic told him that she couldn't have known what the inscription said, but it still hurt him. He consciously dismissed thoughts of rejection as she read the words on each side of the statue. 'Humanity, Sacrifice, Fortitude and Devotion.' He had chosen a quiet bistro, with background music playing quietly enough for them to hear each other speak. His tastes were simple; the prices were reasonable but not cheap. Jodie chose onion soup followed by coq-au-vin, and he chose duck paté as a starter and grilled Salmon for the main course. She shrugged as he asked her what wine she liked, so he ordered a Burgundy. At the end of the meal, the waiter poured the coffee and retreated to his station.

'You're really not spoilt at all, are you?' she said.

He fiddled nervously with the coffee spoon. 'I have little respect for my father, but one area of his life I do respect is his handling of money. He has certain luxury items like his car, the grand piano and his record player but in everything else he's careful but not mean, even to me. I think I've learned a few things from him.'

As he stirred the coffee, Jodie tightened her grip on his other hand, and the strength of the emotion he felt almost frightened him. He took a deep breath, but his heart raced so fast that he felt sure he must have given away what he was feeling.

Jodie changed the subject. They talked a while before he called the waiter over, paid the bill and tipped him discreetly. Bobby helped her into her coat before they left the restaurant and set off for Shaftesbury Avenue. It felt cold after the warmth of the restaurant, but being with Jodie gave him a feeling of warmth which the cold air couldn't quench. Her openness and honesty made him feel alive. When they reached the foyer of the Shaftesbury Theatre, Jodie broke the silence with a question.

'Do you go to the theatre often?'

Bobby grinned; this reply would probably surprise her. 'Actually ... no,' he said. 'I did as a child, but I never enjoyed sitting still that long, and a lot of what we saw was boring.'

He was hoping that *Hair* would be conceptually different to anything he had seen before and would be fast moving enough to keep his attention. He knew that he had nothing to worry about from the time the curtain went up to reveal the main character, Claude, sitting centre stage as the tribe mingled with the audience. This promised to be different. All he really knew about the show was that it was loosely based around the lives of the two writers, and it was quite definitely intended to question the traditions of contemporary western society and suggest the possibility of a gentler hippy lifestyle.

It certainly did that as the cheerful early scenes and even the nude scene at the end of the first act didn't seem out of place.

'What do you make of it?' Jodie asked Bobby during the interval.

'It's different,' Bobby replied.

'And that,' she replied, 'is non-committal.'

He laughed. 'Intentionally,' he said. 'It makes me think, but I'm not sure that everything about the past is bad, or that all of hippy life is that free.'

'I love the music and the characters. I'm not sure I got what the nudity was actually about though,' she said.

'If I remember rightly,' he said, 'the nude scene took its inspiration from an anti-war protest, but I guess it is also about freedom.'

In the second half, Jodie jumped as a monk was set on fire and fled the stage, depicting the protest of Tich Kwong Duuk, who set himself alight in protest at the persecution of Buddhist monks in South Vietnam. One onstage killing after another destroyed the peace presented in the first half of the musical, and Claude himself had to decide whether to burn his draft card or go to war. He went to war.

At the end, as Claude's body lay on a black cloth, the cast sang 'Let the Sunshine in,' and invited the audience on stage, which Jodie flatly refused to do despite Bobby's remark that, 'even Princess Anne went on stage.'

'Well?' she asked him on the way out of the theatre. 'Did you like it?'

He looked pensive and didn't formulate a reply instantly; indeed he didn't speak until they were outside the theatre. 'I would like to have seen it before it hit the commercial theatre,' he remarked. 'It's exciting in what it attempts to do and it certainly succeeds in putting the message across,' he paused for a moment.

'But,' she laughed.

'But I think by going commercial the message of freedom is being exploited, which is ironic somehow.'

He looked up, suddenly aware that she was smiling broadly.

'Sorry,' he said, 'that was a bit heavy.'

She shook her head as she laughed, which made her hair rock rhythmically. He drew her closer to him, so close that he could smell her sweet, floral perfume. He could hardly believe that he had her at last.

'What did you think?'

'Actually,' she grinned, 'I didn't really think at all. I loved the simple raw nature of it, the songs and the atmosphere.' She talked enthusiastically all the way to Tottenham Court Rd, only relaxing once they were on the westbound train. She leant heavily on his shoulder and eventually fell asleep.

He spoke her name gently as they approached West Acton, giving her time to wake up. The cold air hit them as they emerged from the station at Ealing Broadway and she shivered a little. He took his scarf off and wrapped it carefully around her neck. It was a relief to reach the car and despite the totally inefficient heating system, it felt warmer than walking in the cold night air. By the time they arrived home Jodie was almost asleep again. Bobby jumped out of the car outside her flat to say goodnight.

'Thank you,' she said softly as she rested against his chest. He held her tighter and she kissed him sleepily. Whatever else he had messed up in life, he knew he was right about Jodie.

30

'Can't we go home, Jerry?' Jodie pleaded the next Monday evening at the folk club in the city, where they had been invited as guest singers. 'He's so drunk.'

'I'll see what I can do,' Jerry replied without the slightest hint that he had any intention of moving. 'He's even more sociable when he's drinking, must be light relief from reality,' he slurred, leaning too close to Jodie.

She pushed him away. 'If that's light relief, God help him,' she snapped.

'At least he's enjoying himself,' Jerry said.

'Yes,' she spat, 'and in the morning he'll feel more miserable than ever.'

If Jerry had been sober he would have conceded defeat by now, but his judgement was heavily impaired. 'Oh let him enjoy himself,' he slurred.

Jodie began to walk away. 'If you won't rescue him then I will,' she said causing Jerry to recoil.

She approached Bobby gently, looking directly into his glazed eyes. 'Let's go home. Give me the glass, you've had enough.'

He drank the remainder down in one and handed her the glass. 'That's not funny,' she said, suppressing a smile.

'Just one more ...' he said, leaning on her shoulder.

'No more,' she replied firmly, moving away from him.

'Song, I meant,' he winked. 'They've asked if we'll perform one more.'

Jodie let out an exasperated sigh. 'Then can we go?' she begged.

'For you my darling, anything,' he said, leaning on her so heavily that he nearly knocked her over. She pushed him away and raised her eyes in despair.

'I'll sing,' she insisted, 'if you sing, one word won't be

135

discernible from the next.'

Jodie took one look at the band and wondered what hope they had of performing a nursery rhyme never mind a folk song. She walked briskly over to Jerry.

'We're singing one more song and then we're going.'

'Has Bobby agreed?' Jerry slurred.

'Yes,' she answered with a toss of her head as she walked back to find Bobby.

'Jodie's going to sing,' Bobby explained.

'Though God knows how with a bunch of drunks!' she exclaimed.

'Oh come on my gracious, be a little precious,' he begged and then he laughed. 'No, I mean, come on my precious, be a … oh you know what I mean.'

They stumbled through *Let no man steal your Thyme*, but to cries of 'more!' Jodie led them away and Bobby led them back again. 'Play a jig,' she suggested with a sigh, 'then nobody has to sing.'

She watched him as he led them into *The Irish Washerwoman* on the mandolin. How he managed to get his fingers around the notes in his state she had no idea, but she smiled to herself and joined in with the violin. This time as they finished she led him away and he followed.

The club president thanked them over the microphone as they were leaving and Bobby took a bow as they left and nearly tripped one foot up with the other. The occupants of the van were extremely noisy on the way home and Jodie became increasingly irritated. When Jerry arrived at her flat she was relieved and tired.

'I'll get out here and walk,' Bobby announced.

'Don't be such a bloody idiot,' Jodie said impatiently, 'you'd end up frozen to death in the gutter.'

The rest of the band laughed and Jodie walked away.

Neither Jerry nor Bobby made it into college until lunchtime the next day, and Jodie had little sympathy.

'Don't ignore me honey,' Bobby pleaded in the canteen.

'You might prefer it if I did,' she retorted, turning away from him.

Kate strutted up and banged her fist on the table between Bobby and Jerry causing them both to jump. She pointed at Jerry, 'He drove the van home in that state,' she said to Jodie.

'I know. I was in it,' Jodie replied.

'More fool you, I would have got a taxi,' she shouted banging her fist once more on the table.

Jerry held his head and groaned. As she marched off, all their faces registered relief. Jodie sat down. 'She blames you Bobby. She thinks you're a bad influence on Jerry.'

Jerry got up indignantly. 'I find that insulting. Does she think I have no mind of my own?'

'Sit down,' Bobby said with a grin. Jerry sat down and Bobby and Jodie laughed.

Jerry suppressed a grin and got up again. 'I'm tired of her telling me what to do,' he remarked. 'I'm going to give her a piece of my mind.'

When Jodie eventually stopped laughing she offered him words of advice. 'Maybe now isn't the best time to do that,' she said, before adding with a wink to Bobby, 'unless you fancy being eaten alive.'

'I think I'll just have a cigarette,' he said as he got up to go outside. Bobby and Jodie followed him. As soon as they were outside Jerry offered Bobby a cigarette, Bobby winked and produced a joint. Jodie snatched it from Jerry's hand and threw it to the ground, crushing it under her heel. Bobby looked up briefly at Jerry but said nothing. There was an uncomfortable silence for a few moments. Bobby took her hand, which she instantly and angrily snatched away.

'You're serious aren't you?' he asked with an expression of surprise.

'I'm worried,' she replied without looking at him, her tone softer now. He put his arm around her shoulder and with the other hand took the cigarette which Jerry offered him, lighting it from a match with a sly wink unnoticed by Jodie.

As he blew the smoke over his shoulder away from Jodie, Bobby noticed Kate wandering alone across the field. He looked back and nodded to Jerry pointing with his cigarette in Kate's direction. Jerry walked off with a mock expression of fear.

'I'm sorry,' Bobby said as he gently stroked her hair. 'I don't mean to upset you.'

I know,' she replied.

He held her close. 'I promise I'll stop.'

On the other side of the field Kate ranted on at a rather cowed Jerry.

Bobby laughed, 'Should we call in a United Nations peacekeeping force do you think?'

'They'll sort it out,' Jodie shrugged as they walked away. 'Please don't drink like that again tonight,' she begged, serious now.

Bobby kissed her forehead. 'I won't,' he said earnestly, adding, 'I bet Jerry won't either, he wouldn't dare.'

That evening, Jerry was stone cold sober and Kate had come along to ensure his sobriety. While she was at the bar, Jerry leant over to Bobby. 'She gave me a lift,' he declared pointing with his eyes.

'How did you come?' Bobby asked with a mischievous grin. 'Broomstick?' Jerry laughed but Jodie gave Bobby a sharp nudge with her elbow.

Just as Kate returned from the bar the resident group broke into *Drink the Winter Away*. Bobby leant across to Jerry. 'We could *do* this,' he remarked with an evil glint in his eye.

Kate pointed a finger at him aggressively, 'You can *sing* that if you like Barron, but *he* is not doing it.'

Bobby muttered under his breath loud enough for Kate to hear, 'Disguise our bondage as we will, 'tis woman, woman, rules us still.' Jodie kicked him sideways under the table and he shut up. Just at that moment Rick, a quiet student who had played the guitar and banjo for Bobby since the group's inception, came across and put a hand on Bobby's back.

'What are we playing tonight?'

Bobby grabbed the stool behind him, placed it next to his, and patted it. 'We're starting with *Good English Ale.* Well, Jerry isn't because he's not allowed,' he laughed which prompted another kick under the table from Jodie. 'Next we'll sing *The Green Grass,* Tony will bring it in on bass and then we'll play it just as we practised it. After that I've asked to do a solo.'

Jodie joined his conversation. 'What're you playing?' she asked him.

His answer was evasive. 'It's a new song. Rick do you want a drink?'

'Fab thanks. I'll have a pint of Newky Brown.'

'Don't forget your promise,' Jodie called as he set off for the bar.

He winked. He seemed to her to be perfectly happy without drinking heavily and she remarked on the fact to Jerry as she passed him on her way to the front to sing.

'See, he's perfectly sociable without drinking.'

Jerry beckoned her closer and as she did he leant across and whispered, 'Maybe he's using something else.'

Jodie shook her head gently.

'You'd better be joking Jerry, I'll kill him.'

She knew Jerry wouldn't have told her if he hadn't been concerned. She hurried to the front to catch up with the others and they ran through their songs with ease.

Bobby sat on a stool to sing his solo, accompanying himself on guitar. The tune was captivating but the words seemed muddled and meaningless. The wry grin on his face told Jodie that there was something unusual about it.

After he'd finished he leant over to the microphone to announce that Rossini had once said, "Give me a laundry list and I'll set it to music". He could say no more until the laughter died down. 'Well,' he continued, holding up a piece of paper to the audience, 'I found this one at college the other day and couldn't resist the challenge.' He got up, took a short bow, and returned to his seat. Even Kate managed a laugh but she still didn't speak to him. At the end of the evening Jodie gave him a lift home in her granddad's car and instantly began her interrogation.

'What did you take tonight?'

He stalled; a tactic he'd practised over many years. 'What makes you ask a question like that?'

Jodie didn't reply, just waited for him to answer.

'Speed,' he replied eventually.

Nothing was spoken between them for what seemed an eternity to Jodie. She struggled to hide her anger. 'Just this morning you told me you'd stop.'

'You said that you didn't want me to drink tonight,' he said quietly.

She pulled into the nearest lay-by. Her temper was about to explode and she couldn't concentrate on the road. Every muscle tensed. Having turned off the engine she rounded on him.

'Don't treat me like a moron.'

He closed his eyes as if to shut her out. She felt cruel confronting him and after another long interval he opened his eyes and looked directly into hers, unveiling for once his hidden pain.

'You deserve the truth,' he said.

She looked at him and her heart softened again. She reached out her hand and laid it on his arm.

'I can't cope with my dad. I can't cope with the incessant conflict with Kate, and I can't cope with trying to be what you and your granddad expect of me. Everything about my life is discordant. You know the laundry list song?'

'Yeah,' she smiled.

'Well,' he continued, 'laughing is what I expected everyone to do, but it's about my life. The tune was harmonious but is only an external image. The words are what the song is about but they mean nothing.'

Jodie had no reply. She had sensed it, but was still stunned to hear it from his lips.

That night she sat alone, tears were easier alone. In many ways he was the strongest person she had ever known, and in others he was the weakest. She hoped with all her heart that his strength could overcome his weakness, or maybe her granddad was right, perhaps his weakness needed to overcome his strength.

31

Kate marched through the swing doors into the canteen the next lunchtime, bristling with excitement. She pulled up a chair and sat down confidently opposite Jerry.

'You look pleased with yourself,' he said casually.

'I had an interview for a Christmas job and I got it,' she replied jubilantly.

Jodie laughed. 'By the look on your face you're not shelf filling this year.'

'No!' she exclaimed, 'I've landed a plum job in an art studio.'

Jodie looked surprised; jobs in art studios were rare. 'Now I'm impressed,' she replied with a smile, which dissipated the instant she saw Bobby's face.

'The best in Brockton,' she declared. 'I can't believe my luck,' she continued.

Jodie put a calming hand on Bobby's arm but he pushed her away. She knew he'd told her the truth last night; he was close to the edge.

Jerry leant across the table with a look of disbelief. 'You're working for his dad?' he said, as he pointed at Bobby who had pushed the chair back from the table and was about to leave.

'Their conflict is nothing to do with me,' she said forcefully. 'His father is a brilliant graphic designer and I need the experience.'

Bobby said nothing, but Jodie watched as his eyes narrowed and his lips pursed tightly. She waited for the explosion. He slammed the cup back on the saucer, flung the chair aside and walked briskly away.

Jodie called after him, but he ignored her as he pushed open the swing door with nearly enough force to take it off its hinges. Jodie jumped up quickly to follow him, shooting

Kate a glare of contempt as she looked back over her shoulder. He was leaning on the wall outside the canteen lighting up a cigarette. She looked into his eyes. *Whatever can I say to pacify him?* She gently laid a hand on his arm and he flinched; he did this at the slightest touch these days.

'Do you want to talk?' she asked soothingly.

'What good will that do?' he snapped, and she withdrew from him a little.

'I'm sorry,' he said, taking a long drag of the cigarette.

She leant up against his chest and felt him shiver. 'You shouldn't have come out without a coat,' she said hugging him closer to her. 'Let's go back inside. We can sit in a corner away from everyone else.'

He agreed, too passively for her liking. His hand held hers limply as they walked back through the canteen doors and sat down as far away as possible from Kate and Jerry. His distress was undisguised and he was jittery.

'I feel as if I am living in a private hell.' He stopped, and she longed to know just what was going on inside his head. 'Go on,' she urged.

'I keep going in the vain hope that things will improve, but they don't, they just get worse.'

She was way out of her depth. She longed to take him in her arms and tell him that things would be okay, but she had no assurance that they would be.

'Why does it seem so bad, Kate working for your dad?' she asked.

Bobby looked past Jodie to where Kate and the others sat. He sighed and consciously turned back to Jodie.

'She's just like him. That's why I dislike her so much.'

However difficult she found Kate, she was still her friend and flatmate, but for Bobby's sake she didn't interrupt.

'If it was anyone else I would feel that my private hell was being invaded,' he continued, 'but with Kate I feel as if my private hell is being made public. I don't want my humiliation made public.'

What could she say? She pulled her chair closer to his, reached out and took his head in her hand and kissed him slowly until she felt him relax.

They were interrupted by Lena, one of the canteen ladies. 'Oi, you two, d'you mind, we're trying to clear up in 'ere now.'

Jodie laughed and jumped up. 'Come on gorgeous. Let Lena get on.'

They were headed towards the door when Lena called after them. 'Hey gorgeous, is that your jacket over there?'

'Oh yes, thank you,' Bobby replied as he crossed the canteen to fetch it. He was quiet and subdued but at least he could smile again.

Jodie dreaded going back to the flat, she was furious with Kate. When she walked through the door Kate was already ensconced in the lounge.

'Hi,' Kate called cheerily. Jodie took off her coat and went into her bedroom without a word. If she said anything now, she would explode. She sat down heavily on the end of the bed. Her thoughts were interrupted by a firm knock on the door.

She felt ill-prepared to face Kate but said. 'Come in.'

Kate instantly confronted the issue. 'I know you're angry with me, but it's brilliant for my career prospects.'

Jodie stood up, 'I don't give a damn about your career, people matter more.'

'Exactly,' Kate replied, 'his father seemed all right to me, in fact he was very helpful about the areas where I need experience. You really could do so much better than Bobby,' she said.

Jodie consciously sought to control her rising anger. 'Just leave me alone,' she said through clenched teeth.

Kate shrugged as she turned towards the door. 'He's a self-centred, attention seeking, spoilt rich bastard,' she said, slamming Jodie's door behind her.

Jodie lay on the bed and cried. She had spent many hours

easing his stress and hers was beginning to get the better of her. She needed her granddad.

'Hi Granddad,' she said on the phone to him, 'are you busy?'

Her granddad was never too busy to see her, and she was grateful for the lift he offered her.

'What's happened?' he asked intently once they had arrived at the cottage.

She related the events of the last few days, crying intermittently. He patted the seat next to him on the settee and she got up and sat beside him. She shared her fears with him, the stress that Bobby was under, the massive project which had to be completed over the Christmas holidays, the bookings he had undertaken for the group, not to mention running the folk club and working for his dad. Everyone else was looking forward to Christmas, but she knew that Bobby dreaded it.

'I'm worried,' she said, 'he pushes himself more and more and I'm afraid he's heading for a breakdown.' She told him how Bobby had been keeping himself awake with amphetamines and began to sob again.

'Part of me is afraid that Kate's right, but I love him,' she sobbed.

He took a deep breath and let it out slowly, an indication of the lecture to come. She closed her eyes, listening to his words of wisdom.

'But don't forget that Kate doesn't know him as you do.'

'Maybe, but he's got worse since we started dating,' she said with emotion.

Granddad didn't speak in haste and when he spoke there was only kindness in his voice.

'I think things have got worse at home, but maybe he has never had anyone in his life who gave him enough security to dare to face the past until he met you. Maybe he's doing that for the first time, and I guess it's hard not to run away and hide.'

She looked up at him with an anguished look. 'Are you suggesting that it could get harder for him?'

Granddad put his arm around her. 'It's possible.'

Sometimes Jodie felt that the truth was too much to bear.

'He's so unpredictable. When he's fine, he's the most wonderful company, but the next day he can be in the depths of despair.'

She sighed and dabbed her eyes, desperately trying not to let her make-up run. Her granddad sighed. 'When you first knew him he barely acknowledged the pain in his life, but now he admits what he feels. He's longing for his dad's approval and he's almost at breaking point. When he gives vent to his anger it won't be a pretty sight, and when his anger gives way to sorrow and grief it will be heartrending, but maybe he has to break before he'll let go.'

32

Bobby had a sense of foreboding as he approached Jodie's granddad's house. He jumped deftly over the stile where the field meets the road, near the back of Granddad's house, gathered his courage, and knocked sharply on the door to warn of his arrival before opening the door and walking in. He was warmly greeted by Granddad and the glow of the log fire. Granddad offered to take his coat.

'I'll keep it on for a few minutes,' Bobby said, 'it's freezing out there.' He moved close to the fire, took off his gloves and rubbed his hands together.

'We're about to have a sloe gin. Would you like one?' Granddad asked.

Jodie jumped up. 'I'll get them.'

Bobby smiled as he caught sight of Jodie. Today she wore jeans, as usual, and a tie-dye T-shirt, which looked as if it hadn't been ironed. Despite the cold, she had bare feet. He eventually walked away from the log fire.

'How's the doll's house coming on?' he asked as he wandered over to the table in the corner and opened the tiny door at the front of the hand-crafted house.

'You've put lights in,' he exclaimed before Granddad had a chance to reply. 'Do they work?'

'Plug it in and see for yourself,' Granddad said.

One by one he tried all the switches. 'Fab,' he declared as he peered inside. Then he laughed. 'You've wallpapered the walls.'

He turned back to face Granddad. 'Are we going to finish the game of Monopoly?' he asked.

Granddad smirked. 'Jodie's not keen.'

'I bet she's not,' Bobby replied as he strutted across the room to the kitchen and opened the door. 'Carter, you're a coward,' he said without going inside.

She pushed the dark hair back from her face. 'What are you talking about Barron?' she asked in a patronising tone.

He leant against the kitchen doorpost. 'Monopoly,' he replied, gazing at her intently. 'You're scared I'm going to win.' He moved out of the way as she came through into the lounge with a tiny tray.

'I have Mayfair,' she whispered in his ear as she passed by. She put the tray down on the coffee table.

'And I,' he said, leaning over her shoulder in an annoying manner, 'have Park Lane.'

Jodie handed her granddad the glass, put Bobby's down on the coaster on the coffee table and sat beside him.

'Don't be so cocky, Mr. Mouth, get the board out,' she ordered, grinning behind his back. Bobby jumped up and carefully moved the board onto the coffee table.

'He'll cheat, you should be banker,' Jodie said to her granddad.

'I find that offensive,' Bobby replied, looking at her with indignation. 'I don't need to cheat to beat you.'

She shot him an evil glare and he turned towards her and kissed her. She pulled away. 'Then you won't mind proving it,' she said, tossing her hair back behind her shoulders. She reached across Bobby and handed the box to Granddad.

'It was your move Jodie,' Granddad said casually.

'Yes,' Bobby added with feeling, 'you're the old boot aren't you?'

She slapped his arm.

'I was on Liverpool Street Station,' she said, and then she threw the dice.

'Seven,' she said aloud, and moved the boot around to Community Chest. Granddad handed her two hundred pounds as she passed "Go" and then he complained because she hadn't landed on Old Kent Road or Whitechapel Road.

'Take a card,' Bobby ordered.

'Don't rush me,' she said and picked up a card from the pile.

'Doctor's fees pay fifty pounds,' she read.

'The psychiatrist, no doubt,' he laughed.

'Very funny,' she replied as she shot him a supercilious glare. 'Granddad, it's your go.'

Her granddad threw the dice. 'Five,' he said as he moved the car round to Regent Street. 'I'll buy it. Three hundred pounds.' He transferred the money to the bank. 'Now I've got the set.'

After the first hour Jodie got up to make coffee. She still had Mayfair in her possession, and Bobby still had Park Lane.

'You two are very stubborn,' Granddad laughed. 'Would you sell Park Lane to me?'

Bobby looked shocked. 'Certainly not,' he replied. 'I want to win.'

After another hour, in which the stalemate remained, Jodie began to yawn. 'Can we finish another day?' she asked. 'I'm tired.'

Granddad made a note of where all the pieces were, who had what property, and how much money they had. He put the board on the shelf in the cupboard under the stairs as Bobby got up and put his coat on.

'Don't go a minute,' Granddad said, peering out from the cupboard. 'I want a word with you first.' Bobby took his coat off again.

'You don't mind if I go to bed do you?' Jodie asked Bobby.

'Are you staying here tonight then?' he asked her.

'Yeah, I'm borrowing Granddad's car and bringing everything back here for the Christmas holidays.'

He took her in his arms. 'Okay I'll see you tomorrow then.' He kissed her on the cheek. 'You're here so often, I don't know why you don't live here,' he said as she turned to go upstairs.

'I'd rather be close to college in term time,' she replied.

'She'd never get there on time if she lived here,' Granddad said to Bobby as he motioned towards the settee.

149

'What did you want?' Bobby asked.

'Jodie is worried about you.'

Bobby cocked his head to one side and with a quizzical look asked, 'Because of Kate?'

Granddad shook his head lightly, 'Because of drugs.'

Bobby looked away, embarrassed. He wasn't proud of it; he had lost control of life somehow. He had difficulty sleeping at night and staying awake in the evenings.

'Why?' Granddad asked. The question didn't condemn him as it did from his father.

'I haven't slept well lately,' he replied, conscious that he was only telling Granddad half the truth.

'So why don't you talk to your doctor?' Granddad replied, fixing Bobby with a penetrating gaze.

Bobby sighed and looked away to avoid her granddad's gaze, uncertain what to say. *What would he think of me if he knew?* Something in his manner demanded truth. 'My life feels out of control,' he began. 'I can't sleep when I want to, and I need to be awake when we're playing at folk clubs so I control it with drugs.' He glanced up very briefly and waited for the reply.

At first, Granddad simply nodded, then he moved and sat next to Bobby on the settee. He spoke gently but firmly. 'You can't afford to live your life in a state of drug induced energy. Jodie's afraid that you're pushing yourself too close to the edge.'

Bobby's breathing had become shallow; he didn't want to hurt Granddad or Jodie. What he saw in Granddad's face surprised him; there was no anger, only concern, kindness even.

'Can I be really honest?' Bobby asked, knowing his pain was showing anyway.

Granddad nodded. 'I wish you would.'

Bobby continued. 'I've tried so hard to please my dad but he's never satisfied. Part of me wants to give up, but then I feel that maybe I'm just not trying hard enough. In my head I feel that I will never be able to please him, but I can't stop hoping.'

Granddad looked thoughtful and gazed into the log fire for a few minutes before he spoke, slowly and deliberately.

'But you're tearing yourself apart trying.'

Bobby leant back in the chair and closed his eyes, a picture of exhaustion. *How can I just give up, he's my flesh and blood. How can I be so ungrateful for all the things that my dad has given to me and the inheritance of art and music, which I love so much?*

For all his disagreements with his dad over style and content, it was his dad who had taught him so much about technique; he had merely adapted it to suit his own purposes. *What would it cost me to try harder, to give back something to the business, to attempt to please my dad instead of always opposing him? Surely I owe him that.* He jumped up, not wishing to hear any alternative.

'I can't just give up, he's my dad. I owe him so much.'

Granddad replied to him softly. 'You can't be the person that he wants you to be, it's destroying the person you really are.'

Bobby turned briefly to look Granddad in the face. In that moment even the master actor couldn't conceal his confusion and agony, and he knew that Granddad would recognise it.

'Perhaps he's right and I'm wrong.'

Deep inside he was disturbed by the look that Granddad gave him, but whatever the outcome he couldn't just give up; not yet.

As Bobby left, Granddad's words rang in his ears: 'You're making a mistake.'

33

Jerry stood motionless just inside the canteen door plucking up courage. He was torn between Bobby and Kate. He watched Bobby from a distance this morning. *Whatever can I say to him?* He thought, *Surely he's going to consider me a traitor. Let's get this over with.* He walked casually across the canteen and sat down opposite Bobby, glad that they were alone.

'I'm sorry. I had no idea that Kate ...'

'Forget it,' Bobby interjected waving a hand dismissively in front of him. 'It's not your fault.'

'Are you busy on Tuesday, after work?' Jerry enquired.

'That depends what you want and who you're likely to be with,' Bobby replied curtly.

'I just wanted a quiet drink alone in the village.'

'Okay,' Bobby nodded slightly without even a hint of a smile.

He was quiet, lifeless even. Jerry watched Bobby's eyes light up as Jodie entered the canteen. She flicked her hair off her face as she walked with energy across to Bobby and flung her arms around his neck. His eyes met hers as he turned his head; he looked content. She threw her jacket over the back of the chair beside him and laid her bag on the table. Despite the energy she displayed, Jerry noticed dark shadows under her eyes.

'Will you bring me a doughnut if you're getting a drink?' Bobby asked.

'Sure,' she replied.

Jerry smiled but he was worried. He didn't want to be angry with Kate, but he was glad that she was going home for the weekend before starting work on Monday; he could just about manage to stay civil with her until Saturday morning.

After eating the doughnut, Bobby got up to leave.

'I want to get on with the sculpture. I'll see you later.'

Jodie blew him a kiss and he smiled. Jerry was grateful; he'd been waiting for a chance to talk to Jodie alone.

'He's so jittery,' Jodie said, opening up an opportunity for Jerry.

'I've never seen him this bad,' Jerry said, leaning across the table.

Jodie said nothing, just stared at him as if she was looking through him. Eventually she spoke. 'Is it my fault?' she asked, looking away from him.

Jerry reached his hand across the table and placed it on hers. 'I didn't mean to infer that. You are the only ray of light in his life.'

'Thank you Jerry,' she said with a smile.

'Honestly,' he insisted, 'his eyes light up when you enter a room.'

'Yeah, but sometimes I don't know how to cope with him.'

Her eyes were welling up. He didn't want to cause her unnecessary anguish but he wanted her to face the truth. It would be hard, if not impossible, for Bobby to trust him now. Just as he was about to speak, Kate came into the canteen and marched over to them.

'Excuse me,' Jerry said with abnormal politeness, 'but I'm having a private conversation with Jodie.'

'I can see that,' she replied, shifting her gaze too obviously to Jerry's hand on Jodie's.

Jerry felt Jodie move her hand slightly and he defiantly tightened his hold. He surprised himself, and he could tell by the expression on Jodie's face that he surprised her too. He had never spoken to Kate like that before and her anger was evident as she walked away. He removed his hand and ran his fingers through his long curls. 'Sorry Jodie,' he ventured. 'Where was I?' He picked up where he had left off. 'I've seen the pattern over many years. It takes him roughly three days to get over a violent attack, less if it's verbal but this is something else. He's been like this for over a week and I don't see any signs of it abating. It'll only get worse when he

153

starts working for his dad.'

Jodie stroked the back of her neck. She had always seemed strong and courageous in the face of Bobby's suffering. She was clearly struggling to speak. 'Last night we played Monopoly and he was relaxed and good fun. But he's not listening to my granddad at the moment.'

'I know,' Jerry replied. 'He told me himself that there is no point discussing the problems with your granddad because he can't act on the advice.'

She smiled but it was a weak smile. 'You'd better go, Kate is not looking too pleased,' she said. 'Thank you for being honest.'

Jerry hoped that she had what it took to stand by Bobby but he couldn't be certain any more.

'Finished your tête-à-tête,' Kate snapped as Jerry sat down opposite her.

The weekend suddenly seemed a long way away. He looked away, desperately trying not to over-react. 'You didn't stop to consider the implications for anyone else, did you?'

Kate looked at him defiantly. 'It isn't anyone else's business. Bobby doesn't like it because he's spoilt.'

Jerry slammed his fist on the table, ignoring the pain it sent through his hand and the silence that fell on the canteen as his anger got the better of him. Kate looked stunned but he couldn't stop now. 'Don't you dare call my best friend spoilt,' he said. 'You are the one who's had life easy, you can't begin to imagine his pain because you've never really suffered.'

He stormed out leaving Kate looking bewildered. He caught up with Bobby in the art room. Bobby picked up on Jerry's disquiet.

'Are you alright?' he asked as Jerry sat down heavily.

'No,' he replied gazing into the distance, 'I just lost my temper with Kate in the canteen.'

Bobby let out a long low whistle. 'Not good for the super-cool image.' He wiped his hands on his apron and turned his chair around to face Jerry.

'Listen,' he began. 'I'm touched that you defended me, but I don't want you to do anything on my account. You must have had good reason for going out with her, though God knows I can't see it. Don't feel you *have* to be angry with her.'

Jerry managed a faint smile and nothing more than, 'Thank you.' He respected Bobby for his kindness and his ability to overcome, but increasingly he was worried about his future.

34

Bobby was delighted at the success of Rick's end of term Christmas party at his parents' house in Brockton, although in reality it could hardly have failed since it had been advertised by the entire folk group. Rick wasn't as extroverted as the rest of The Cobwebs, but to Bobby he was indispensable.

For the first few hours the party buzzed with music and talking, and Rick served drinks and changed the records. By midnight the party began to fade. A few people had left, some had departed to the kitchen and others had disappeared into the bedrooms. Finally, there was room to dance.

'Come on,' Bobby said, taking Jodie by the hand and attempting to drag her up from her seat on the floor.

'Wait until someone else has started,' she groaned.

'Somebody has to be first,' he said, pulling her to her feet.

Those who could still stand joined in for a while, but by 2am even the most energetic were beginning to flag and at 3am Bobby sat strumming Rick's guitar and singing *Chimes of Freedom*.

Jodie laughed as she interrupted the song. 'How do you do that? It sounds just like The Byrds.'

'Oddly enough,' he replied, 'I practice.'

She looked at him irritated and slapped him on the arm. 'I realise that. I didn't learn the violin by staring at it either,' she replied.

He laughed at her suppressed anger. He loved her indomitable spirit; she could be kind and compassionate but underneath she was tough.

With pursed lips she rephrased the question, 'Technically speaking, how do you make that sound?'

He forced himself to keep a straight face. 'Sorry, I can't resist it,' he said with a genuinely apologetic expression. 'It isn't a good thing to do because I strain my voice in my throat. So there's a chance I'll destroy my voice before I'm thirty, but I'll probably be dead by then anyway,' he shrugged.

At that moment Kate came in with a tray of mugs which she placed down on the coffee table at the side of the room. She glanced across at Bobby with her hands on her hips.

'So,' she said patronisingly, 'are you planning on smoking yourself to death, drinking yourself to death, overdosing on something or simply getting beaten to death?'

Bobby winced before replying caustically, 'Poisoned by your tongue in all probability.'

Jodie watched him anxiously but he merely winked at her as he continued to strum quietly until he felt drowsy. He put down the guitar and fell asleep with his head on her lap, oblivious to the ensuing argument.

She stroked his head gently, whispering to him. 'You sleep baby, you're safe here.'

Kate shot her an angry glare. 'For goodness sake, there's no need to be melodramatic. He's in more danger from his own stupidity. He probably will be dead by the time he's thirty and most likely by his own hand if you ask me.'

Jodie's reply was almost a whisper. 'Well I didn't, and I don't believe he will be dead by the time he's thirty.'

She turned her head away from Kate's gaze and Jerry smiled kindly at her. 'Neither do I.'

'Thank you,' Jodie said.

With Jerry's help, she gently lifted Bobby's head from her lap onto the giant cushion next to her, before laying her head down beside him.

She woke before him in the morning and helped Rick to clear the night's devastation. 'Will your parents mind the mess?' Jodie asked.

'They knew what to expect,' he replied. 'If I find a box will you collect up the empty cans and bottles while I collect the glasses?'

'Sure,' she replied as she began to pick up cans and bottles. After she had searched the entire house, she plonked the box down on the breakfast table in the kitchen. She looked around for a tea towel and began to wipe the glasses.

'Is Bobby okay?' Rick asked.

She looked up at him twice before concluding that she could trust him. 'Not really. I think the speed is making him worse.'

Rick nodded thoughtfully. 'Is there anything we can do to help?'

She shook her head. 'I don't think so.'

She tried to hide her face as she wiped tears from her eyes but Rick noticed and put his arm around her to comfort her, unaware that Bobby had appeared in the doorway.

'Jodie?' Bobby spoke her name, clearly shocked at what he saw. He looked from Rick to Jodie and back again with fire in his eyes. He turned on Rick and punched him in the shoulder. Rick tripped over a chair as he attempted to back away with a look of bemusement on his face.

Jodie screamed at Bobby and grabbed hold of his arm, physically trying to restrain him as he pushed Rick back against the wall.

Jodie forced her way between Bobby and Rick. 'Hit me too,' she shouted at Bobby, 'then you could be just like your father!'

He squinted at her through angry eyes and turned to walk away with his fist still clenched.

Rick called after him with more strength than Jodie would have thought he had in him.

'Neither Jodie nor I would be that thoughtless or cruel to someone we care about. Her tears were for you, I was merely comforting her in your absence.'

Exhausted with stress, Jodie collapsed in tears. 'Sometimes you make me so angry,' she said, shaking her dishevelled hair back from her face. She took the expression of accusation on his face personally, and felt it deeply. She wanted to help him, but she couldn't even cope with herself right now. She sat down on the kitchen chair and laid her head on her arms, on the table.

Rick headed for the door looking Bobby in the eye as he left. 'You owe her an apology. She worships the ground you walk on. Too much speed mate, it's making you paranoid,' he added accusingly as he walked away.

When Bobby approached Jodie, she pushed him away, got up and walked across to the other side of the kitchen. 'Get away from me,' she shouted, turning her face away from him.

'Jodie,' he ventured softly, 'I'm sorry.'

She collapsed in tears again and he drew closer, stepping back as she rounded on him.

'Go away!'

He sat in the lounge with his head in his hands.

Jerry attempted to console Jodie but she sent him away too. 'Just leave me alone,' she said.

It was a while later that Jerry attempted to enter the kitchen again.

'Leave me alone,' she said again.

'Jodie.' She recognised the voice that gently called her name. Her granddad pushed past Jerry and moved closer to her. She got up and fell into his arms.

'Thank you,' he said to Jerry, who had started to walk away.

Eventually the crying subsided as Granddad held her close. 'I think you'd better come home,' he said.

Granddad loosened his grip on Jodie and motioned to a chair as she described the events of the last twelve hours. He moved close to her and sat down, taking her hand in his. Her tired puffy eyes looked into his penetrating gaze and he smiled. 'Bobby has never made himself totally vulnerable to anyone. He just can't trust.'

He gently squeezed her hand. 'He wants to trust, but the people he should have been able to trust betrayed him.'

Jodie nodded gently, her eyes almost closing with

159

exhaustion. 'All right,' she said weakly with a heavy sigh, 'I'll talk to him.'

'Let me talk to him first.'

Bobby quietly strummed, not even putting down the guitar as Jodie's granddad entered the room. Everyone else retreated.

'You can't hide behind the guitar, the music or anything else,' Granddad said.

Bobby sat up and put the guitar down beside him.

'Thank you,' Granddad said as he leant forward in the chair.

'I think you need to ask yourself whether you really want to learn to trust, because you'll go a long way to find someone as devoted to you as Jodie.'

Bobby nodded. 'I know that, in theory ...'

Granddad interrupted him sternly. 'Maybe you're denying yourself the love of others, in a vain attempt to gain the love of one who can't give it. Come and see us in the morning.'

Bobby nodded as Granddad got up to leave.

'Granddad?' Bobby called as the old man reached the door. Granddad turned around with his hand still on the door handle. Bobby continued. 'Do you think she'll let me apologise?'

Granddad nodded. 'Make it brief, I want to take her home.'

Bobby followed him into the kitchen sheepishly. She took a few steps towards him and he quickened his pace towards her, embracing her as he reached her. 'I'm sorry,' he whispered softly.

'Come on Jodie,' Granddad urged as he left the house with his arm around her.

'Thanks again, Jerry,' her granddad said quietly, as he passed him. 'I'm glad you rang.'

35

Bobby arrived at Jodie's granddad's house at 10.15am. Granddad's hushed tones as he opened the door told Bobby that Jodie was still asleep, so he tiptoed into the lounge. He didn't take off his coat or stop to admire the progress in the doll's house as he usually would.

'Have a seat,' Granddad said.

Bobby kept his gaze firmly on the ground as he sat down.

'Why have you stopped talking to me?'

Bobby hated the way her granddad did that. For a moment he was dumbstruck, jittery even. He wanted to speak but struggled to get the words out.

'I keep having flashbacks. They only last seconds but ...' His voice failed. He closed his eyes, running his fingers through his hair as Granddad replied slowly, deliberately.

'You mean flashbacks in time?'

Bobby nodded, 'I've always remembered certain things that he did to me but these are worse, really awful memories.'

'That's good,' Granddad exclaimed.

'No,' Bobby replied, distressed. 'I want to forget but no matter how much I drink or what I take, I can't get rid of them.'

Bobby held his head in his hands now as Granddad moved to sit next to him.

Granddad spoke with strength in his voice. 'Those memories couldn't surface until something inside told you it was safe.'

Bobby's eyes didn't stop moving and his mind was working overtime. 'They've only begun recently.'

Granddad spoke to him firmly, 'If you face them, then they'll have no hold over you.'

Bobby nodded gently without a word.

Jodie appeared, still in her dressing gown. She ran her

fingers frantically through her unbrushed hair. 'I must look a sight, I didn't realise you were here,' she said to Bobby as she turned to go back upstairs. He got up and walked towards the staircase.

'Don't go. You still look beautiful to me.'

'Flatterer,' she smirked, but she came back downstairs anyway. He put his arms around her as she reached the bottom of the stairs.

'I'm such a fool,' he declared.

She tightened her hold on him. 'Me too,' she replied.

Bobby leant back and looked at her carefully.

'What?' she said nervously.

'Nothing,' he said with a smile, not wishing to expose his innermost thoughts. She looked much younger without make-up, innocent even. Seeing her like this he didn't want to let her go. He wanted to hold on to her and protect her, which he thought was ironic, since what she most needed protection from was him.

'Bobby?' Jodie said softly.

'Yes honey,' he replied, almost absently.

'Do you think we should go to see Rick?'

'Not now', he said, and he felt her tense. He paused before continuing, 'Not until you've got dressed.'

She pushed him away and hit him playfully.

'I'll get dressed,' she said as she turned around and ran back upstairs. Now he was sure she'd forgiven him for last night. She blew him a kiss. 'I love you.' He smiled on the outside but on the inside he wanted to cry. *I know it's true but I wish it wasn't for your sake. I don't deserve you. If you knew the extent of the darkness in my soul, you wouldn't love me. I'm terrified that whatever I do now I will hurt you. If I could die you would recover, maybe there would be some hope, but alive ...*

His train of thought was interrupted by Granddad. 'Bobby?' he said and by the look on his face, Bobby guessed that it wasn't the first time that he had asked the question. Bobby almost looked through him.

'Sorry Granddad. What did you say?'

Granddad laughed aloud. 'Do you want anything to eat?' he asked again.

'No thanks,' Bobby replied. 'I had toast before I came out.'

There was silence for a few moments but eventually Bobby broke it.

'I don't know why I got so angry last night. I'm afraid of losing Jodie. I don't know how I'd cope without her.'

Bobby got up and walked towards the window, gazing out. It was a long while before Granddad spoke.

'You need to cope with yourself first. You'll always find it difficult to love someone else if you don't love yourself,' Granddad said.

'After what I did to her last night, I hate myself,' Bobby replied. 'But I do love her, I really do love her,' he said as he turned around to face Granddad.

Granddad looked up at him. 'If you try to hold a butterfly in your hand, you'll kill it. If you keep a frog in a jam jar it will die.'

'You're right,' Bobby said, gently nodding his head. Out of the corner of his eye, he caught sight of Jodie coming downstairs. She walked across and stood beside him and he put his arm around her shoulder. Neither of them spoke for a long while but the silence wasn't uncomfortable. Jodie spoke first.

'Okay let's go. Rick deserves an apology.'

Bobby took Jodie's hand. He mouthed, 'Thank you,' to her granddad as he left.

They made the journey to Rick's house in Granddad's car. It was a peaceful journey and when they arrived Rick was gracious.

'I'm just glad you sorted it out,' he said, 'you two were made for each other.'

Bobby smiled, but he wasn't sure that Rick was right. He adored Jodie, but he was certain that he was ruining her life.

36

'Put that cigarette out!' Colin shouted the moment he entered the design studio on Monday morning. 'Now!'

Bobby's reply was sulky. 'Sorry,' he muttered, although he wasn't.

He stubbed out the offending article on the inside of the grey metal bin at his side, before making a Nazi salute behind his father's retreating form. He had put in an hour's work before the rest of the staff appeared and when Kate arrived he steadfastly ignored her in a deliberate attempt to make her uncomfortable.

Undeterred she marched up to his desk. 'I'm here, so you might as well get used to the idea,' she said as she stood with one hand on his desk and the other obstinately on her hip. 'Now where do I need to go first?'

He looked up slowly from what he was doing, with a supercilious air. 'That,' he said with emphasis, 'is hardly the way to treat someone if you want their help. I suggest that you start by telling Hitler that you're here. He's in his bunker.'

He waved his hand in the general direction of his father's office and continued with what he was doing. About twenty minutes later Kate reappeared with Colin.

'Bobby,' Colin called from his office doorway, 'come here.'

He rose to his feet slowly and walked casually across the studio; the best he could manage by way of insult was to keep his father waiting.

'Yes?' he replied with as much dignity as he could muster. Colin put a hand on Kate's shoulder, an expression of kindness which he never afforded to his son and it angered Bobby intensely, indeed so intensely that he missed what his father said. 'I beg your pardon?' he replied distantly.

'Pay attention,' Colin snapped. 'I said, take Kate down to

the stock room and show her where everything is kept. Then report back to me.'

He had no choice but to comply. As he showed her around the stock room he spoke casually to her.

'I don't know why he makes such a big deal of this. Everything is stacked in alphabetical order. I can't imagine a single sheet of paper having the audacity to allow itself to be stacked in the wrong place on his shelves.'

Kate managed a slight smile. 'It must be a nightmare when you get deliveries,' she remarked.

'A tedious bore,' he replied. 'He has a major delivery this afternoon which I imagine I will be sorting.'

He went through everything he could think of, described their uses, and was about to leave when he suddenly turned around. 'Any questions?'

She looked less confident in this environment and her reply was almost nervous. 'I expect I'll think of them later.'

'Then ask them later,' he retorted, 'but remember, I don't mind helping you, but if you attempt to make my life difficult, I can do the same to you and probably with much greater effect.'

With that he went back upstairs to the studio and she followed. He knocked on his father's office door and opened it before his father had a chance to reply.

'Wait outside,' his father snapped.

Bobby sighed. He was desperate for a cigarette to calm his nerves and he'd only been here an hour and a half. Eventually his father opened the door, causing Bobby to almost jump to attention; he hated the way that he did that.

'What do you want Kate to do next?' he asked.

Colin addressed himself to Kate. 'Take a seat at the desk there, Kate,' he said, pointing to the other side of the studio. 'I'll be there in a few minutes. Don't worry, it takes time to get used to everything.'

He turned to Bobby. 'Come in,' he said curtly. 'I want you to take this information about this sports club and design them an advertising leaflet. Just do a few thumbnails first but make it snappy because they want a couple of ideas to look over this afternoon. Then go to lunch and be back …'

'In time to sort the delivery,' Bobby interrupted him and was half way to the door when Colin called him back.

'Listen, young man,' he said, 'time is money and you are more than twice as quick as anyone else when you put your mind to it.'

If Bobby hadn't known his father better, he would have mistaken it for a compliment. In an effort to please his father, he chose to ignore the fact that it was *his* time and his *father's* money. His attempts to keep on the right side of his father paid off and his father appeared pleased, if a little shocked, at the compliance.

By the next day the dutiful son act was beginning to take its toll. He was tired, irritable, and chain smoking whenever he wasn't working. By 11am on Tuesday, when he was meant to be designing a cover for an album, he was leaning up against the wall in the backyard, smoking. He knew that discovery would incur his father's wrath, but he didn't anticipate being hunted down. As soon as his father appeared, Bobby saw the menacing look in his eye. He dropped the cigarette, stubbed it out and instinctively moved away from the wall. His father spoke through clenched teeth, pointing in the direction of the studio.

'Go to my office.'

Bobby desperately needed the old bravado but he felt jittery and weary. He hadn't intended vexing his father, he had simply wanted to calm his nerves. His dad kept him waiting in the office, which he assumed was a psychological ploy to increase the tension. If that was the case then it was successful. His father walked through the doorway and sat down at the imposing desk, leaving Bobby standing.

'Well?' he asked aggressively.

'I'm sorry,' Bobby said with genuine humility, 'I just

needed a cigarette.'

Colin stood up and marched around to the other side of the desk and Bobby flinched.

'Give them to me,' his father demanded with his hand out. Bobby could feel his hand shaking but tried desperately to disguise it. He took the cigarettes out of his pocket and handed them to his father who promptly threw them on the floor and stamped his heel on them. Bobby showed no emotion as his father dismissed him, but he was furious.

'Get on with your work,' his father snarled.

For the rest of the day Bobby didn't put a foot wrong and by the time he caught up with Jerry in the pub in Dernham, he was a nervous wreck.

'I've really tried,' he told Jerry, 'but I just can't do it. Because of that one incident he wouldn't let me have a lunch break and I've just finished. I've been working since 8.30am without a break.'

Jerry offered him another cigarette. 'That's ten hours,' he declared, counting on his fingers before lighting Bobby's cigarette with a match.

'Ten and a half,' Bobby corrected.

He took a long slow drag of the cigarette. 'One more drink, then I must go. Jodie's coming round at half eight.'

After another pint and a quick game of darts, Bobby left for home.

'Your dinner's in the oven,' his mother said feebly, 'I expect it's a bit shrivelled up by now.'

He shrugged. 'That's okay, I'm not really hungry.'

She launched into a lecture about the importance of regular, balanced meals. Bobby just wanted to be left alone and to get away from his father, who was sitting reading at the kitchen table. Bobby's patience snapped and he rounded on his mother.

'Okay!' he shouted as he moved towards the door into the hallway. 'You've made your point.'

Colin looked up from his book and turned around. 'Get

back here and sit down … and don't shout at your mother.'

Bobby returned and sat down at the opposite end of the table muttering, 'Sorry, that's your prerogative isn't it?'

He assumed that his father hadn't heard because he merely looked up and went back to his book. Bobby found the food unpalatable at the best of times.

Jodie aided and abetted his escape by arriving early. She knocked at the front door and Bobby's mum let her in. Breezing into the kitchen she ordered, 'Come on Bobby, let's go to the pub.'

He got up in the knowledge that his father wouldn't challenge Jodie; for some reason he never did.

'I have to change. I'm not going out like this,' Bobby replied.

After a few minutes Jodie called up the stairs. 'Hurry up.'

Colin looked up from his book as Bobby appeared. 'Don't you mind going out with him looking like that?'

He addressed his question to Jodie, but she recognised the provocation aimed at Bobby and replied instantly.

'I love a man in velvet. I probably won't be able to keep my hands off him all night.'

She stroked his burgundy flares as she led him to the door leaving Colin speechless.

The evening was restful and Bobby's anxiety subsided. Not a word passed between them as they walked home that evening by the side of the river. He wrapped his arm around her shoulder and she leant gently against him. They had almost reached his house when Jodie spoke. 'Call around at the flat after work tomorrow and we'll go out.'

Bobby yawned as he stopped and held her in his arms under the private lamppost at the entrance to his neighbour's house. 'We close half-day on Wednesdays and Saturdays but I have no idea what time he'll let me go,' he said.

She leant close to him and whispered in his ear, 'I'll wait', and then added, 'You look tired. I'll see you tomorrow.'

She left as soon as they reached the car and he watched her

disappear from view. He knew his serenity wouldn't last, but right now he felt content. He went in through the front door, called goodnight and went upstairs. He lay on his bed and fell asleep with thoughts of Jodie filling his mind.

37

Bobby's mum knocked softly on his bedroom door at seven o'clock on Wednesday morning.

'Bobby,' she called.

It took him a while to answer, and when he did he was a bit irritated.

'What is it?' It was still dark and he squinted at the alarm clock before exclaiming in surprise. 'Good grief Mum, it's only seven o'clock.'

She spoke softly, almost apologetically.

'Your father's not well. He wants to see you.'

Bobby dragged himself out of bed, grabbing his dressing gown from the hook on the back of the door and fumbling a little over the bolt.

'He's been sick all night,' his mother explained.

'He's not dying I suppose,' he replied as he tied his dressing gown.

His father was propped up in bed with a bowl at his side. An acrid smell of vomit filled the room. Despite the sickness, his father was only marginally subdued as he barked instructions.

'Hannah will be in but you'll have to do my work.'

The reply had not even a hint of sympathy. 'I'm sure I can sit in your chair all day.'

Colin had all the signs of erupting anger and Bobby felt a twinge of conscience. 'All right,' he said raising his hands in front of him as if to protect himself. 'I'm only joking. I'll do what I can.'

Bobby sat back in bed planning the day. It was the worst possible time of year. At Christmas the studio was in a constant state of frenetic activity. The one advantage was that his dad wouldn't be able to control him all day.

He arrived at the studio at the same time as Hannah and

unlocked the door.

'Where's your father?' she asked with concern.

'He's been sick all night,' Bobby replied.

'Oh gosh, do you think we can manage without him?' she asked.

'No choice,' Bobby said with a shrug as he swung open the door through to the studio.

He stood in his father's office and lit up a cigarette.

'Does he have a work list for today?' Bobby asked as he hunted through the piles of papers on his father's desk. She opened the top left hand drawer and produced a list of jobs to be completed. He nodded acknowledgement and quickly assigned tasks to each member of staff. At 9am the rest of the staff arrived and the studio was quickly in full swing. Bobby was sitting on the edge of Kate's desk helping her design a poster for a disco, when he was interrupted by Hannah.

'I'm sorry to interrupt you but I have a manager of a company on the 'phone wanting to know if we can print all his advertising for him at short notice.'

Bobby jumped off the desk quickly. 'I'll be back,' he said to Kate. He turned to Hannah. 'I'll take it in Dad's office.' When he returned he sported a jubilant expression as he bounced over to Hannah's desk, talking fast.

'If I can have these figures put into an estimate as soon as possible, I'll take them over there this morning. The guy's been let down and needs everything done fast.'

She took the paper from his hand and began to work on it immediately. Meanwhile, Bobby stopped to see how Kate was getting on.

'Brilliant,' he said, surprising himself a little. 'I'd be inclined to reduce the size of the main text a little, make the word "disco" stand out more.' She turned around as he went to walk away.

'What I wanted to do was distort the characters of the word "disco," to make it dance a bit, but I'm not sure how.'

He took up a pencil and a piece of paper and roughly drew a numbered grid with a ruler, writing the word "disco" inside it. Then he drew a distorted grid freehand and filled in the letters. 'Like that?' he asked without waiting for a reply as he saw Hannah approach him.

She handed him the estimate and he leant on the corner of Kate's desk to sign it, before folding it carefully and placing it in an envelope.

'Oh damn!' he exclaimed, thumping the corner of the desk and talking to no-one in particular. 'I can't ride over there on a motorbike and turn up in a leather jacket.'

Simon handed him his jacket and Kate looked up from her work. 'Do you need a chauffeur?' she asked.

He nodded gently. 'Thank you, I hope to see the managing director myself.' As he looked up he saw Hannah watching him.

'Hannah?' he said awaking her from her daydream. 'The 'phone's ringing.' She jumped up and answered it. He lit another cigarette.

'Let's go Kate. I'll help you with the poster when we get back.'

On his way across town he thanked her.

'If we can get this order now, they'll probably put more work our way,' he explained, before suggesting that she come in with him if she was really interested in graphic design, as, "customer relations are an important aspect."

'Thanks,' she replied as she parked the car in the tree lined avenue. He pushed open the heavy front door and stopped off at the reception desk to get directions. They went up the elegant stairs to the first floor office and after a short wait Bobby spoke to the Managing Director personally.

'This is obviously important,' Bobby said after a brief conversation, 'so I'll get the leaflets to you tomorrow morning and everything else by Friday.'

The Managing Director stood up and reached out to shake his hand. 'That's brilliant, thank you.'

'Good, thank you for your time,' Bobby replied with almost a bow.

As he left the office he felt like sliding down the sweeping banister, but he walked down the stairs like everyone else. He got into the car with a spring in his step.

'Now at least the old man should be pleased with me,' he said.

Kate looked sceptical. 'Provided you can make the delivery on time,' she said with a shrug.

He looked at her, incredulous.

'I'll have to work this afternoon, that's all,' he said.

Arriving back at the studio, he motioned to his father's parking space at the front of the building. 'Thank you, the motorbike and leather jacket would definitely not have been the right image.'

Soon after he'd gone into his father's office, Hannah knocked on the door. 'Come in,' he called. She entered looking agitated. 'All these should be signed by your father,' she said, holding out a pile of letters.

He took them from her hand. 'It's okay, I'll sign them.'

He quickly signed them on behalf of his father, R.S.W. Barron p.p. Colin J. Barron and handed them back to her. She looked a little stunned.

'Aren't you going to check them?' she asked. He leant back in the chair and laughed. 'I don't imagine you make mistakes after working all these years for *him*,' Bobby declared.

Hannah laughed. 'By the way, you did a good job with that order.'

Bobby beamed. 'Thank you.'

He followed her out of the room and headed for the kettle. 'Anyone for coffee?' he asked.

Simon got up and took over. 'I'll do that, you've got enough to do.'

At twelve o'clock everyone left and he set about producing the leaflets. At half past two, having finished the work, he had just sat down for a quiet cup of coffee and a cigarette when he heard the bell go. He looked towards the door. *Who could be calling at this time on a Wednesday?* 'Jodie?' he said with surprise, raising his eyebrows and then, after choking on the smoke he had just inhaled, he added, 'I forgot.'

'Kate said you'd be here,' she said as she sat on the edge of the desk where he rested his feet. With great effort he raised himself up and sat beside her.

He leant over and whispered, 'I love you.' She kissed him, before jumping off the desk with an energetic spurt.

'Let's go for a stroll by the river. Come on,' she ordered.

'Yes Ma'am,' he replied with a salute.

'You cheeky rat,' she said as she reached out a hand to hit him.

He caught her arm and pulled her towards himself and kissed her. Suddenly she pulled away from him. 'You're distracting me, let's go,' she said sternly, and then she added, 'and don't forget to lock up or Old Man Barron will be cross.'

'You really are mischievous aren't you?'

He laughed, and began to chase her round the studio. She ran into his father's office and sat down in the imposing chair.

'How dare you come in here without knocking,' she shouted menacingly as he entered the room.

He vaulted the desk nimbly in order to catch her just as she stood up. She held her hand to her mouth and screamed. 'Bobby, no!' and then breathed a sigh of relief as he miraculously missed the piles of papers and grabbed hold of her as she collapsed in laughter. 'Let's go,' she suggested, 'before you do any damage.'

After shutting the papers away in cupboards and locking his father's office door, he emptied the rubbish into the main bin outside the front door. Then he unplugged all the electrical equipment and locked the main doors before they left. He felt her eyes on him as he locked up.

The afternoon passed quickly, too quickly he thought. As they arrived back at the studio hand in hand he casually looked at his watch.

'Oh my goodness, it's five o'clock.'

'And?' she asked.

'Well ... ' he said, flustered and patting all his pockets in search of cigarettes, 'the old man will be expecting me to play for choir practice tonight and it starts at six o'clock.'

He eventually located the cigarettes in the inside pocket of his jacket, and sheltered from the wind behind an oak tree as he lit up. He said goodbye to Jodie at the office, where she'd left the car, and then he raced home.

Rushing through the door at twenty-five past five, he flung the crash-helmet down on the wooden floor and hung up his jacket. His mother appeared looking flustered.

'I know,' he said impatiently, before she had a chance to speak, 'the choir practice.' Then he added under his breath, 'He should have had slaves not children.'

His mother flinched but said nothing as he disappeared into his room to change out of his work clothes. He arrived at the church late and breathless and hung his jacket just inside the door into the north transept. 'Sorry I'm late and sorry it's me. My father's sick, more sick than usual, I mean,' he said with a grin and the choir smiled back at him. 'I'm sure you've sung all this often enough before. Let's run through the pieces quickly,' he suggested, as he took his position at the organ console.

After one hymn, the *Magnificat,* and two anthems, Bobby came down from the organ to talk to the choir. 'Any problems?' he asked. Eventually Dennis spoke up. He wasn't the brightest, but Bobby had known the grocer's son for a long time.

'With that last anthem, I always try to come in at the wrong place,' he said looking down as he spoke.

'You have to come in on a half beat, look ...' Bobby pointed to the score. 'I used to count the beats in my head, still do if it's difficult. Like this.'

He counted Dennis in by beating time with a pencil on the pew. Bobby flinched at the memory of his father beating time on his fingers with a ruler when he got it wrong. 'We'll try it again after a break,' Bobby suggested putting a hand lightly on Dennis's shoulder. 'That okay?' Bobby asked and Dennis nodded as the Reverend flew through the main door looking flustered. He spoke without looking around.

'I'm so sorry I'm late Mr. Barron I've …'

Bobby laughed out loud causing the Reverend to turn around mid-sentence.

'Call me Bobby, please,' Bobby said to him with a grin.

Rev Turner sighed, 'Oh hello Bobby.'

'My dad's sick,' Bobby explained. 'We're just about to take a break.'

Rev Turner patted Bobby on the shoulder as he passed by. 'You mean you want a cigarette?'

Bobby grinned. 'Well that too.'

Bobby knew the score; his father expected Rev Turner to be there in time to hear the practice. God alone knew why.

'Okay now Dennis?' Bobby asked him privately at the end of the practice.

'Yes thank you,' Dennis replied, beaming up at him.

As the choir and the vicar left, Bobby stayed behind playing the old instrument. He didn't play it often these days. When he'd finished, the church echoed with the click, click, click of the stops as he pushed them in one by one. He climbed down quietly, not wishing to disturb the sacred silence. He stood still in front of the altar looking up at the cross. Hearing footsteps he turned around.

'Jodie,' he said, surprised to see her. 'How long have you been here?'

She looked distant, thoughtful. 'I was here for some of the practice. I came to hear you play.'

'Did I meet your expectations?' he asked with a wry smile.

She looked at him in a strange manner that he couldn't

understand as she moved close to him. He wrapped his arms around her as she spoke. 'I was just beginning to think that I understood you a little, and then you play like that.'

He smiled.

Rev Turner walked slowly back into the church humming to himself, unaware that he had company. Bobby smiled and put a finger to Jodie's lips, before suddenly letting out a deep growl, which made the vicar jump. Jodie slapped Bobby on the arm, but the vicar smiled, a warm friendly smile,

'Don't worry,' he said, 'I have to put up with his tricks if I want his services from time to time.'

'No, no,' Bobby corrected mischievously, 'I put up with your services from time to time.'

'Well I'd appreciate it if you'd put up with them more often,' he said with a smirk.

Bobby patted him on the shoulder as he turned to leave. 'Don't worry Rev, the expert will be back soon.'

Rev Turner adopted a more serious tone. 'Listen,' he said, raising a finger to Bobby as if reprimanding one of his choirboys, 'there's more to being a church organist than playing the right notes. Dennis wants you to play again.'

Bobby laughed. 'Yes, but Dennis isn't too bright is he?'

Jodie put her arm around his waist and he put his arm around her shoulder, resting heavily on her. 'The vicar's right,' she said.

Bobby shrugged. 'Oh I don't mean it,' he said, but his final, lingering thought was less positive. *There's no way I can ever hope to come up to my father's level of perfection.*

38

Bobby was clearly busy when Kate arrived at the studio the next morning. She coughed; she still hadn't got used to the strong smell of the ink.

'Hi Kate,' he said without stopping work as he glanced up at the clock. 'You're early,' he observed, collecting together bottles and paper and implements.

'I thought you might need a hand.'

'Thank you,' he replied, and made a point of looking up from what he was doing this time; she appreciated that.

'I know this is a bit cheeky, but could you make me a cup of coffee?' he asked, a little hesitantly Kate noted.

'Sure.'

While she made the coffee in the tiny kitchen area she thought about the last few days; she had to admit that working for Bobby was easier than working for his father. When Colin was there the studio revolved around him, but when Bobby was in charge, it centred around the work. He seemed to sense what was needed and just do it.

'Thank you,' he said to her as she put the coffee down beside him, and suddenly he sensed her interest. 'Have you seen the Rota print in action before?'

'Only something similar at college, but a bit older,' she replied.

He picked up the coffee as he leant heavily on the desk, deep in thought. 'Okay,' he said slowly, furrowing his brow as he sipped the coffee. 'The principle's the same but the machinery is better than at college. In business we can't afford to make mistakes.'

Hannah came through the door. 'Good morning,' she said wearily.

Bobby looked up briefly. 'Are you all right?'

'Just tired,' she answered slowly. 'How's your father?'

'No idea,' he said; there was no animosity in his voice and no interest either.

He turned back to Kate and continued his explanation. 'This is much quicker than the old Heidelberg Platen, but it's useful to be able to use both.'

She watched him with a mixture of admiration, envy and surprise. He was much better at teaching than his father. She was having second thoughts about him. *Maybe I'm wrong; perhaps what I thought was arrogance was enthusiasm.* The rest of the staff arrived and the studio buzzed with activity. Bobby called to Simon the instant he walked through the door. 'Could you get me more ink from the stock room?'

Simon looked briefly over Bobby's shoulder and quickly fetched the ink. Kate noticed the respect Simon had for Bobby. On his return, Simon threw a bottle of ink at Bobby. He caught it deftly. 'Thank you.'

The litho was set up and ready to go when Hannah interrupted him. 'Your father's on the 'phone.'

He looked annoyed at the intrusion but picked up the receiver anyway. 'I can't stop, Dad, I've got the litho set up and I've got a lot to do.'

He was clearly angry at the response he received and Kate couldn't help listening in.

'Because I've got tickets to print. I took a call yesterday from a managing director of a company who had been let down by another studio. I promised him the goods quickly and I've got a very large order and hopefully ...'

His father obviously interrupted him and Kate watched the excitement drain from his face, replaced by anger, and in that moment she knew that she'd been wrong. He put the receiver down without a word, walked into his father's office and shut the door. She could see through the frosted glass door panel that he had laid his head on his arms on the desk. She was fighting herself. *Shall I go to him or will I only make it worse?* He had always seen her as an enemy, not as a friend. She couldn't stand doing nothing. The studio seemed to hold its breath as she knocked gently on the door. She got no reply so she entered anyway. He looked up slowly, dejected and forlorn.

'Leave me alone,' he pleaded, turning his head away from her.

She moved around to the other side of the room so that he couldn't avoid her gaze. 'I can't do that,' she replied.

'Please go away,' he begged, with his eyes closed.

She wouldn't give up that easily; she put a hand on his arm. 'What did your father say?'

He got up and faced away from her and just as suddenly he turned around in an angry outburst, his face contorted with rage. 'He said, "I should bloody well hope so, what the hell do you think you're there for," so now you know.' He shrugged as if he didn't care but she could see he was terribly hurt and she knew how much work he'd put into that order. 'Then he said, "If you were a decent son you'd help me all the time, not just when I'm ill, but you're a selfish swine".' She felt remorse; she had judged him without any idea of his life, assuming that because of his father's reputation, Bobby had to be in the wrong.

'Did he not even say thank you? She asked softly.

'Thank you!' he exploded, arms spread. 'My father has never said, "Thank you, Sorry", or "I love you," to me. Do you know why?' he shouted.

She hoped it was a rhetorical question because she was dumbstruck.

'Because he isn't grateful, he's never sorry, and he doesn't love me, but that's my fault isn't it?' he said with heavy sarcasm. He turned away again with pursed lips.

She hated to intrude on his private anguish. His breathing was fast and shallow as he desperately sought to gain control.

'I'm sorry, I was wrong.'

'What do you mean?' he asked, looking puzzled.

She sighed. 'Oh don't make me spell it out. I was wrong on just about every count. You are hardworking and reliable, you don't deserve what you get from him and I mistook your fervent enthusiasm for arrogance and your sense of humour for flippancy. I'm sorry.'

She looked away from him feeling ashamed and wishing that he would say something to break the silence that hung between them. It had taken courage to admit her mistakes and it made her feel extremely vulnerable. He had a right to be angry with her. When she looked up he was staring at her, calmer now.

'Thank you,' he said, and a flicker of a smile crossed his face. 'But I do have a bad temper eh?' he added, breaking the awkward air between them.

Kate gave a casual shrug. 'Nobody's perfect.'

He raised his eyebrows with a look of mock surprise. 'Not even you?' he asked as he took a cigarette from his pocket and lit up.

'Not quite,' she whispered, 'but please don't tell anyone.'

'All right,' he agreed. 'Oh damn it, the litho.'

He quickly left the office and was stopped briefly by Hannah. Kate didn't hear Hannah's question but Bobby's reply was dismissive.

'I'm okay, thank you.'

He gave Kate instructions with just as much detail and help, but the spark had gone out of it and suddenly she could understand what Jodie had tried to tell her; Colin was the problem, not Bobby.

'You know what?' Kate began, back at the flat that evening.

'What?' Jodie said, somewhat distracted by the magazine article she was reading.

'You were right about Bobby.'

Jodie looked up from the magazine the instant she registered what Kate had said.

'Colin really hurt him today,' she said with a pained expression.

'Oh was he back so soon?' Jodie replied, almost disinterested.

'No, he rang him. Bobby worked hard to ensure that the business got a new customer's order, and his dad just dismissed it.'

Kate was distressed by the events of the day. 'I've never seen him hurt like that.'

Kate wouldn't have blamed Jodie if she had said, "I told you so," but she didn't. If the tables had been turned Kate knew that she would have said something. As she lay down to sleep that night, Kate was haunted by visions of his face, the pain and rejection deeply etched and the sorrow she had seen in his eyes. *How could I have missed it before? His father has broken his heart*, she thought, *and he's breaking his very spirit.*

39

Bobby dragged himself out of bed the instant the alarm clock went off on Saturday morning. If he could get a lift with his dad it would save him coming home to drop off the motorbike. Finishing half day and going Christmas shopping with Jodie made the day seem more bearable. He splashed his face with cold water to speed up the waking process and appeared in the kitchen with five minutes to spare. As he picked up a slice of toast and headed for the back door his father called him back.

'Sit down,' he barked. 'Eat breakfast properly.'

Rather than begin the day on the wrong foot, Bobby complied. His mother put a cup of coffee in front of him and he glanced up, 'Thank you.'

He planned to say nothing during the journey to town, to ensure that he didn't say the wrong thing. He answered his father's questions with simple yes or no replies. They arrived at the studio early but when he leant on the wall and attempted to light up a cigarette, his father pushed him inside.

'We'll start now,' he said sharply, pushing Bobby by the shoulder towards the door.

Bobby gave a sigh of resignation and went inside. *Just half a day*, he reminded himself.

Colin threw a pile of papers on Bobby's desk without saying a word.

Bobby stared at his father's retreating form. '*Could you make a start on these please*', *would be nice.*

'You'll have to answer the phone too,' his father added.

'Is Hannah sick?' Bobby asked.

Apart from Colin, Bobby was the only person capable of covering for her.

'Mind your own business and get on with your work,' his

father snapped.

When Kate arrived, Bobby was on the 'phone.

'Yes that's fine ... okay let me make a note of that, Wednesday at the latest ... that's no problem, a thousand leaflets ... yes, that will be at the same price as last month ... thank you for calling.'

He looked up from the telephone to see Kate laughing at him. 'It's not funny,' he said turning away.

He moved the top letter aside and picked up the next. Kate leant across to him. 'You make an attractive secretary,' she laughed, and he made a swipe at her but she ducked.

'Hello, yes, Barron's Design,' he said, swiftly turning his attention back to the telephone. 'I have your order here but you make no mention of a delivery date ... okay, that's fine yes. Thank you,' he replied, scribbling on the bottom of the letter whilst balancing the receiver under his chin.

He perched on the edge of the desk as he worked his way through countless queries. Glancing at the next letter on the pile, he suddenly realised that the delivery date on the letter was Monday. He picked it up and re-read it. With a look of consternation, he jumped up and took it to his father's office, rushing in without invitation.

Colin banged his fist hard on the desk. 'How many times have I told you?'

'This is important,' Bobby interrupted.

'I don't care how important it is,' his father yelled. Bobby walked towards the door.

'Suit yourself,' he shrugged.

'Come back here,' Colin shouted.

Aware that the conversation would be audible to the entire studio, Bobby lowered his voice whilst maintaining his condescending tone. 'I'm trying to help your business,' he said. 'It obviously needs it,' he muttered under his breath, which caused his dad to rise angrily from his seat. Bobby threw the paper down on the desk in front of his father, halting his advance.

Colin picked up the letter, skimmed through it quickly and threw it back onto the desk with a look of alarm, sitting back down heavily as he spoke. 'You'll have to do it, Bobby.'

He was almost, but not quite, pleading with him, which gave Bobby a modicum of pleasure. This was as close as his father would ever get to grovelling.

'I may be a genius,' Bobby ventured slowly and deliberately, 'but I cannot design the leaflets, print them and pack them ready for Monday, answer the telephone, ring through queries, type the invoices and finish all the filing in one morning. With the Litho out, it will take me two hours just to print the leaflets and I'm going Christmas shopping with Jodie this afternoon,' Bobby said impatiently.

Colin stood up and walked around the desk. 'Then you'll have to cancel it,' he said.

Bobby backed away from his father, desperately trying to hide his fear and acutely aware that there was nothing but the wall behind him, but he was determined not to give in.

'Why can't *you* do it?' Bobby asked, sidling towards the door.

Colin moved fast and kicked it shut in fury, before approaching Bobby slowly and deliberately. He pushed a finger into Bobby's shoulder as he glared into his eyes.

'You will stay until it's done,' he ordered.

Bobby was close to exploding. 'I wish I'd put the bloody letter in the bin.'

He turned to walk away but his father barred his route, pushing him roughly against the wall with his fist. As he spoke, he banged Bobby's head against the wall in time with the words.

'Don't you dare swear at …?'

Bobby interrupted out of courage born of anger. 'You are such a selfish ...'

Colin slapped him around the face before he had a chance to finish. Bobby held his face and walked away in case he did something he might regret. He was still shaking as he sat down at Hannah's desk, painfully aware that the staff would have heard every word, and worse still, the slap. He closed his eyes briefly to regain his composure and to hide from the shame and humiliation, took a deep breath, and picked up the persistent telephone, 'Barron's Design,' he said. Out of the corner of his eye he could see Kate watching him. She smiled at him, but he looked away, embarrassed.

'That's only approximate. I can send a written estimate in the post if you like. Thank you for ringing,' he said.

He put the receiver back on the hook. Then he had a brainwave and took it off again, before laying it down on the desk. Now he could work without interruption. He heard Kate laugh quietly and looked up, putting a finger to his lips. She shook her head and carried on with her work, smiling to herself.

After twenty minutes he returned the receiver to its rightful place and it rang instantly. 'Barron's Design,' he said, suppressing a laugh as he looked up at Kate. When he came off the phone and looked round again Kate was throwing yet another piece of paper in the bin in frustration. He got up from his desk and went across to her.

'What's the problem?' he asked.

'Your dad told me to keep practising with the airbrush, that practice makes perfect.'

'Bloody idiot,' he retorted as he took the screwed up paper out of the bin and spread it out in front of her. 'It's too wet I think,' he said.

'And?' she replied.

He took a rough piece of paper from the side of her desk to demonstrate.

'You're probably holding the airbrush too close to the paper, which creates a sort of puddle. Other thing is to make sure that you keep it moving, watch.'

She raised her eyebrows heavenwards and watched with an expression of disbelief as he moved the airbrush expertly over the paper, creating a smooth effect. 'Okay, I'll try again,' she said.

He stood upright with a supercilious look on his face. 'Practice makes perfect,' he said haughtily and strode back to Hannah's desk.

At 11.30am Colin passed through the studio, casually putting the keys down on Bobby's desk. 'I have to see a client in the city,' he said.

Bobby stuck up two fingers behind his father's back as he left, and as the doorbell rang signalling his departure, the rest of the studio relaxed. The next time Bobby answered the phone, he had his feet on the desk and a cigarette in one hand. Within five minutes of Colin leaving, Simon had brought Bobby a cup of coffee.

'Thank you,' Bobby said.

'I wish you were in charge all the time,' Simon remarked.

Bobby's response was instant. 'I don't, it bores me to tears.'

'But you're good at it,' Simon said, turning back briefly.

'Practice makes perfect,' he mimicked for the second time today, displaying more resentment than humour.

At five to twelve he looked up at the tardy old clock on the wall. 'Okay, everybody, go!' he said, stubbing out yet another cigarette.

Simon whistled to himself as he gathered up the mugs and washed up. Kate packed everything away and cleared her desk, before approaching Bobby tentatively.

'Bobby?' she said quietly.

His reply was a little impatient. 'What Kate? I've got a lot to do.'

'Shall I type the invoices for you?' she said, without looking at him.

He waved a hand dismissively. 'Oh don't worry, Herr Hitler is very particular about his invoices.'

She sat on the corner of his desk, forcing him to look up from his work. 'Don't be so bloody-minded,' she said, looking only marginally taken aback as Jodie appeared by the desk.

'Hello, Jodie,' Kate said, changing her tone entirely. 'I didn't hear you come in.'

'Obviously,' Jodie replied sharply.

Kate explained the situation to Jodie, while Jodie leant across the desk to give Bobby a kiss.

'Let Kate do them,' Jodie said.

Kate jumped off the desk and walked around to the other side. She leant over Bobby's shoulder to talk to him. 'Show me how to do one and I'll finish them. I spent all summer one year typing invoices.'

'Thank you, I didn't mean to be ungrateful,' he said.

He looked up briefly. She was better as a friend than as an enemy. He showed her one example, and in twenty-five minutes she had completed the whole pile. 'Shall I put them in envelopes and address them?' she asked him.

'Absolutely not,' he replied emphatically. 'I'm not doing *more* than he asked.'

Kate smiled. 'You don't believe in going the second mile then?'

Bobby leant on the desk and took another drag of his final cigarette before he replied, 'He already sent me the second mile.'

She grinned. 'Do you want me to file this lot?' she asked, picking up a pile of papers and dropping them back on the desk. 'Or is it easier to do it yourself?'

'Easier to do them myself,' he said lifting up the pile of papers and dropping them in the rubbish bin beside him.

'You can't do that!' she said, alarmed.

'I'm only joking,' he said, 'it would take longer to explain the system than to file them. You go.' Reluctantly, she went.

'I hate the bastard,' Bobby said to Jodie as he flung the telephone directory across the room. 'I have to finish setting this up and run off two thousand bloody leaflets.'

She picked up the directory and then stood behind him running her fingers through his hair, which caused a shiver to run down his spine. 'Don't worry. I'll wait,' she said.

'Woah, please don't do that, I can't concentrate,' he said shrinking away from her. 'Do me a favour will you? Go down to the newsagents and get me ten Embassy.' He produced a pound note from his trouser pocket and handed it to her. She sat down on the desk right beside his work. 'How many have you smoked today?'

He let out a protracted 'Well ...' before continuing. 'I didn't have any until dad left at half-past eleven, but I've been trying to catch up ever since,' he said with a grin.

She folded the note and put it in her purse as she jumped down off the desk. He leant back on the desk in weariness as she left, and by the time she returned he was asleep. She called his name softly. 'Bobby?' There was no flicker of response, so she moved closer and gently slid the paper out from under his arm. She still had it in her hand when he stirred.

His heavy eyes struggled to open until he suddenly registered where he was. 'Damn,' he said jumping up from the chair. 'I wanted to get finished quickly.'

Jodie put the design back on the desk and handed him the cigarettes.

'I was just wondering if I could run them off myself,' she smiled.

He fumbled nervously with the cigarette packet as he opened it, lit up, and took a long drag. He closed his eyes, holding his head in his hands. He desperately wanted to hide his anger from Jodie.

'I wish you'd give up,' she said quietly.

'Smoking?' he asked with a look of surprise.

'Not the smoking, chasing after that bastard's approval.'

He flinched at her harsh words, but picked up the design and carried on working, saying only, 'He's my father.'

'Do you even know what a father is?' she snapped.

Bobby didn't reply, but carried on working.

He shook his head as if waking himself up and in a short

time he was ready to print.

'I'm sorry,' she said eventually, lowering her eyes, 'I didn't mean to be angry with you.'

It hurt him but he wouldn't show it.

'Why can't you see what he's doing to you?' she sighed. 'Anyway,' she shrugged, 'if you do the filing I'll feed the paper in here?'

He nodded agreement. Few words passed between them and the tension didn't evaporate until they'd left the studio and arrived in the city centre.

'So,' Jodie said after parking the car, 'where are we going to shop?'

Bobby seemed more relaxed now. 'I don't mind. What are you looking for?' he asked.

She moved closer to him and he put his arm around her shoulder. 'Something for Karen and Neil, my sister's twins.'

'So you want a toy shop?' he asked casually.

Jodie grinned. 'I'm sure they'd love it but it would be a bit expensive,' she retorted.

He drew her closer to him and laughed.

'So what do the idle rich buy each other for Christmas?' she enquired, not revealing the hidden question of how to decide what to buy for him, something she'd been pondering for weeks.

He let out a protracted 'Well ...' before continuing, 'I buy whatever I want. I've had a necklace put away for Mum that she admired when we were on holiday in France, which may cause trouble with Dad, he prefers British.'

'Hmm, except holidays,' Jodie quipped.

'Oh that's a brilliant argument,' Bobby said. He talked her into stopping for a late lunch, which meant that it was past three o'clock before they even began to shop.

'What will you buy your dad?' she asked cautiously.

He replied instantly. 'A Parker pen and a time bomb, in separate packages. I shouldn't want to damage the pen.'

'Why waste money on the pen?' she asked. 'Just give him

the bomb first.'

He laughed.

'And Elaine?' she enquired.

He stopped to look in a shop window. 'I can't think of anything imaginative, so I'll probably buy her a Stones album, she hasn't got *Let it Bleed* yet.'

Jodie sighed, he made it all sound easy and yet she couldn't think of anything to buy her granddad. Maybe Bobby would have an idea. 'So what could I buy for Granddad?' she asked, desperate for suggestions.

He thought for a moment, furrowing his brow. Suddenly he looked up and spoke as if a light had been switched on. 'An electric kettle, he's always making coffee,' he said positively. She shook her head and smiled as he casually took out a cigarette and lit up.

'All right Mr Cleverclogs, so how do I know what to buy for my sister's twins?'

He arched his eyebrows as he turned his face towards her. 'I'm not the Christmas shopping adviser you know.'

'That's a pity,' she said, adopting a look of disappointment.

'Okay,' he said, dragging her off in the direction of a large department store, 'I try to listen all year but in this case that won't work because you don't see them so …' he drew out the final word for effect, 'you have to do it another way. Ask yourself questions, how much do I want to spend? Shall I buy them something the same, or different? Do they have any particular interests? Do I want to buy a toy or something useful?'

'Stop, stop,' she said, raising a finger to his lips. 'I obviously haven't done enough research.' She wondered what she could buy for someone who took choosing a gift so seriously. She couldn't resist asking, 'Do you know what you're buying for me?'

'I've had yours a while,' he replied nonchalantly.

'What is it?'

He turned an imaginary key in the lock on his lips. She

shook him playfully, laughing. 'Tell me, tell me.'

'No! You can wait until Christmas like everyone else,' he scolded, putting his arms around her. Jodie pushed him away.

'We haven't actually bought anything yet,' she exclaimed.

With Bobby's exhaustive help, Jodie finally settled on an Airfix plane for Neil and a book on camping for Karen. When they had finished shopping, they piled everything into the car.

'Jodie, do we have time for me to drop in and give Dale his Christmas present? I may not see him before Christmas, so I brought it with me.'

She continued organising the contents of the boot as she replied.

'Yeah, I can't be long though.'

'Thanks.'

She parked outside Dale's house and followed Bobby down the alleyway that led to the steps down to the basement flat. Bobby rang the bell and waited for Dale to answer the door. It creaked open.

'Bobby!' Dale exclaimed with obvious pleasure. He spoke with a slight slur and tripped over the doormat as he stood back to let them in. Bobby watched with a smile as Jodie's hand lingered in Dale's. He looked a sight. His vest hung loosely on his too-skinny frame, his hair desperately needed a wash, and his arms were covered in scars from years of heroin abuse.

'Happy Christmas,' Bobby said, handing Dale a beautifully wrapped present. Dale looked pleased and embarrassed simultaneously.

'Thanks,' he said slowly, without looking up. 'I haven't got you a present yet.'

'Then don't,' Bobby said in animated fashion. 'I buy presents because I want to and it gives me great pleasure to give away the old man's money.'

Dale laughed and placed the present on the kitchen worktop.

'Coffee?' he offered.

'We can't stop, we're on our way home,' Bobby replied. 'I hope to see you before Christmas, but I thought I'd give you the present in case I don't get the chance.'

'It's lovely to see you,' Dale said.

Few words passed between Bobby and Jodie on the way home and as she dropped him off at his house, she thought about the events of the day. He was delightful away from his father and she was determined to make him see the effect his father was having on him, before Colin destroyed him completely.

40

'It's pagan,' Colin spat.

'So is Christmas,' Bobby shrugged.

'Well it seems to me,' Colin raged, 'that your definition of *wassailing* is roving from pub to pub getting more and more drunk.'

Bobby tried to stay calm but failed dismally. 'I might be missing something here,' he said with mock humility, 'but I fail to see how sitting in self-righteous judgement gives you the moral high ground.'

Colin jumped up and Bobby flinched. He hadn't intended arguing again but he was tired, his defences were weak, and it seemed to him that everything he tried to do came under fire from his father.

'If you want to sing traditional songs then you can come and sing Christmas carols at church this evening,' his father declared, pacing the floor as if waiting to pounce.

Bobby turned sideways on the settee and put his feet up before answering matter-of-factly, 'I *am* going to the carol service. I'm reading a lesson.'

His father motioned angrily to him to get his feet off the settee. 'Couldn't Reverend Turner find anyone more respectable?'

Bobby got up casually and moved to the door, 'Obviously not.' He walked away before he was tempted to say something he might regret. He'd sat in his room for half an hour when Jodie arrived, and when he heard the doorbell he ran downstairs two steps at a time to meet her. As he opened the door she took a step back in surprise.

'Wow, dig that,' she said with a smile, before taking hold of him by the lapels of his extraordinarily smart suit and pulling him towards her. She kissed him before asking the question which must have entered her head the second she saw him.

'Why the smart gear?'

'As much as I would enjoy wearing the leather jacket to upset my father, I wouldn't want to offend the Rev.'

They arrived early at the church, positioning themselves close to the front. Jodie rested her head on Bobby's shoulder. 'Are you tired?' he asked her softly.

'A bit,' she replied with a smile.

The service took the usual form of nine lessons and carols and as Bobby began his lesson, he stood at the lectern and read,

"The people that walked in darkness have seen a great light: they that dwell in the land of the shadow of death, upon them hath the light shined." The last two words faded away as he stood staring at the Bible on the lectern in front of him. He didn't notice his father's angry glare as he turned around from his seat at the organ, or his mother's look of anxiety, or Jodie's grin. He looked up and saw Rev Turner returning his look of interest with a smile. Having remembered why he was meant to be reading it, he began again and read fluently to the end of the passage.

As Bobby and Jodie were leaving, Rev Turner thanked him, adding with a smile, 'Maybe we all need to reflect more on what those verses really mean.' He then enquired, 'Are you staying for mulled wine and mince pies in the hall?'

Bobby lifted his index finger to his lips before saying in hushed tones, 'We're off wassailing now, but keep it quiet, it's a bone of contention between me and my father.'

The vicar called after him. 'If you're in the area in the next hour, call in and sing to us while we're having our mince pies and mulled wine.'

Bobby gave him the thumbs up sign and left with his arm around Jodie's shoulder. Quarter of an hour later, they met up with the rest of the group outside the Three Crowns Inn and went inside to sing. Village friends had swelled the usual group to ten. They sang *The Holly and the Ivy,* with Jerry playing the melody on the harmonica. The locals soon picked up the tune of the chorus as it danced to the rhythm of the accordion and the harmony of Jodie's violin. With no introduction they broke into *The Wassailing Bowl*, beginning with a drum beat. Encouraged by Bobby, the local people soon joined in the refrain. After a quick drink at the bar, they collected money for Biafran refugees and departed for the church.

'I took you at your word, Rev,' Bobby said.

The vicar opened the door wide to let them in. 'What are you going to sing for us?'

'*A Virgin Unspotted*, followed by *The Joys of Mary*,' Bobby said. 'And then if you don't object we'll take round tins for Biafra.

'That's a good idea,' the vicar replied.

'Can I use the piano?'

The Rev Turner cringed. 'You might regret it,' he replied uncertainly.

Bobby laughed and put the accordion down by the old piano. He tinkered on it for a few moments, shrugged, and after a brief introduction by the vicar, they began to sing *A Virgin Unspotted*, with Bobby accompanying on the piano as Jodie played them in on the Irish whistle. Most of the villagers joined in the refrain but his father left, with his mother following meekly behind. Bobby couldn't hide his exasperation but smiled again when he caught Jodie's reproachful look.

At the end of the first song, he got up, picked up the accordion and the wassailers began *The Joys of Mary*, with male voices bringing in the first verse. They gradually added instruments until on verse four Jodie put down the tin whistle and picked up the violin. They all looked a little surprised as, on the fifth verse, old Stan, a local man, picked up the whistle and began to play a high harmony. After much applause, the group joined the villagers for mince pies and mulled wine. On the way out Bobby placed a hand on the vicar's shoulder.

'That piano needs tuning,' he stated plainly.

The vicar looked up at him and nodded slowly with a thoughtful look before responding. 'I don't suppose that's one of your talents is it?'

He looked hopeful but Bobby laughed and shook his head. 'That's a skilled craft.'

He stopped briefly, desperately trying to remember a name. 'Roberts,' he said suddenly. The vicar looked a little bemused and stared at him as if waiting for more information.

'Eric, I think it is,' Bobby said after a moment's thought. 'He's a brilliant blind piano tuner. His wife drives him everywhere. He doesn't charge a lot but he takes longer than most so Dad got rid of him. I don't think the piano's been the same since.' He looked into the Rev's eyes with a deadpan expression. 'Dad would know his telephone number if you asked him.'

His face broke into a mischievous smile, enjoying the worried look on the vicar's face, until suddenly he lost his composure and laughed.

'Don't worry Rev,' he said patting him on the back. 'I'll find it in his telephone book when he's not around.'

The vicar laughed. 'Thank you Bobby,' he said, before looking oddly at old Stan who was following the young wassailers.

Stan beamed with pride as he answered the quizzical look in the vicar's eye. 'They asked me to come along and play the tin whistle.'

Bobby slung the accordion over his shoulder and turned to wink at the vicar as he left. 'Don't fret,' he teased, 'we won't let him get drunk.'

Stan hit Bobby on the leg playfully with his walking stick. 'Get away with you, you young rascal!'

Bobby jumped as if to avoid further beatings, before whispering to the Rev, 'He used to go wassailing in the village as a boy, or so he says.'

After an hour singing around the village, the little group saw home a very happy old man before returning to the pub. Jodie and Kate left after just one drink and gave a warning to Bobby and Jerry not to drink any more. By the time they finally left, Jerry and Bobby were a little worse for wear. Bobby slipped quietly into the house and up the stairs, locking the door quickly behind him.

41

Colin looked at the boy with disgust on Monday morning. Bobby drank only black coffee and had no breakfast. Colin had no energy to fight him. The run-up to Christmas would be frantic and he needed all his strength to contend with the workload. Even Bobby seemed to sense the urgency once they were at work. Colin kept him busy all morning.

'Bobby, get the platen ready to do those fashion show leaflets, the litho's working flat out.'

'Sure, I'll be finished here in ten minutes,' Bobby replied.

The boy was almost amenable.

'Has Kate got time to watch, Dad?'

'Colin shrugged. 'You'll both have to stay late if she does.'

Bobby raised his eyebrows at Kate, who nodded and jumped up.

On his way across the studio, Hannah intercepted Colin. 'There's an urgent call for you,' Hannah said sombrely. 'I've put it through to your office.'

He nodded a thank you and went into the office with Hannah, closing the door behind them. He lifted the receiver. 'All right Sister, thank you, I'll be there as soon as I can.' He had known that with his father in heart failure he wouldn't live long, but it broke his heart. Now he would never know the acceptance he had craved and he was worried that if he had to keep on leaving work early, Bobby would get suspicious.

As he sat at his desk he reminded himself of happier days, long ago, but as hard as he tried, the sad memories continually sought to intrude. His mother had been the strong one, but he hadn't realised it until she died. He was brought back to reality by Hannah.

'Is he worse?' she asked, pulling up a chair beside him.

Colin simply nodded, 'Probably only hours.'

'I guessed as much,' she said softly.

She sat in silence for a moment but a smile gradually dawned on her face. 'I was remembering today ...' she began, 'how your father used to gaze at your mother when she played the violin.'

Colin smiled briefly, but it was a sad and distant smile and his mind was all over the place. 'My mother was the reason I became a perfectionist at music, I've never told anyone that. I never had time to grieve for her. I learned the music to her memory.'

Hannah laughed and nodded. 'I always knew that. I remember my mother watching you return from church one day, she said, "His mother would have been so proud of him".'

'She would,' Colin agreed, nodding slowly, close to tears. 'But if she had lived I guess I wouldn't have been so motivated.'

'True,' Hannah conceded, as she looked up at the clock and added, 'You'd better go.'

He got up and brushed himself down with his hand, as if to shake off the past, before picking up his suit jacket from the back of the chair.

'I'll join you when I've finished here,' she said softly.

He put on his jacket as he walked towards the door, adopting a controlled, professional look as he entered the studio. As he walked towards the side room he overheard Bobby talking to Kate.

'To start this old beast up you need to stamp hard on the pedal ... no really stamp, like this.'

Colin heard the thud and the platen started up. He put the keys down in front of Bobby.

'I'll be back later, I've got a call to make,' he said abruptly as he turned away towards the door.

'Dad, you know I can't do all this without you,' Bobby protested. 'I'll be here all night.'

Colin turned around briefly. 'That will keep you out of

200

trouble,' he replied.

'That's not fair,' Bobby moaned.

'Just do as I say,' Colin said in frustration.

He had to get to his father and he couldn't explain it to his son. As he turned to walk away, Colin caught sight of Bobby saluting him behind his back in the reflection of the glass in the door, and swirled around fast enough to catch him for once. He strode across the studio at such a pace that the boy took a step backwards.

'I'm sorry,' Bobby said quickly, his eyes wide with fear.

Colin pointed in his face, so close that he could see the slight twitching in his son's muscles. 'Just do as I say,' he repeated through clenched teeth. 'Do you understand?'

'Yes,' Bobby muttered, looking aside.

'Yes sir,' Colin said poking him in the shoulder.

'Colin?' Hannah called to him. 'You'll be late for your appointment.'

He strode quickly out of the studio, down the stairs, got into his white Mercedes and drove off. He dreaded these visits. He'd spent so many wasted years believing that his father would change and now it was too late. If he had known when he was young, what he knew now, he would never have wasted his life, but in those days he had hope.

The twenty minute drive seemed over in a flash. He parked the car in the Royal Hospital car park and locked it carefully before walking slowly to the ward. It would probably be the last time. He knocked on the half-open door of the sister's office and she beckoned him in.

'We've moved your father into the room opposite. She pushed the office door shut with her hand. 'He won't live long now. I'm surprised he's survived this long.'

'Thank you,' he said matter-of-factly.

'You can stay as long as it takes,' she replied kindly.

'Thank you,' he replied again and left the office. He crossed the corridor to his father's room and pulled up a chair. *Imagine dying*, he thought to himself, *in the knowledge that you wasted your whole life.*

Apart from a slight rising and falling of the chest, his father was motionless. Each breath seemed more laboured than the last and he gurgled slightly. Colin watched, detached and emotionless. About an hour after he arrived, Hannah joined him. They sat in silence until his father breathed his last breath. Colin made a decision in that moment to break away from all that had destroyed him for so long. He took hold of his father's hand and squeezed it tight.

'Thank you Dad,' he said as he got up to fetch the sister, 'you've finally taught me something worth learning.'

Hannah looked up into his face and caught his eye, but he didn't explain it to her and after a few minutes they left. There were changes he needed to make to his life.

'Do you want to come back for coffee?' Hannah asked.

Colin shook his head. 'No thanks. I'd better check up on Bobby.'

Bobby and Kate had almost finished the tickets when Colin walked back into the studio at 5.30pm.

'When you've finished what you're working on, you'll need to pack up tomorrow's deliveries. It needs doing tonight,' Colin said as he turned to leave again.

Bobby stood up and turned on him with angry sarcasm.

'Oh that's all right. I thought it might be fun to work until midnight just for good measure. Anything else you'd like me to do?'

Colin moved towards him. He could see Kate's fear but that wasn't his primary concern. He pinned Bobby to the wall, one threatening finger pushed into his chest. Kate jumped up, clearly distressed. Colin turned to face her without moving the finger that psychologically held Bobby captive.

'You go,' he said angrily.

He saw the boy directing her towards the door with his eyes. Colin attacked Bobby the second Kate had left. 'How dare you show me up like that!' He held Bobby by the shirt collars now and slammed him backwards against the wall. He let go, and Bobby fell on the floor. Then he kicked him hard in the side. Bobby eased himself up and spoke quickly,

'If I have a headache tomorrow I won't be able to work,' he said, the anger evident in his eyes.

'Don't leave here until you've finished,' Colin said as he turned and walked out of the studio.

He slammed the door behind him without hearing Bobby's retort. 'I hate you, I hate you, I hate you, you son of a bitch!'

42

By the time Christmas Day arrived, Bobby was exhausted. He needed to feel relaxed in order to face a day at home. There was no hope of escaping until the evening unless he got up early. On Christmas Eve he had set the clock for seven o'clock and was up and dressed by half past. He put on his coat and scarf and headed towards the river.

It was still dark and a beautiful winter mist hung over the river. Peace flowed over him as he wandered to where the river cascaded over rocks and babbled incessantly. He stood still and studied an icy spider's web before continuing his walk over the bridge that held so many memories from childhood, both good and bad. He remembered playing 'Pooh sticks' with his mother, and going on picnics with her when his father was working, and he remembered his father hitting him because he dropped his school cap in the water as he walked back from the village school. He did up his coat and thrust his hands into his pockets.

At eight o'clock he lit a cigarette and turned back towards home. As he turned the key in the lock, he could hear movement and guessed that his mother was preparing the turkey. After hanging up his coat and scarf he crept into the kitchen but his mother heard him.

'Good morning, happy Christmas,' she said.

Her tone was flat and her voice shaky. He sensed that he was intruding. She didn't turn around to look at him, so he walked over to the sink where she stood peeling potatoes. He took the knife and the potato from her shaking hands and laid them on the draining board. 'Is it my fault that you are so unhappy?'

Her eyes were red and swollen. He had always despised her weakness, but today he pitied her misery. She didn't reply so he drew his own conclusions.

'I'm sorry,' he said softly.

He picked up the knife and began to peel the potatoes. He quickly finished them and when he had worked his way through sprouts, carrots and parsnips, even his mother managed a smile. 'There are things I can't tell you,' she said.

There was something even more desolate and hopeless in her demeanour this morning. By the time his father appeared, most of the meal was prepared and the table was laid for dinner.

'Happy Christmas,' Bobby said, attempting to sound genuine.

'Good morning,' his father offered. It was formal and polite.

'Where's Elaine?' Colin asked his wife.

'I'll go and see,' she replied quietly.

'You've done enough already Mum,' Bobby said risking a rather pointed glare at his father. 'I'll go and call her.'

He called Elaine and she appeared, just as Colin left for the church.

'Don't be late!' Colin shouted as he left.

Bobby saluted, but not until his father had closed the door behind him. His mother trudged slowly upstairs but after a few minutes Bobby began to get agitated. He didn't want to upset his father on Christmas day. He called up the stairs. 'Mum, are you coming?' When she appeared, her eyes were red and puffy. She'd clearly been crying again. He said nothing as they left the house but once he'd closed the door behind them, he caught her up and put his arm through hers as they walked briskly to the church. Elaine walked ahead and sat in a pew close to the back of the church, so Bobby followed her and his mother sat down next to him. Her anxiety was worse than usual and more than once Bobby had to find the place for her in the order of service. She didn't sing as she normally would and Bobby was quietly worried about her. He was lost in his own thoughts and had no idea what the vicar said in his Christmas address.

The service was brief and at the close, Dennis came over to Bobby with a wide smile and a present in his hand.

'Thank you for helping me', he said as he handed Bobby the package.

'Oh thank you Dennis,' he said with obvious delight, 'you didn't have to do this.'

'I wanted to,' he declared and skipped away.

'It meant a lot to him,' Dennis's mother whispered.

As they left the church, the vicar shook hands with Bobby. 'You've certainly made a hit with Dennis.'

Bobby merely shrugged.

Colin turned around and looked Bobby up and down. 'Same wavelength,' he remarked.

'Probably,' Bobby replied, suppressing his anger.

Rev Turner placed a hand on Bobby's shoulder which Bobby acknowledged with a smile, belying his true feelings.

For the rest of the morning he helped his mother in the kitchen to avoid his father. Even polite conversation was difficult.

The exchange of presents was polite but formal and the presents they gave him were impersonal. Much to his relief, his father decided to go for a drive alone after the Queen's speech, as he did every year. Bobby sprawled on the settee. At four o'clock he decided to walk to Granddad's cottage to give Jodie and her granddad their presents.

'Mum, I'm walking over to Jodie's and then I'm going to see Jerry on the way back.'

His mother was sitting in an armchair talking to Carl and Elaine. 'Yes, love,' she replied.

He didn't imagine they would miss him since they had hardly seemed to notice that he was there. He donned his coat and scarf and set off across the field. He felt more isolated at home with the strangers he called his family than he did out here alone. When he reached Granddad's cottage he was contented, smiling even. He knocked on the back door and walked in.

'Hello, happy Christmas,' he said as he laid the presents down on the table and took off his coat and scarf. He was cold and tired but the atmosphere was warm and alive as he sat on the floor by the fire next to Jodie.

'Are you cold?' she asked, moving closer.

'I am but I'll be okay in a minute,' he replied.

Granddad reappeared with coffee before Bobby realised he'd gone. He put the tray down on the coffee table and handed Bobby a mug. 'Are you impressed by the speed of my new kettle?' Granddad asked him.

'Oh absolutely,' Bobby laughed as he warmed his hands on the outside of the mug. He sat for a while without saying a word, just staring at the Christmas tree. It was completely opposite to the one his father had decorated. He put the coffee down on the floor and got up to take a closer look. Up close it was a veritable hotchpotch, even the angel on the top was made of odds and ends attached to a small blonde doll. He motioned to the tree and turned to address Jodie. 'Tell me,' he said.

She got up and stood beside him. 'Everything has a memory,' she said, 'bought in a place we have visited, or made from something we found, or it's something significant from the past.'

'Such as?'

Jodie removed a small knitted woollen sheep from the tree. 'This,' she said, handing it to him. 'My mother knitted it from wool we found caught on the bushes in a field in Ireland.' She took it from him and carefully placed it back on the tree. 'My mother brought this shell back from Australia. We decorated it, pierced a hole in it and hung it on the tree.'

Bobby gazed at it. He had another question in his head. 'Do you have mementoes of bad as well as good?' he asked, feeling like an intruder in her memories. Jodie looked surprised.

'Of course.'

She leant across him and took down a bell on a ribbon.

'This belonged to the family cat. When he died we kept the bell.'

He longed to know what other memories were immortalised in the tree, but he didn't dare ask. The tree was decorated with joy and laughter, heartache and pain, and it wasn't his business to know.

'It's beautiful,' he said, staring at it. He had always tried to forget pain, but here was joy and pain in balance, all part of the passage of time.

Jodie sat down on the settee and Bobby sat down next to her.

'I nearly forgot,' he said jumping up again. I brought presents.'

He bounced over to the table and handed them a parcel each. Both parcels were carefully wrapped with ribbon and hand-made bows.

Granddad gently fingered his parcel. 'They look too beautiful to open.'

Bobby grinned. 'That would defeat the purpose.'

Granddad removed the navy-blue ribbon and un-wrapped the gold paper. He held up a portrait of Jodie. 'You remembered. It must have been weeks ago I said I wanted one.'

'I have to admit,' Bobby offered, 'I was quite interested in the subject myself.'

'Don't be so embarrassing,' Jodie said sharply, but he detected a hint of pleasure in her voice. She was carefully trying to slide the ribbon from her parcel without it losing its shape. He laughed.

'It's stapled underneath the bow.'

'Typical,' she muttered under her breath and took it apart before carefully removing the black paper. She lifted the lid of the box and unfolded the white tissue paper. As she took out the dark green, satin mini-dress, he could see her hands shake. She lifted it out of the box and stared at it.

'I can't.' She shook her head fiercely. 'I can't take it. It's too … I can't.'

She looked away from him and he was hurt. Granddad rescued him.

'Jodie it's beautiful.'

'It's too expensive.'

Bobby took a deep breath. 'From the time you saw it in London I had to have it. I knew it would suit you and I wanted you to know that, to me, you are worth every penny of it. Anyway, I've bought it now and it won't fit me.'

Jodie smiled as she lifted it out of the box again. 'It *is* beautiful,' she said at last, accepting both his explanation and his gift. 'Thank you.'

The cost had never crossed his mind; it was only money after all.

'You make me feel mean,' she said shyly, 'because my gift has cost me nothing.'

Granddad contradicted her. 'I would say that your gift has cost you very dearly.'

Bobby was already unwrapping the present that Granddad had given to him, a penny whistle hand-made in Ireland.

'Brilliant,' Bobby said, 'the genuine article.'

He played it a little before declaring that he would need to practice before he could use it seriously. Jodie handed him a small box, neatly wrapped in hand-dyed paper. He untied it carefully, looking at her fleetingly with an expression of wonderment. He lifted the lid and opened out a folded piece of paper.

'A broken heart on a makeshift chain,' he read, and lifted the tissue paper to reveal a polished wooden heart with a break down one side. It had obviously been hand-crafted. The black leather thong, which was threaded through a hole at the top, was a little frayed and he guessed that it was old. He laid it across the palm of his left hand and fingered it lightly as he looked up briefly at Jodie before continuing to read. He began again.

'A broken heart on a makeshift chain;
a symbol of love, torn apart by pain.
When nothing will comfort you in your grief
and weeping won't come to bring relief;
when the well of tears seems dry and shallow
and the ground of your heart is hard and fallow,
don't close up your heart to the love that would soften
and tenderly heal, as it waters you often
with showers of kindness when you feel all alone;
don't ever give way to a heart of stone.
So even though darkness has clouded your way
and fear overwhelms you night and day,
still keep your heart soft, though it's wounded and broken
and remember this heart, which is simply a token
of love.'

He wanted to say something, but nothing seemed appropriate. He could feel his heart racing as he cradled it in the palm of his hand. His breathing was fast and shallow. *How could she bear to part with it?* He gently stroked the smooth polished wood with the index finger of his right hand and looked up at Jodie.

'Your granddad is right Jodie. Your gift *did* cost you a great deal. Thank you.' She took it from his hand and put it over his head, gently tucking it under his shirt. He re-folded the poem, placed it back in the box, and got up to put it in his coat pocket along with the penny-whistle.

'What are you going to eat?' Granddad asked. 'If you don't eat some of the Christmas cake it will last until Easter.'

It was almost nine o'clock when Bobby got up to set off for Jerry's house. Jodie offered to drive him there. He was glad of the lift; the wind was bitterly cold as he opened the back door of the cottage. When they arrived at Jerry's house, Bobby leant across and kissed Jodie on the cheek.

'I've always hated Christmas,' he said softly, 'but I will never forget this one, thank you.'

As Jerry opened the front door, Bobby was struck by the noise, and a blow-out.

'I really dig that hat,' he laughed pointing at the Christmas cracker hat on Jerry's head.

'Okay everyone,' Jerry announced as he dragged Bobby into the lounge by the sleeve, 'Bobby will attempt to pin the tail on the donkey'.

The house seemed crowded and noisy. Jerry took Bobby's coat before blindfolding him with his own scarf and handing him the tail and pin.

'Okay, here I go,' Bobby said before confidently pinning the tail on the donkey's ear, to the howls and shrieks of the little ones.

'Good try,' Jerry declared. 'Well, not very good actually. Grandma won that, here's your prize. Toffees, they'll take a long while to suck'.

She tried to whack him with her stick but he jumped out of the way.

'Time for a drink,' Jerry announced next, which Bobby guessed was an excuse to stop for a while.

'That's enough games. I'll never get the girls to bed,' Jerry's mum said.

Sarah appeared at Bobby's side.

'I know what you want,' he laughed, 'You want me to play you a song?'

'Yes,' she said hopping on one leg excitedly, 'on this'. She produced a mouth organ from behind her back.

'Wow,' Bobby said. 'Where did you get this?'

'From Jerry,' she said with a smile.

'Of course, he plays this doesn't he?' Bobby said returning the smile and putting his hand out to her. 'Let's have a try.' She handed it to him and bounced up and down with delight as he played to her.

Jerry slumped down on the settee, Bobby sat beside him and Steve, Jerry's stepfather, offered them both a cigar. Steve's relationship with Jerry was not quite paternal and yet,

Bobby observed, they were much closer than he was to his father.

'I'd better go,' Bobby said after a while, 'if Dad's back he won't be pleased with me.'

Jerry drew back in surprise. 'Back from where? It's Christmas Day.'

Bobby shrugged. 'He went for a drive in the car.'

Jerry raised one eyebrow and cocked his head to one side.

'Bit odd don't you think?'

'He likes to be alone. He goes for a drive every Christmas,' Bobby said, putting on his coat and retrieving his scarf from the chair by the tail-less donkey.

As he walked across the village, his mind raced. *Jerry is right. It is a bit odd.* His mother's words from this morning rang in his ears. "There are things I can't tell you ..." As he neared home, Bobby began to reach some uneasy conclusions, but he put them out of his mind, they were ridiculous.

43

Colin had never known the business to be as frantic as it was right now. He could have done without it as he finalised the arrangements for his father's funeral. It would have been less complicated if his children had known the truth, but they had no idea that his father existed. He just hoped that Bobby believed his story about an important business meeting in the city.

The handful of people at Joe Barron's funeral that Tuesday morning was a pitiful sight. It saddened Colin that the passing of a life should be so insignificant, and yet he had struggled to write a few words to help the vicar. *What could be said about a drunk who had not only wasted his own life, but had brought such misery to his children?*

The vicar from Joe's estate had clearly had practice at speaking to a handful of people, and carried off the proceedings with a dignity far beyond the call of duty. Colin cringed at the organ playing as they rose to sing the first hymn, but it had a certain irony since his father had always mocked him for playing the organ.

Max, who was standing next to Colin, dropped his hymn book, almost losing his balance as he attempted to pick it up. Colin silently handed him his. He turned and caught Grace's eye; she raised her eyebrows but said nothing as the hymn finished and they sat down.

The vicar showed his gift for fiction writing, since he had succeeded in turning a few indifferent notes into a creditable eulogy. As Colin knelt to pray he felt a deep sorrow wash over him; not a sorrow at his father's death, but at his father's life and a grief that he had wasted so much of his own. His mind began to wander. *What will my family say as they stand around like this at my funeral?* Hannah placed a hand on his shoulder but he didn't look up; this was private sorrow. He quickly regained his composure, even managing to sing the final hymn.

As he walked to the graveside only minutes later, he felt oddly detached. He put up his umbrella and held it aloft for Hannah and Grace who took it gratefully. Leaving them behind, he sprinted to the sprawling yew tree, which provided temporary shelter from the teeming rain. Max made no attempt to keep up.

'What a waste of a life!' Colin exclaimed louder than he intended, as he walked away before the bemused vicar had finished the committal. Max was so distraught that he got a bit close to the edge of the freshly dug hole and had to be held back by Grace. Colin took a few deep breaths and returned to the graveside.

'Thank you vicar,' he said at the end, and walked slowly back in the rain to the chapel of rest where he had left the car. He slowed his pace slightly until Hannah and Grace caught him up. Max staggered along behind.

'Can I give you a lift home?' he offered, although Hannah's terraced house was only a few streets away. 'I'm giving Max a lift,' he continued.

'That would be lovely,' Hannah replied, 'I feel quite cold now.'

Hannah and Grace got into the back of the car, leaving Colin to bundle Max into the passenger seat. As Colin climbed in behind the wheel, he caught sight of Max removing a hip-flask from his pocket. Colin leant across and snatched it out of his hand. 'Give me the lid,' he demanded with his free hand outstretched. Max handed it over and Colin put it back on the hip-flask, placing it in the side pocket, out of Max's reach. He pulled up outside Max's house and helped him out of the car and bundled him through the front door; he'd had enough for one day.

'I don't know how you put up with him for so long,' he said to Grace as he turned the key in the ignition. 'Do you think you'll go back to him?'

Grace shrugged. 'I can't say right now,' she said. 'I'm taking my time resting at Hannah's house at the moment.'

'Do you want to come in?' Hannah asked Colin as he turned the corner into her street.

Colin shook his head. 'I have to get back to the studio.'

'You really should have the rest of the day off,' Hannah said, scolding him.

'Maybe,' he shrugged, 'but I've left Bobby in charge.'

Hannah caught his eye in the rear view mirror and looked at him sternly. 'He's perfectly capable of running the studio.'

Colin winced. It was true, but he didn't trust what Bobby would say about him to the staff, and no doubt the boy would be smoking all day, which was a safety hazard. He stopped the car outside Hannah's house and she and her sister got out. Hannah was cross with him, he could sense it.

'You're right,' Colin called to her as he got out of the car and locked it. 'I will come in,' he said, as he remembered his promise to himself at his father's deathbed.

He hung up his coat in the hall and went through into the lounge. It always seemed warm there, but then the company wasn't as cold as it was at home.

'I'll make a pot of tea,' Grace offered and Hannah nodded. 'Thanks,' she replied.

Colin and Hannah were silent for a while. Eventually she spoke. 'Maybe your father's greatest fault was that he had been desperately in love with your mother.'

Colin didn't look up at Hannah. Their families had been friends for as long as Colin could remember. 'He never thought about me or my brothers,' he replied with anger.

Hannah returned the anger. 'When will you ever forgive him?'

'He ruined my life,' Colin retorted.

'You did that all alone,' Hannah snapped as she shot him a killing glare and looked away.

'I had no choice,' he replied sadly.

'There's always a choice,' Hannah said with feeling,

swaying slightly and sitting down on the settee.

Grace came in with the tray and placed it on the coffee table.

'Are you all right?' she asked her sister.

Hannah took a deep breath. 'Yes,' she said quietly. 'I feel a bit faint.'

'I'm sorry, I shouldn't have got angry,' Colin said softly.

Hannah didn't look up as Grace sat down beside her.

'I know you're right,' he said to Hannah. 'Today made me realise that I don't want to live in regret anymore.'

Hannah forced a smile, but she looked weary to Colin.

'Take tomorrow off,' he ordered.

As soon as he finished the tea he left and returned to work. As he walked through the studio door, he caught sight of Bobby smoking.

'I can't trust you for five minutes, can I?' he barked, as Bobby swiftly extinguished the cigarette.

'I've done all the work,' Bobby said casually, 'and more.'

'Good,' Colin replied sarcastically. 'I'll find you some more then, if you've run out of things to do.'

The telephone rescued Bobby.

'Good afternoon, Barron's Design,' Bobby said in his professional voice.

Colin couldn't fault his son there; whenever a customer was involved he was polite and professional.

'Just a moment, he's right here. I'll put him on.'

He handed the phone to his father.

'It's Scott's Funeral Directors,' he said without feeling.

'I'll take it in my office, put it through,' he ordered.

Colin took the call in his room, relieved that he had returned in time to take the message. At least that was one secret that was now dead and buried.

44

Jodie knew that New Year's Eve had been a traumatic day for Bobby. It had triggered something, maybe some memory, but she couldn't get close to him. He'd been cold and unresponsive all evening, but he covered it with the old arrogance, only becoming quiet when a group of them had discussed New Year's resolutions.

On the stroke of midnight, just as they broke into *Auld Lang Syne*, she saw him leaving the hall. She followed him, glancing around quickly to decide which way he'd gone. She called after him but got no reply.

Guided only by the light of the moon, she buttoned up her coat and wrapped her scarf tightly around her neck. She cursed him as she stumbled down the path in her high-heeled boots and finally caught up with him by the side of the river. He sat in silence on the bench by the lamppost.

'I found this glass slipper. My prince left it when he fled at midnight,' she said. He looked up but his smile was feeble and he quickly resumed his slumped posture. She sat beside him and cuddled up close but he didn't move.

When he finally spoke, it was barely above a whisper. 'I can't do it anymore,' he said, despair in his voice.

He took a joint from his pocket and lit it, something which he wouldn't normally do in front of her, and she resisted the urge to reprimand him.

It was a long while before she answered, she felt out of her depth. 'It's all right,' she said in a kindly tone. 'I don't care whether you sing or not'.

He took a swig from his beer bottle before rising to his feet angrily and turning on her. 'You really don't understand do you?' He threw the bottle aside and it shattered on the wall behind him.

The unkindness in his tone pierced Jodie. She had tried her

best to understand.

'I'm not talking about singing. I can't cope with life.'

He thrust his hand into his pocket and produced a handful of amphetamines. She stared in disbelief for a moment, feeling sick in the pit of her stomach. She struck his hand, scattering the tablets.

'I thought you loved me,' she said, trying to quell the anger. 'I am courting you, but you are courting death.'

He glanced up at her. 'I've never loved anyone more.'

Refusing to let him see the tears in her eyes, she got up and walked beside the river. He followed her slowly, lifelessly.

'This isn't about you Jodie. I can't keep on like this.'

She didn't care if he did see her tears now, she was hurt and angry as she turned and faced him. 'I thought that your life and mine were inextricably linked,' she said, 'and now you tell me that I mean so little to you ...' her voice faltered. 'How did you think I would cope? What did you think it would do to me? Or didn't it even cross your mind?'

She began to walk away from him but he held her back by the arm.

'Do you want the truth?' he asked and she nodded, unable to speak. 'If you really knew what was in my heart you wouldn't want to know me at all. I could never be worthy of you Jodie, and your granddad doesn't need me sapping his energy and losing my temper with him just because he tells me the truth.'

She felt a failure. Despite all her effort, she had failed to communicate her love.

'How many times do I have to tell you that I love you?' she raised her voice. 'Do you think that I'm some kind of angelic being who will be tainted if I get close to you?' she attacked him angrily. 'Suicide is not courageous, it's cowardly. You are afraid to face the truth. Your father doesn't love you, has never loved you and will never love you.' She thrust her hands in her pockets and sat down heavily on the bench.

Bobby exploded; she could see fire in his eyes and wanted

218

to run, but she would not allow the fear to dominate her - how could she after the lecture she had just delivered? He towered over her with arms flailing and hair tossing from side to side, then he turned to her, sneering his riposte. 'So you used to be my girlfriend and now you've become my psychiatrist.'

She got up as she spoke to him. '*Used* to be your girlfriend? Are you saying it's over Bobby?'

He didn't reply, just kept his gaze on the water. Inside she felt such hurt and rejection, such total devastation. As she walked towards the hall, she hoped with all her heart that he would follow but knew in the depths of her being that he wouldn't. It wasn't until she reached the car that the tears began to fall. She drove through the mists of her own tears to the comfort and kindness of her granddad.

'I don't know,' she confided to her granddad, 'if I have the courage to love again.' He put his arm around her and she smiled despite her deep sorrow. Her granddad had always known when words were meaningless.

The quiet knock on the door the next morning woke Jodie's granddad. He unbolted the door and looked surprised to see Bobby.

'Come in,' he said, opening the door wide.

Bobby's expression was pained. 'I'm sorry. I hurt her.' He kept his eyes fixed firmly on the ground.

'Yes you did,' Granddad said, 'you hurt her very much. Did you want to see her?'

'Yes please,' he replied, unable to look her granddad in the eye.

'Have a seat. I'll see if she's awake.'

Granddad gently tapped on Jodie's door and then opened it slightly. 'Bobby's here to see you,' he said as he peered round the door.

She didn't look him in the eye. 'I don't want to see him,' she said.

'I think he's here to apologise,' her granddad said.

'I don't care what he's here for. I don't want to see him,' she said, and despite her granddad's pleading she stood her ground.

'I'm sorry Bobby but she won't see you,' Granddad said.

'I just wanted to apologise,' he offered.

'Don't push her Bobby,' Granddad said.

'Will you give her this for me then?' Bobby said, handing Granddad a gold bracelet with hearts on it.

'I will,' Granddad said, nodding lightly. 'Aren't you meant to be at work?'

Bobby laughed. 'We came to an agreement. I agreed to work all day Saturday if I could take a couple of hours to come round here now.'

'I'm sorry you had a wasted visit,' Granddad said as Bobby left.

45

'Dale's dead,' Elaine announced matter-of-factly at breakfast on Sunday. Bobby spluttered coffee everywhere and got up to wipe himself down with a dish cloth.

'You could have said it more kindly,' her mother said.

Elaine shrugged with an expression of disinterest, as Bobby sat down again.

'How?' Bobby asked, his hand shaking so much that he could no longer hold the coffee cup.

'OD'd on heroin, the place was crawling with police last night.'

Bobby felt sick. He walked away with his mother's voice echoing in the distance. 'You haven't finished your coffee.'

He sat at the desk in his room shaking. In desperation he took a bottle of whiskey from the wardrobe, and drank a little to calm his nerves, and then he drank a little more. He had no idea how long he'd been lying there when he was aroused by a knock at the door. He could hear it but he couldn't move. Eventually the door opened.

'Bobby?' He heard Jodie's voice as if she was far away, and her distorted face drifted in and out of focus. He wanted to ask her what she was doing here but he couldn't form the words.

'I came to say that I forgive you, and to thank you for the bracelet. Your mum told me about Dale.'

He closed his eyes, and she took hold of him by the collars, lifting his head off the pillow with some difficulty.

'How much of this have you had?' she said, letting go of him and picking up the empty whiskey bottle.

His face was contorted with pain, but she got no answers. 'Did you want to be next?'

He shook his head lightly from side to side without lifting it from the pillow.

'I don't care,' he said, though the message took a long time to get from his brain to his mouth.

'Why didn't you ring me?' she said, as she stroked the downy fair hair on his arm. He tried to open his eyes again but failed.

'I love you, you fool,' he heard her say, but he couldn't co-ordinate a response.

He heard her speak, as if into a cloud, then he felt his eyes closing again.

When he woke up, Jodie was still there and a streak of light from the street lamp rested on the bedcovers.

'How are you honey?' He was grateful that she spoke softly; his head wasn't treating him kindly.

'I'm sorry,' he ventured, anxiety etched on his face. 'Why did you come back?'

'I love you,' she said.

He didn't want her to see him like this. His hands shook slightly and he was perspiring heavily. He needn't have worried about her response, she stroked his hair and kissed his head lightly, before picking up the flannel from the washbasin, dampening it with cold water, and gently wiping his forehead. All he read in her expression was concern and kindness.

'You can't work tomorrow,' she declared.

'Oh that's okay,' he replied sarcastically as he sat up slowly, 'I'll ask Dad for compassionate leave.'

She smiled, and he apologised.

'I'm sorry,' he said, 'I didn't mean to snap.'

She sat beside him and leant across to kiss him. 'I won't stay,' she said softly. 'You need to rest. I'll come back tomorrow evening. Don't drink, Bobby,' she pleaded. 'It won't help.'

He fell asleep again almost as soon as she left the room, and awoke in a dishevelled mess on Monday morning. After switching on the bedside lamp, he forced himself out of bed and peered at himself in the mirror. 'You look a bloody mess,' he told his reflection, as he ran his fingers through his hair. After a shower, he got dressed, put on his coat, and went down to the end of the garden for a cigarette.

He survived work that Monday simply because he couldn't argue. He couldn't concentrate, so for once in his life, the more mundane the task was, the better he liked it. He'd lost. He knew he'd lost. He couldn't even kill himself successfully and he'd lost the will to fight. He trudged through his meaningless day in a dull grey haze.

When Jodie arrived in the evening he was almost asleep. He forced himself to sit up.

'It's okay,' she said, turning to leave, 'you sleep.'

'No, take me for a walk,' he requested, grabbing hold of her arm.

'That makes you sound like a dog,' she laughed.

'I feel like a dog,' he said. 'I should have known something was wrong. I saw him last week. He told me never to touch the stuff.'

She took his hand as they wandered beside the canal. Nothing she said would convince him of his innocence. Most of the time they wandered in silence; everything but nature's sounds stood morbidly still under the village moonlight.

'I'm sorry I haven't been much help,' she said as she was about to leave.

'Just being here helps,' he smiled.

He kissed her gently and she left. His weary body fell instantly asleep that night and he woke late, rushing into work at the last second.

'You were almost late,' his father said.

Bobby sighed. 'But I wasn't,' he replied, but there was no energy in it. His father made it clear that he expected Bobby to be back to normal, but as the day drew on his work became increasingly inferior, and at times unfinished. 'Concentrate!' his father shouted at him in front of everyone. 'Keep your private life out of your work.'

Bobby winced, but he hadn't the energy or the will for a confrontation. It would be easier to block out the pain than to cope with his father's wrath. For the rest of the day he put every ounce of his energy into concentrating on his work, but by the evening he was a nervous wreck. Jodie was baby-sitting, so his only answer was to drink. He drank until he felt sick, and then fell asleep on top of the covers.

When he awoke on Wednesday, his father's angry face was glaring down at him. 'Dale's mother is on the phone. It better not be trouble.'

As Bobby sat up, he clutched his head and groaned, instantly cursing himself for his indiscretion. After dragging himself up to a standing position, he threw on his dressing gown and walked slowly downstairs.

'Hello,' he said softly, more because it would hurt his head to raise his voice than for respect for Dale's mother. 'I am so sorry, I still can't believe it.' He slumped on the floor in the hall against the wall. 'Yes Mrs. Connor. I'm working half-day today. I'll come round this afternoon.' He nodded, though she obviously couldn't see it. 'Yes, I'll see you later.'

The instant he hung up his father shouted to him. 'Hurry up.'

Bobby pulled himself to his feet. 'You'd better not be late for work,' his father continued.

By the time he reappeared, his father had left for work. Unable to face breakfast at home, Bobby stopped off at the village shop and bought an apple.

'Are you on your way to the studio?' Ernie asked him as he handed him the change.

'Yes sir,' Bobby replied politely.

'Haven't you had breakfast?'

'No sir.'

'Here,' he said, handing Bobby a cup of tea. 'You have this one, there's plenty more in the pot.' Ernie was silent for a moment and then looked back at Bobby.

'Are you all right Master Barron? You're not normally this

quiet.'

Bobby smiled; a weary smile. 'A good friend of mine just died.'

'Oh I'm terribly sorry,' Ernie said, raising his hat in respect. 'You shouldn't be goin' to work.' Then he added, 'Oh, your father don't agree I guess.'

Bobby smiled; a real smile this time. He didn't reply, he didn't need to, and once he'd politely finished the far too sweet tea, he left for work to ensure that he wasn't late.

46

Hannah arrived at the studio before Colin on Wednesday morning. She unlocked the doors and cupboards, and restocked Colin's office as she always did, but today she sat and waited for him.

She heard the soft purr of the engine as his car drew up and gazed at him out of the window with admiration. He had always been the brightest kid on the estate. The studio bell rang and her heart beat fast as she heard him on the stairs.

'Hannah?' he said, startled as he leant on the doorpost of his office. She shot a forced, nervous smile in his direction whilst avoiding his gaze. Colin shut the door and sat beside her, taking her hand in his. 'It's positive isn't it?' he whispered.

Hannah's eyes met his for a brief second but she looked away as she nodded gently. 'I'm sorry, I should have known better.'

'This is my doing. I never loved Mary. I'm sorry,' Colin said.

She gripped his hand. It felt so strong, so tender, so right, but it was so wrong.

'It's okay,' she said, laying aside all that she felt and desired. 'I've been awake all night thinking about it and I've made a decision. If you'll help me financially, there's a clinic not far from the estate where …'

'Absolutely not,' Colin interrupted, slamming his free hand down on the filing cabinet beside him.

Hannah jumped and then broke down in tears. 'I can't,' she sobbed as she let go of his hand, got up, and walked towards the window which overlooked the town. 'I'm thirty-nine, I just can't do this alone.' Her tears turned to anger at him now. It wasn't him who would have to tend and nurture the child, and struggle alone.

He got up and took her hand. 'I've been thinking too, in fact I've done nothing else since you told me that you could be pregnant. My marriage is as much of a millstone around Mary's neck as it is around mine. I'm leaving her. '

Colin let go of her hand as he heard the bell ring. 'That must be Bobby. Say nothing. I'll settle it with Mary tonight,' he said as he walked towards the door.

'No Colin, don't,' she replied, raising her voice.

As Colin left the office, Bobby walked through the studio door.

'I don't want to hear any more about it,' Colin said firmly to Hannah.

He threw Bobby the keys. 'I'll be out of the office this morning, lock up when you leave,' he ordered as he left.

Bobby looked puzzled, his eyes flitting between Hannah and his father's retreating form. She looked away as she saw him approaching, hoping to hide her recent tears.

'Are you all right?' he asked her, and he gently laid a hand on her shoulder, just as his father would. She winced slightly but merely nodded, unable to reply for fear of crying. She watched as Kate arrived and talked with him.

'Are you okay?' she heard Kate ask.

Bobby nodded. 'I'll cope,' he replied. 'I'm staying with Jodie's granddad on Thursday night. He offered as soon as he knew that Dale's mum had asked me to speak at the funeral, but I protested. Jodie talked me into it.'

'You'll be better there than at home,' Kate said to him.

Hannah winced at the harshness towards Colin but she felt compassion for Bobby. She knew him well enough to know that with a sensitive spirit like his, he would be deeply upset. She knew it because it was the same spirit that had once dwelt in his father.

At mid-day, Bobby locked up and wandered to his motorbike. He wasn't in a hurry to see Dale's mother. *Whatever can I say to her that is meaningful?* In reality, her numbness made it easy. Bobby agreed to say a few words at the funeral on Friday, and soon afterwards he left. Now all he had to do was get the morning off work. Today didn't seem a good day to ask, but he couldn't leave it any later. He asked at dinner.

'Oh Colin, he can't let poor Mrs Connor down can he?' his mother said.

Colin turned on her.

'Oh shut up whittling. All right,' he snapped, turning to Bobby, 'but I expect you back afterwards.' Bobby said nothing.

Colin left the table first and as Bobby got up he stopped to help his mother clear the table, grateful to her for once. That evening he lay in his room desperately trying to think what he could say at the funeral of a friend who had just turned twenty-one. He fell asleep.

All Thursday he struggled through work. He felt a little better than he had for a couple of days but when Kate called him across he still plodded wearily. 'What's the problem?' he asked.

'Your dad asked me to design a flier advertising the new Chinese take-away using this typeface, but I can't tell which one it is or even what size the font is.'

He took the example card in his hand. 'You can measure the font ... about thirty,' he suggested, 'but you can tell the typeface by the lower case "g", now try.'

Relieved, Kate smiled. 'Thanks,' she said as he returned to his desk.

Colin came into the room. 'Have you finished that brochure design yet?' he asked Bobby.

'I'm working on it now,' Bobby replied without looking up.

Colin marched away as he replied. 'I want it on my desk within the hour.'

By the end of the day Bobby was exhausted and relieved to be staying with Jodie's granddad for the night. He sat on his motorbike outside the studio, leaning on the handlebars. *However will I get through the next twenty-four hours?* he asked himself. He took a deep breath and started the bike up. The traffic was heavy and it took him a long time to get to the main road to Granddad's house but at least he was welcome there.

'I'm glad Jodie convinced you to change your mind. You don't want the faintest possibility of an argument with your father tonight,' Granddad said as Bobby took off his leather jacket.

'You're right,' Bobby conceded. 'And I still have to work out what I'm going to say.'

The evening was relaxed and Bobby went to bed early to think. As soon as he'd written the eulogy, he fell asleep, emotionally and physically exhausted

47

On the morning of the funeral, Bobby awoke from his best sleep in years, though what he awoke to was still daunting. He sat at the breakfast table drinking a cup of coffee. This morning, he regretted agreeing to speak at the funeral.

'How do you feel baby?' Jodie asked, mussing his hair gently.

'I can't do this,' he cried with a deep sigh. He looked up at her like an anguished child. 'Dale's mother said that he had massive amounts of heroin in his bloodstream. He wouldn't have made a mistake like that.' He was close to tears. 'He did it on purpose.'

'Why do you think he did it?' Jodie asked, sitting beside him.

'Dale and I laughed our way through our pain in the early days, and he coped okay when his dad left, but the morning after his stepfather moved in he changed. He became nervous, he stopped smiling and laughing, and he wore a look of terror. He never spoke about it.'

Bobby broke down in tears.

'If only ...' he sobbed, lying down on his arms.

Granddad moved Jodie to one side and spoke soothingly to him. 'Sometimes there's nothing we can do.'

Jodie glanced at her watch. 'We'd better be going,' she said anxiously.

'I have to do it. I have to do it for Dale,' he said, getting up and moving with determination towards to the door.

It seemed a long way to the church on the outskirts of Brockton, as if time had slowed and everything held its breath in mourning for a young life cut short. Bobby felt weak as they walked the few yards from the car park to the church. As the usher on the door shook his hand limply and offered him an order of service and a pitying smile, he wanted to run.

Deathly silence and the stone cold atmosphere greeted him as he stepped inside the church. Everyone was silent and still, as if rigor mortis had set into the living as well as the dead. They walked slowly down the aisle to the seats reserved for them near the front. Throughout the brief service Bobby laid his head on his hands, as if in prayer.

The coffin rested on trestles at the front of the church, with white lilies adorning it. There was something surreal about it; Bobby wouldn't be surprised to wake up and find that it was all a nightmare. He awoke from his musings as the vicar called his name.

He stood at the lectern silently for a moment to gain his composure. He had told no-one that he had written a poem, not even Jodie.

'Oh gentle, gentle friend,
  too tender for a cruel and loveless world
  that lends no comfort to tormented souls,
  but binds the son of anguish and despair
  while setting free oppressors everywhere.'

His voice grew in strength as he continued,

'Justice mocked you from afar
 and yet, you never turned an evil eye
 or sought revenge, when others would have tried.
 Another's battles you would seek to fight,
 making light, of the darkness of your night.'

He caught Dale's mother's eye as he began the next verse, and she held his gaze for a moment.

'Oh sweet, kind comforter,
 you often took my pain upon yourself
 and calmed my aching heart with gentle words,

231

or stilled my raging anger with a touch,
a tiny gesture which has meant so much.'

He stopped for a moment but Jodie urged him on with her eyes.

'Crushed by life's cruellest blows
you shrouded fear and sorrow's deepest woes
beneath a mask society condemns.
What could such faceless people know of grief
which fills your head at night without relief.'

His voice grew stronger as he began the final verse.

'Rest on my dearest friend.
Leave now the battles and the strife to us,
who take the mantel of your justice cry.
We'll never lay it down and never rest,
until we have set free the poor, oppressed.'

He blinked back tears as he left the lectern and returned to his seat, leaning heavily on Granddad, who whispered, 'Well done,' but the kindness and softness caused him to weep again, and at the sight of his weeping, others wept too.

Bobby stayed with Jodie and her granddad as they walked to the graveyard, until looking over his shoulder, he realised that Dale's mother was alone. She looked frail and vulnerable. *Where are the family? Why is no-one here to support her?* He caught her up and took her arm. He didn't really hear the words of the committal, he felt detached somehow. As they left the graveside, Dale's mother was driven away alone. When he arrived back at the gate to the graveyard, Jodie and her granddad were waiting for him in the car. They drove back to the cottage in silence.

'Thank you,' Bobby said, 'I'd better get back to work.'

Bobby took out a cigarette, but his hands shook so much

that he couldn't co-ordinate the actions needed to light it.

Granddad put a hand on his shoulder. 'Jodie's made a lovely vegetable soup, why don't you stop and have some and then go back to work?'

'I don't want to make him angry,' Bobby replied, but he put the cigarette back in his pocket and turned towards the door, following them inside.

'It won't take long to warm it up,' Jodie said.

Bobby took off his coat and sat down beside the fire with his eyes closed. Before the soup was ready he was asleep. Jodie called him gently when she brought the soup in. She put the tray down on the coffee table beside him and tried to rouse him. He sat upright as he realised where he was.

'What time is it?' he asked.

'It's okay,' she replied. 'You only nodded off for a few minutes. Here,' she said as she picked up the tray and handed it to him.

'Thanks,' he said softly, forcing a smile.

'Bobby?' Granddad said cautiously, sitting down beside him as he repositioned the cushion. 'I want to ring your father.'

'No, don't do that!' Bobby exclaimed, agitated.

'I'd rather you didn't go back to work this afternoon.'

Bobby became agitated. 'He'll go mad.'

Granddad smiled a mischievous smile. 'Oh, I think I could persuade him.'

Bobby shrugged, too exhausted to argue, so Granddad picked up the phone.

'Hello ... Mr Barron? Yes that's right it is ... Yes he is here ... no I really don't think he's well enough to work this afternoon. I'm sure it is very busy, yes, but if I take him to the doctor to get a certificate he'll be off longer.'

Bobby couldn't hear the reply but Granddad held the receiver a long way from his ear.

'He'll be back tomorrow ... yes I promise.'

Bobby choked and had to get up to get a glass of water.

When Granddad appeared at the kitchen door, he sported a satisfied grin. Bobby broke into a real smile for the first time since the funeral.

'Thank you,' he said.

Bobby and Jodie went for a walk in the afternoon and spent a quiet and relaxed evening together. He slept peacefully through the night, but he was nervous in the morning at the prospect of facing his father. Granddad embraced him and whispered to him alone. 'Come and see me again tonight.'

With a weary nod, Bobby left.

48

'That,' Colin said through gritted teeth, 'was a disgraceful piece of manipulation.'

Bobby didn't raise his eyes from the floor of his father's office. 'I'm sorry,' he said. He'd lost the will to fight. The submissive attitude took his father aback momentarily.

'That's what happens if you mess around with drugs,' his father stated sternly without sympathy. Bobby flinched but he hid it from his father.

'I hope it teaches you a lesson, now get on with your work,' his father said handing him a pile of work that Bobby could see instantly would take him well past the normal Saturday half-day, and probably into the evening. He didn't reply and after Colin left at lunch-time, Kate came across to him.

'What the hell are you doing back so soon?' she asked.

'I can't fight him anymore,' he replied despondently.

'You can't just give up,' Kate protested.

'You should have gone by now,' he said, and then ignored her until she left; he didn't want to discuss it any more.

'I still want your love, Dad,' he called to the silence. He laid his head on his arms and cried as the emotions of the last few days and of many years overwhelmed him. When he finally lifted his head it was with a new resolve to be the son that his father wanted him to be. He forced himself to concentrate on the next piece of work on the pile. Two hours later he had completed the work to perfection.

It was already late so he rode straight to Granddad's house. Jodie was baby-sitting again tonight so he would have her granddad to himself. The welcome, the coffee, the seat by the fire, all the familiar gestures of kindness awaited him, but he was restless, and consciously tried to stop the nervous flickering of his eyes.

'What's the matter?' Granddad asked him.

Bobby stared blankly ahead. His voice was weak and lifeless. 'I feel as if I'm about to step off the edge.' He looked troubled, his eyes pleading with Granddad.

After a moment of silence Granddad spoke calmly.

'What happened the day you came here as a child?' he asked.

'I don't know. I don't remember,' Bobby replied sharply as he got up and paced the floor, lighting yet another cigarette.

'Why don't you sit down?' Granddad said softly.

Bobby sat down on the edge of the chair.

'Once you have told me you will understand,' he said gently but firmly.

'I don't remember,' Bobby repeated harshly. He jumped up again, this time turning away from Granddad and looking intently out of the window.

'Until you accept that you are totally incapable of making him love you, you will never be free,' Granddad said.

Bobby stubbed out the half-smoked cigarette in the ashtray with great force.

'I need to prove myself to him. I owe him that. I'm tired of listening to everyone. I'm going to do it alone now.' He grabbed his coat and scarf and walked out slamming the door behind him, stopping outside the door to put on his coat and light yet another cigarette. Now he would work hard in the studio and on his return to college he would drop fine art and the folk club. 'From tonight I will be the son he wants,' he said aloud as he walked across the field.

As he opened the front door at home, he could hear his parents arguing in the kitchen and was determined not to get drawn in. *Have I really caused so much friction in the family?* He put his head around the kitchen door.

'Excuse me ...' he said politely, 'do you still want me to play the organ in the morning?'

Colin raised his eyebrows. 'Er ... yes, okay. It's the early service.'

Bobby smiled. 'Okay,' and went straight to his room.

His sleep was restless as usual but he got up early, dressed smartly and played for the early service as he had promised. The day went smoothly as Bobby complied with his father's wishes. Whatever he felt, he would do what his father requested. It was the only way to receive his father's love.

That evening when Jodie arrived she kissed him on the cheek; it felt more dutiful than loving. He made coffee, carried it on a tray to his room and set it down on the corner of his desk. An uneasy silence hung between them but eventually Jodie spoke.

'Why, Bobby?' She looked hurt and he doodled nervously on a scrap of paper. He hadn't intended hurting either of them, but he couldn't handle their disappointment. He could hear shouting again downstairs. He closed his eyes and sighed deeply as he flung the pencil across his desk. 'I wish they'd stop it,' he exploded in exasperation.

'Why?' she persisted, more gently this time, but with no less pain in her eyes or her voice. He took a deep breath.

'I have to do it alone Jodie. I'll do whatever it takes.'

Jodie stared at him, shaking her head in disbelief. 'You're chasing the wind.'

She turned aside, looking aimlessly out of the window, calmer now. 'Sometimes you can be incredibly stupid for someone so bright.'

Anger rose from deep within him. *How could she begin to understand?* So many thoughts were clamouring for his attention that he couldn't hear anything, but he'd heard her call him stupid; he'd heard that many times before but never from Jodie. It pierced his heart and he lost his temper.

'It's all right for you isn't it. You can stand there and judge my life. Listen to them.' He waved his hand in the direction of the door. 'It's every night these days. That's my fault,' he said, pointing to himself.

She interrupted him, angrier than he'd ever seen her before. 'How can it possibly be your fault? You'll end up as bitter and angry as he is.'

She looked away from him and he felt her rejection deeply. He greeted rejection as he always had, defensively. 'How the hell would you know?' he shouted, though she stubbornly refused to look him in the eye. He lit a cigarette and inhaled deeply, desperately trying to calm himself.

She turned and looked him angrily in the eye this time. 'All I know is that my granddad loves you and you've walked away from him. You're a fool.'

Bobby erupted, speaking through clenched teeth, his face contorted with rage. 'It's so bloody easy from where you stand isn't it?'

He picked up the half full coffee mug and flung it full force at the door. Coffee flew across the room and the mug smashed into pieces. Jodie covered her face with her hand to protect herself before turning towards him. He faced the window, ashamed. When he finally looked up she placed a hand on his arm but he pulled away. She stepped back as she called his name, questioning and anxious. 'Bobby?'

He stared at the door where the coffee still dripped onto the pile of broken crockery. In that moment he loathed himself. He physically shook, terrified of his anger, terrified of himself.

'Go,' he ordered her. 'Just leave.'

She looked at him with awful anguish in her eyes. 'Bobby?' she said again with that same questioning anxiety, and he could see tears in her eyes.

He looked away. By dragging her into his wretched life he had hurt her. He destroyed every life he touched. When he turned around she was leaving and he could hear her sobbing even above the clattering of the broken crockery as she opened the door. He was devastated.

'I've become as monstrous a bastard as he is,' he said aloud to himself. As he stared out of the window he could see Jodie's sorrowful silhouette leaning on the steering wheel of her granddad's car. He knew she was crying.

'I can't allow myself to hurt her anymore; she'd be better off without me,' he told himself sadly with resolve. He took writing paper and his fountain pen from the drawer of his desk and sat down to write her a letter, beautifully written in his usual hand.

Dearest Jodie,

I am sorry that I ever drew you into my pitiful life. I have hurt you so much and I will regret that all my days. I have no hope for the future and I'm not prepared to destroy you. I believe that it is best for you if I break off this relationship and put you out of your misery. I hope that you will find someone worthy of you,

All my love, Bobby

He folded the letter carefully and reached into the drawer for an envelope. He felt numb as he placed the letter in the envelope. He had no idea how he would bear life without her. His head pounded but he had to do it now, he had to relieve her of the agony.

He went downstairs in his leather jacket, picked up his crash helmet and keys, and left. Arriving at her granddad's road, he left the bike at the end of the row of cottages and quietly slipped the note through the letterbox.

49

Kate had only rung Jodie that Sunday night to ask a favour. She hadn't expected her to be in, she'd only intended leaving a message. She stormed into work the next morning and laid into Bobby, without noticing how subdued he was.

'How could you do that to her?'

Kate's eyes narrowed as she leant aggressively across his desk, heavily invading his personal space. She was so angry that she could not, indeed would not, allow his pain to penetrate her heart.

'I did it for her, not for me,' he said passively, without stopping his work.

'You're a selfish bastard,' she shouted at him, banging her fist on the desk, totally unaware that Colin was stood behind her.

'Kate,' Colin shouted, causing her to jump. 'How would it look if a customer walked in here now?'

He cocked his head on one side, awaiting an answer, but continued before she had a chance.

'I agree with your sentiments,' he said glaring at Bobby out of the corner of his eye, 'but not with your means of expressing them. Get on with your work.' He turned to Bobby, pointing to his office, 'You, in there now.'

Kate felt guilty. The look that Bobby shot her as he rose wearily to his feet was not one of anger, but of betrayal. He didn't utter a word in his defence, his spirit seemed crushed, and in that moment she knew that he hadn't broken up with Jodie for his own benefit. He looked back at her as he entered the office and his eyes condemned her. All she could hear was an angry tirade from Colin, not a word from Bobby. Normally he would make some attempt to defend himself, but today he was silent, broken. He needed her support not her condemnation. She jumped up impulsively and knocked at Colin's door. He opened it angrily.

'Go away, I'm busy.'

She put her foot in the way so that he couldn't shut the door.

'It was my fault not Bobby's,' she insisted.

'Get on with your work,' he demanded, and pushed the door hard until she moved her foot.

She was angry with Colin and angry at herself for acting impulsively. When she finally heard the office door open, she looked up with an expression of contrition which was totally lost on Bobby; he didn't raise his eyes from the ground. He walked over to his desk, scribbled on a sheet of paper, picked up his jacket, and walked out without looking back.

Kate couldn't concentrate now, all she could think about was Bobby, and when Colin entered the room half an hour later, she couldn't look him in the eye.

'Where is he?' Colin shouted to nobody in particular, as he crossed the studio to Bobby's desk.

'He left,' Simon offered without emotion.

Colin's eyes scanned the scribbled message. He picked it up and screwed it up, clenching it in his fist. His eyes narrowed and his nostrils flared as he threw the note into the rubbish bin. 'He'll pay for this,' he said under his breath, as he passed by Kate's desk.

He stopped briefly to talk to Hannah, and then returned to his office to gather his belongings before leaving. Kate could no longer take the strain; she laid her head down on her arms on the desk and cried. It was Hannah who came to her side to comfort her.

'It's not your fault, it's a long-standing battle.'

Kate's words were punctuated with sobs. 'It wasn't his fault, I was angry with him for breaking up with Jodie last night.'

Kate was startled by Hannah's response. She spoke quietly, shocked. 'He broke up with Jodie? No wonder …' Hannah's countenance changed to one of alarm. 'Oh God no,' she said, shaking her head and taking hold of Kate's arm, 'you have to do something.'

She took Kate into Colin's office and sat down. Hannah was breathing heavily, attempting to compose herself. 'It's history repeating itself,' she whispered, as she leant back in Colin's chair and closed her eyes in distress. She opened them again and looked straight at Kate. After a deep sigh, she began slowly, but with determination.

The tale Hannah told left Kate flabbergasted. Colin's father had been a violent alcoholic, and it had been Hannah who was Colin's sweetheart, not Bobby's mother. Colin had tried repeatedly to help his father, always hoping that this time he would stay sober, but always disappointed by broken promises. Eventually, he felt that he could offer Hannah no future except heartache and pain, and he broke off the relationship and slept with Mary, Bobby's mother, on the rebound. Mary's ensuing pregnancy trapped him forever in a loveless marriage. His life descended into anger, bitterness and duty. He had a duty to Mary. This bastard child had come between him and the woman he loved.

Kate stood up, struggling to take it in and whispered, 'So Colin never loved him, Bobby never stood a chance.' She stood up, staring out of the office window, the sunlight picking out the autumn shades in her long auburn hair.

'Why did he marry her? Why did he never leave her, if that was how he felt?'

Hannah shrugged, barely able to speak. 'Duty,' she said eventually, 'and that's what he expects from everyone else.' Tears filled Hannah's eyes, but she quickly wiped them away. 'I've often watched Bobby, the likeness to Colin when he was young is so striking. He's sociable, excitable, enthusiastic, sensitive, and yet tortured and angry.' She broke down in tears and this time it was Kate who comforted *her.* She pleaded with Kate through reddened eyes.

'Talk to him, Kate, he's wasting his time with his father. Tell him the truth.' She grabbed hold of Kate's arm. 'Don't let this happen again.' Kate promised not to, left the room and returned to her desk. She felt uneasy when Colin returned and went into the office, where Hannah had stayed. She could hear animated discussion and Hannah's tearful words. Eventually, Colin emerged, threw Simon the keys, and left.

The day dragged; Kate longed to escape the studio, to tell Bobby what she knew, although she guessed that he would never want to speak to her again. When she finally got away she headed for Jerry's house. He seemed to have a sort of instinct where Bobby was concerned.

'Hurry up, hurry up,' she said to the front door as she waited on his doorstep. Jerry was never in a hurry. She rang the bell again, launching into an animated explanation the second he opened the door.

'Cool it babe,' he said casually. 'I can't take it in at that pace.'

Once inside, she stopped and took a deep breath, and only then did she notice his attire. He was dressed in a t-shirt and dungarees, and his long, curly hair was tied back off his face. 'What are you doing?' she asked him, changing tack briefly. He looked down at his clothes and up at her again.

'Er, decorating,' he replied. 'Now would you mind backing up, slowing down, and telling me what you came to tell me?' Then he replaced the cigarette in his mouth.

'It was entirely my fault really ...' she began.

'... I doubt that, but carry on,' he said with the cigarette still in his mouth.

'Last night I rang Jodie to ask her a favour ...' She recounted the story to him, and when she finally came to a conclusion he let out a deep sigh.

'Actually ...' he said as he took another drag on his cigarette. 'I'm not surprised.'

Kate looked startled and was about to speak, when Jerry beat her to it.

'I suggested to him at Christmas that there was something

odd going on, but he thought the idea was preposterous.'

Kate looked at him with wide, pleading eyes. 'But I don't know what to do with the information.'

Jerry laughed aloud as he stubbed out the cigarette in a saucer. 'You mean you don't want to do what you have to do.'

Kate got up and paced the room. 'I'm frightened of how he'll react.'

'To you or to the information?'

'Both,' she replied, sitting down again.

Jerry walked across the kitchen and picked up the 'phone. 'I'll see if I can get hold of him.' He dialled the number as he spoke, turning away as the call was answered.

'Hello, is Bobby there please?' he asked politely, which suggested to Kate that Colin had answered the phone. Jerry held the receiver away from his ear. Kate could hear the ravings from where she sat, and saw the colour drain from Jerry's face before he put the receiver down. 'I hope we can find him before his father does,' he said softly to Kate. 'His dad is a total nutcase.'

Kate's eyes followed him earnestly as he sat down again, nervously tapping an unlit cigarette on the edge of the saucer in front of him.

Her face was taut with anxiety. 'Where do you think he is?'

He put down the cigarette and took her hand in both of his. 'Don't worry,' he said, 'Bobby's a survivor. I'll get changed and we'll go and see Jodie's granddad.'

She got up and sat down three times, asking herself over and over again why it was that she always acted first and thought afterwards. When Jerry appeared at the foot of the stairs, Kate looked up as if she had just returned from another planet.

'Are you coming? I'll drive,' he said.

She didn't argue with him, but as they drove away she felt fear in the pit of her stomach. *What would Bobby say when he saw her?* She knew she'd gone too far this time; she had destroyed his final hope of reconciliation with his father.

Kate's forced smile faded when she realised that Bobby was not at Jodie's granddad's cottage. Jodie's granddad ushered them inside, and Kate related the day's events to Granddad. Granddad listened attentively, giving only a knowing nod from time to time. 'So it's my fault,' she concluded.

This time Granddad shook his head, leant towards Kate and fixed his eyes on hers. 'He was going to find out one day.'

Kate was certain that Bobby wouldn't see things quite that way.

'Listen,' Granddad continued, 'he knows where we are if he needs help.'

Kate was unconvinced; indeed she was certain that he wouldn't come looking for her unless he had a shotgun.

Jerry looked up at her, 'Mum will be back by now, we'd better go.'

She stood up and crossed the room to pick up her coat. Granddad got up and stood beside her.

'I'll let you know if I hear anything,' he said.

'Thanks,' she said.'

Granddad gave her a kindly wink, as if to tell her not to worry, and they left.

Back at the flat she was concerned at Jodie's apparent disinterest. She had erased him from her life as if he had never existed. Kate tossed and turned, tortured as she tried to sleep that night. Tomorrow she would see Bobby and she would have to tell him the truth. She woke up in the night and heard Jodie in the kitchen. She knew Jodie's heart was broken, but how long could she go on denying it to herself? She heard Jodie's bedroom door shut, and finally allowed herself to relax. Tomorrow he would listen to the truth. Maybe then things would change forever.

50

Bobby rode to his retreat by the river in total desolation. He had tried everything to gain his father's love, but he'd failed. He had never felt so completely without hope as he did now. He had neither the courage to live nor to die. He leant back against the damp tree and shut his eyes. All he felt was indifference. When he awoke it was almost dark. He got up drowsily and brushed himself down before heading back to the motorbike. He got as far as Dernham church before he realised that going home wasn't a wise option.

He stopped the bike outside the church and wandered through the graveyard, trying to consider his best course of action. Apology wouldn't work; his father would never give him the opportunity for that. He tried the old church door; it was open so he stepped inside. The bad memories of the public humiliation by his father in this place were outweighed by the kindness of a few of its members and of the present vicar. He walked slowly down the aisle until he stood, once again, looking up at the cross which hung high above the altar in the apse. He knelt at the altar rail as he had many times before, but this time he cried out from the depths of his heart.

'Why, God, why?' he cried aloud to the god he no longer believed in. His cries were disturbed by the sound of soft footsteps and as he turned around he saw strange shadows playing in the half-light of the church before he heard Rev Turner's voice.

'I'm sorry, I didn't mean to disturb you.'

He rose to his feet as he spoke and stepped back from the altar. He knew that if he faced the vicar his tears would be visible even in this light.

'Don't go,' the vicar said, sitting down on the front row of the choir stalls. He signalled to the space beside him.

Bobby didn't want to break down; not there, not then. He hoped that the Rev didn't see him as he wiped a tear from his face.

'Come and sit down,' the Rev beckoned. He spoke with gentleness. 'Why have you rejected the people who care about you?'

'Who told you?' Bobby asked, puzzled.

'You forget; I know Jodie's granddad.'

'Oh yes,' Bobby said forlornly, gazing at the ground. 'I couldn't go on hurting them,' he said eventually. 'I couldn't do that to Jodie, anybody else, but not Jodie.' Tears ran down his face but it didn't seem to matter anymore.

'Don't you think,' the vicar continued, 'that you hurt them more by taking away their right to stand by you?'

'I was constantly disappointing them.'

He got up and paced the floor in front of the altar before suddenly rounding on the vicar. 'I have to do what's right by him. "Honour your father and mother", isn't that what you say?' he snapped angrily, turning his face away from the vicar. He stood and faced the cross again, hiding the shame of his failure from the vicar. He felt a calming hand on his shoulder. Rev Turner was slow to answer.

'I have never said those words in your presence for fear that you would be unnecessarily burdened by a misinterpretation of them.'

'He says it to me,' Bobby spat.

'Your father?'

'Yes.' Bobby's voice was a whisper.

'He must be a very unhappy man.'

'I bloody well hope so,' Bobby exclaimed.

The vicar continued, 'He runs his life by duty but he's forgotten how to love.'

Bobby stepped back and looked up at the vicar with anger in his eyes. 'Do you expect me to feel sorry for him?' His voice echoed around the stone church.

'Of course not,' the vicar replied gently. 'I just want you to be free of him. It's time you had a life of your own?'

Bobby said nothing. Something rang true in the words that the vicar spoke to him. He walked away and sat in the nave alone, resting his head on the pew in front of him. He was so life-weary, so worn out. After a while the vicar moved and sat beside him. 'It was never your fault Bobby. He tries to control us all but he takes out his anger on you.'

Bobby sat up and turned to face the vicar with a look of anguished defeat.

'I can't do it anymore. I can't be the submissive son he wants.' There were tears in his eyes again.

Rev Turner smiled. 'I'm glad to hear it.'

Bobby didn't return the smile, or even meet the Rev's gaze. Where could he find the courage to tell Rev Turner what he was thinking? This was the first time he had admitted his feelings to himself, never mind sharing them with the vicar.

'What is it, Bobby?'

Bobby took a deep breath and looked away, unable to face the vicar as he spoke. 'Rev?' he said tentatively, addressing the vicar informally, as if talking to a friend. The vicar nodded, urging him to continue.

'I'm afraid,' Bobby said eventually. 'Until I met Jodie and her granddad I never stayed still long enough to find out what I feel, but they have brought to the surface all sorts of feelings that I had never acknowledged before, which has sent me into deeper turmoil.'

He stopped and looked up, aware that Rev Turner was studying his face but saying nothing.

'Go on,' the vicar urged.

'Sometimes I think I hate my father and yet I feel so guilty about it that I can't bear to admit it.'

He looked away again, ashamed of his thoughts and feelings. How could he sit here with this godly man and admit to such evil thoughts? He got up to leave to spare the vicar the embarrassment. 'I shouldn't have said that. I'd better go before I say ...'

The vicar took hold of his arm as he interrupted him. 'No. Stay. Of course you are angry with him. Sometimes I get so angry with the way he talks to me before a service that I don't know how I make it through the morning.'

Bobby sat down again and looked up at him, stunned. 'Do you, honestly?'

'Bobby I'm human, and your father is one of the most bitter and angry people I know.'

Ashamed, Bobby closed his eyes as he said quietly, 'When I was younger I used to hear him go out in the car and I'd pray to God that he would crash it and die. That's a terrible thing to think isn't it?'

'But understandable, you didn't know another way to cope with what you felt,' the vicar replied.

'What can I do?' Bobby asked in a whisper.

'I would go and see Jodie's granddad.'

'What if he won't see me?' Bobby's question was anxious, but he was calmer now.

The vicar placed a comforting hand on Bobby's arm, 'He will.'

Bobby sighed as he got up to leave. 'I'll go tomorrow after work. I mustn't keep you any longer, I'll see you Sunday,' Bobby said with a weak smile.

As Bobby left, the Rev raised one eyebrow as if to say that he would believe it when he saw it. Bobby smiled.

51

As Bobby walked out into the darkness it engulfed him. Part of the memory of his time at Granddad's house as a child returned to him and he ran to the motorbike as if he could outrun the memory. He rode faster than he knew was safe, fighting thoughts, fears and anger.

As he entered the house he could hear shouting, and his spirit sank. He took off his jacket and walked straight past Elaine, who was standing nervously in the hallway, and went upstairs. He put on a record to drown out the arguing and lay back on the bed, thinking about his conversation with the vicar. His father came upstairs and banged on the door, shouting at him to turn it down. He turned it off and as the arguing got worse, he entertained suicidal thoughts again. Nothing would ever change.

'No dad, don't!' he heard Elaine shout, followed by a blood curdling scream, 'Bobby,' his sister yelled.

By the time he reached the bottom of the stairs, Elaine was paralysed with fear. He moved her aside in order to get to the kitchen.

'Quick!' she cried as he passed.

He turned back to her briefly as he pushed up his sleeves. 'I'll stop him for good this time.'

The tone was sinister and she tried to hold him back, but he shook his arm free of her grasp and tore into the kitchen, raging with strength he never knew he had as he pulled his father away from his mother.

'What kind of a bloody coward hits a woman?'

He took advantage of his father's shock to push him hard, back against the wall.

'Tell me,' he demanded, prodding his father in the chest in the same way that his father had done so often to him. Anger overtook his fear. He was out of control, cold even, nothing could stop him now. Colin reached out and slapped Bobby so hard around the face that he stumbled long enough for his father to grab him by the collars.

'Mind your own business, you worthless bastard?' he said through angry clenched teeth, almost lifting him off the ground. He tightened his grip on Bobby's collars and flung him backwards against the Welsh dresser sending crockery clattering and smashing around him.

He heard his mother scream, and looked over to see a curled up wreck cowering in the corner. Colin turned momentarily to tell her to stop whining, and Bobby seized the moment. He leant over and grabbed a knife from the knife block on the work surface next to the dresser. Elaine shouted hysterically, before turning her face to the wall.

'Bobby, no,' she yelled.

Colin sneered at him, shaking his head. 'You really are insane aren't you?' he goaded.

Bobby returned the insult. 'Maybe it's hereditary. This mess is yours not mine,' he said, pointing with the knife from one parent to the other. 'You blame me for everything, anything rather than accept that it's your own bloody mess.'

He drew closer to his father with the knife poised.

His mother looked momentarily stunned, but quickly adopted a calmer tone. She got up and moved towards him with her hand outstretched. 'Drop the knife, honey,' she said calmly. 'Maybe you're right, perhaps we should talk about this. Give me the knife.'

Her hand was outstretched towards him as he looked up at her and back at the knife, dazed and disorientated, like a sleep-walker awakened. He fixed his eyes on his mother and saw the sheer terror beneath the calm exterior. As he stared at the knife in his hand, his expression altered from anger to anxiety. *What have I become?*

'God no,' he cried out, collapsing to his knees as he flung the knife across the kitchen. It slid across the red tiles, spun round and came to a halt at the other side of the room.

His father instantly grabbed hold of him by the collars again, and he heard his mother scream.

'Colin, no.'

His whole body was thrust backwards as his father lifted him forcibly off the ground. He felt himself lurch, felt the thud as his head hit the wall, felt the agonising pain, and heard his sister's scream fade slowly into the distance.

52

Bobby woke up choking. It was difficult to swallow, and every time he coughed his head was in agony. A nurse removed the plastic airway and explained to him where he was.

'You're in hospital. You were unconscious.'

He tried to sit up but he hadn't enough strength. It sent excruciating pain through his head and he retched. He lay back down, clutching his head. After a few deep breaths, he closed his eyes again until the pain gradually subsided.

'Do you want something for the pain?' the nurse attending him asked.

Bobby held his head with his hand again. He spoke through his daze and uncertainty.

'I don't know …' he replied.

The nurse touched his arm, 'I'll be back in a minute.'

His body felt weak as he tried to move and his brow furrowed with pain. He felt a hand stroke back the hair from his face and as he strained to focus, he realised he was looking into the eyes of Jodie's granddad.

'Hello,' her granddad said tenderly. 'You just missed your mother. She couldn't stay long because your sister was waiting in the car.'

Bobby nodded silently, unsure what to think.

'She says that if your father won't give you financial help through art college, then she will. She's had money put away since her mother died,' Granddad said.

'Good for her,' Bobby replied with heavy sarcasm.

Granddad put a hand on Bobby's arm. 'Whatever you think of your parents right now, you should accept any financial help they offer. I can give you a home and food, but if they have the money to get you through college I would accept it if I was you.'

Bobby sighed. 'I guess you're right.'

The nurse returned and Granddad moved out of the way. 'How are you feeling?' she asked.

Bobby's voice was no more than a whisper. 'My head's agony if I sit up.'

'It will be painful for a little while yet,' the nurse said. 'Let me look at your eyes.'

Even the light from the pen torch hurt his eyes. The nurse checked his pulse and blood pressure, and wrote on the chart attached to the clipboard at the foot of the bed. She pulled the curtain around the bed and gave him an injection for the pain. As soon as she had gone, Granddad moved the chair closer.

'Do you remember what happened?' Granddad asked.

'I remember some of it but my mind is a blank about how I ended up in here. I remember that Dad cornered mum and Elaine called me ...' He stopped talking and looked puzzled. 'How did you know?' he asked. 'What day is it?'

'It's Tuesday afternoon. Doctor White spoke to Rev Turner and he rang me this morning. He told me about your talk with him last night.'

Bobby smiled, but he knew very well that Granddad would recognise the mask. He fought back tears.

'I'm sorry,' he whispered. 'I really thought I could make him love me.'

He could hold back the tears no longer. 'As I left the church, having decided to come and talk to you, I had the most horrendous flashbacks. I wanted to run back into the church to tell the vicar but I couldn't, I felt as if I was going mad.'

He stopped, unable to speak; even his breathing was laboured.

'Go on,' Granddad urged.

'I ran down the path to the motorbike hoping to outrun the memories and then raced away wondering if I had the courage to ride into a wall, but I didn't. When I got home I went upstairs, but the screaming and shouting was getting more and more violent. All the hope that I'd found talking to the vicar vanished. When I saw what Dad had done to Mum, I lost control. Something inside me snapped. I would quite happily have killed him.'

As the injection began to take effect, his speech became slurred and he drifted off to sleep. Granddad got up and whispered gently to him before leaving to get a cup of tea.

'Your body will survive I'm sure – it's your heart I'm worried about.'

53

Sleep eluded Kate as she tossed and turned on Monday night. *How can I tell Bobby? And how will I be able to face Colin tomorrow?* She went through every possible response, to every possible comment. 'I owe Bobby the truth,' she said to the darkness before finally falling into an exhausted sleep.

She was jittery and on edge in the morning. As she got out of bed she glanced in the mirror, brushing her fingers through her hair. She couldn't eat. As she sat drinking a glass of orange juice, she decided to apologise to him at work that day and arrange to meet him at the pub to talk. When the phone rang she jumped.

'Hi, Kate here,' she said in her telephone voice. 'Jerry,' she sighed with relief. He was just checking that she was okay.

The call was brief, but boosted Kate's courage. She thought about Jerry as she brushed her hair, and masked the dark circles under her eyes with make-up. *He is a special kind of guy.*

As she approached the studio door she hesitated, took a deep breath and pushed it open. Bobby wasn't there.

'Where's Bobby?' she asked Hannah quietly.

Hannah looked distraught but whispered, 'He's in hospital.'

Kate felt sick. 'You're joking, what's wrong?'

Hannah busied herself with letters on her desk. 'He had an accident last night, he's unconscious.'

'Colin hit him, didn't he?' Kate said loudly.

'Keep your voice down,' Hannah whispered. 'He's in his office. They had a fight, I don't know any more.'

'Right,' Kate raged, 'I'm going to see him.'

'Kate, no!' Hannah called after her, but she was too late; once Kate had made up her mind, hell itself would have difficulty stopping her. The studio fell silent as she knocked furiously on the office door.

'Come in,' Colin called impatiently. She had hardly closed the door before she laid into him.

'What did you do to him? He never asked to be born, but you went out of your way to destroy him. I won't work for a bullying son of a bitch like you.'

She gave him no time for reply, simply turned angrily on her heels, walked to her desk, took her coat and left. As she walked out of the door she had an immense feeling of relief. Bobby had lived with this atmosphere all his life, a vulnerable child bullied to the point where, even now, he had no power to escape.

She was angry and determined as she drove to Jerry's.

'Nice dressing gown,' she quipped as he answered the door. She pushed past him into the house.

'It's seen better days,' he smiled, and then suddenly registered, 'I thought you were at work!' he exclaimed.

'I just quit,' she announced as she pulled out a chair from under the kitchen table and sat down. Jerry sat next to her.

'Why?' he asked calmly.

Kate's eyes narrowed with anger. 'Because I'm not prepared to work for a son of a bitch who bullies his son and puts him in the hospital …'

Jerry interrupted her, anxiously, 'What's happened?'

Kate looked him in the eye, 'They fought last night. Bobby's in hospital, unconscious.'

Jerry stared in stunned silence. 'Will he be okay?' he asked at last.

'I don't know, I didn't wait to find out,' she replied, angry again.

'So why are you here?' Jerry asked. 'Did you just walk out?'

She looked at him impatiently. 'Of course not, I knocked on Colin's door and told him that I wasn't prepared to work for a son of a bitch who bullies his own son and puts him in the hospital.'

She spoke matter-of-factly, interrupted only by Jerry

257

spluttering the remains of an almost cold cup of tea.

'You didn't say that *to* him?' he asked.

'Yes, then I quit,' she said.

Jerry began to laugh and Kate looked puzzled. After one or two attempts he stopped laughing long enough to explain the cause of his amusement.

'Bobby would have loved to have seen that. No-one stands up to his dad.' Jerry said. We'd better go and see him.'

'He's unconscious,' she replied impatiently. 'I'll ring the hospital tomorrow and we'll go then if he's conscious.' Suddenly she thought. 'I wonder if Jodie's granddad knows.'

She tried to ring him more than once but got no reply. It was ten o'clock before she got hold of him. After a short conversation about Bobby's condition, Kate asked Granddad, 'Have you told him about his father?'

'No,' Granddad replied, 'I think you should do that.'

Jodie's granddad agreed to visit a bit later the next day to give Kate and Jerry time alone with Bobby.

By the next afternoon Kate had lost none of her resolve, she strode ahead leaving Jerry lagging behind as usual. 'Come on,' she said in an impatient matronly tone as he stubbed out his cigarette on the wall outside the entrance. Kate paced the corridor as they waited to be allowed in. She reached Bobby's side room ahead of Jerry and quietly put her head around the door.

'Hello Bobby,' she said gently.

He looked startled and turned away from her, crying out in pain as he did so. Kate didn't know what to do.

'Go away,' he said; his voice weak but determined, 'I have nothing to say to you.'

Jerry came to her rescue. 'She's got something to tell you that may help.'

Kate could sense Bobby's anger.

'Get out!' he shouted this time, causing him pain. It also brought the ward sister swiftly across the corridor.

'You mustn't get excited,' she said.

He turned his head away like a guilty child and tried to hide his anguish. 'I don't want to talk to her,' he replied.

The sister led them to the door and whispered softly, 'We have to respect his wishes I'm afraid.'

Kate nodded, burying her feelings of frustration. They wandered back to the entrance hall.

'Lend me 2p, I'm going to ring Jodie's granddad,' Kate said.

Jerry tried to talk her out of it but without success. 'All right,' he said eventually, tossing her a coin. He didn't go with her to the phone box, but she was happier when she returned a few minutes later.

'He's on his way,' she said.

Granddad arrived about twenty minutes later, a little out of breath. 'Sorry to keep you waiting, I couldn't find anywhere to park. Come on then, let's go and see him. I'll go in first and call you when I've spoken to him.'

Kate had always seen Jodie's granddad as a soft touch; someone who Bobby could control and get his own way with, but as he spoke to her now she saw that it was his strength on which Bobby relied, not his weakness on which he preyed. Jodie's granddad treated Bobby like a son. As her thoughts came to their conclusion, so did the journey along the corridors. She was fearful as they approached his room, comforted only by Granddad's hand on her shoulder. With the door left ajar, Kate could hear most of what Granddad said to him.

'Why wouldn't you listen to Kate?' he asked Bobby.

'I've got nothing to say to her,' she heard him snap back.

Kate noted a change in Granddad's tone, the tenderness had turned to an air of authority that she had never heard him use before. As she looked through the door she could see that Granddad had his hand on Bobby's arm as he looked into his eyes and spoke firmly. 'You need to hear what Kate has to say.'

'She caused this,' he blurted out angrily.

Kate cringed as she heard Granddad's reply. 'She regrets her part in this, but it isn't her fault. Just hear what she has to say.'

He caught her eye and nodded to her to come in. She saw Bobby flinch, and deliberately turn the other way. She didn't hear what Granddad whispered to him, but he turned back slightly towards her without looking her in the eye. He seemed like a frightened child. As she unfolded the story she could feel him recoiling. *What must it feel like to realise that neither parent really wanted him, and that in his father's eyes he had come between him and the woman he truly loved?*

Bobby turned away again, gripping the pillow tightly with one hand. She knew from his breathing that he was sobbing, long before she heard the groans that preceded the crying. As he broke into uncontrollable sobbing, Granddad nodded to them to leave. Kate turned briefly as she left the room, but all she could see was Granddad with his hand on Bobby's shoulder, comforting like a father. She closed the door quietly as she sat down by Jerry in the entrance to the ward, wiping away her own tears.

'Do you think he can survive this?'

He put his arm around her and replied as only Jerry could, 'If you want my honest opinion, I don't think he would have survived if it hadn't happened. Now he can get on with his life.'

Kate jumped up quickly when she saw Granddad approaching.

'Is he okay?' she asked nervously, wracked with guilt.

Granddad nodded lightly. 'He will be. He wants to see you but go gently, he's very fragile.'

As she entered the room, Bobby turned towards her and extended his hand. She took it and spoke to him, feeling deeply ashamed and fixing her eyes on the bedcover.

'I'm sorry it was me that had to tell you. It would have come better from a friend.'

She tried to move away but he gripped her hand harder. He spoke to her almost in a whisper as she looked up at the strained smile on his worn and tired face.

'It had to be you Kate because you have the guts to tell me the truth, but I'm sorry you lost the job.'

She sat on the edge of the bed and he let go of her hand.

'I didn't lose it. I told him I wouldn't work for a son of a bitch who bullied his son.'

Bobby laughed, before congratulating her. 'Well done. I hope you didn't give him time to respond.'

She looked at him with a mock superior air. 'I know you've never had a great deal of respect for me, but I'm not stupid.' She said goodbye feeling more peaceful, though painfully aware that for Bobby, the revelation was only the beginning of his healing.

'Thank you, Kate,' he said. 'You're a good friend.'

She broke down as she left the ward, tears of sorrow for Bobby, and relief that their friendship had been restored.

'I knew you didn't need to worry,' Jerry said gently. 'There's more to Bobby than anyone imagines, but he'll need support now. That reminds me, where's Jodie?'

Kate looked worried. 'I don't know.'

54

Granddad had stayed later than usual at the hospital visiting Bobby and Jodie was angry with him. When he came through the door that evening she jumped up quickly, hiding her heart in activity. She offered to get him something to eat but he declined.

'No thank you,' he replied, 'I'd rather talk.'

'I was just about to have a bath,' she said.

Her granddad looked straight at her and held her gaze. 'That's a lame excuse.'

She said nothing in case her words gave away her anger, but she felt her breathing alter.

Granddad broke the silence. 'I know you're angry with me so let's talk about it.'

Her resolve to hide it from him dissolved and her anger erupted, more violently than she thought possible.

'After all I did for him he hurt me, and he hurt you too, so why should you help him now?'

Her granddad's silence spoke volumes. He took out a rather shabby leather-bound photograph album from the sideboard and handed it to her. She held it in her hand without opening it. 'Look at it,' he said, sitting down again.

She slammed it down indignantly. She knew what was inside, she could remember every photograph and it brought back memories of the state of her heart at every stage until she recovered from her own trauma. She knew his eyes would penetrate her, so she kept her angry gaze on the floor.

'I believe in the person he can be,' he said.

Jodie looked up at him briefly and he added quickly, 'And you are being dishonest with yourself because you are afraid of what you feel.'

She picked up the photograph album in a fit of rage and threw it across the room. Her granddad said nothing, merely looked at her. 'All right,' she said impatiently, 'I can't cope with him. I won't let him rip me apart again.'

He patted the cushion next to him on the settee and she moved to sit by him as she began to cry. 'At least that's honest. But couldn't you show him that you still care?'

She shrugged. 'I don't want to go alone.'

'We'll go together,' he said.

After a simple casserole dinner, which her granddad had left in the oven earlier, they spent a quiet evening reading beside the log fire until bedtime.

Jodie's mind wouldn't let her sleep for a long while that night and it was late when she eventually drifted off. The next morning she was awoken by a loud knock on the door. It was light; in fact it was a bright sunny morning. She got up out of bed and stretched as she casually glanced down at the clock. *How the hell can it be eleven o'clock?* She cursed herself for the wasted time. *If only I could get out of seeing Bobby this afternoon I'd have time to get some work done.* As she pulled open the curtains, she noticed the police car outside and felt her stomach lurch. It hadn't even crossed her mind, but of course it was obvious that the police would want to know what had happened. *What if Bobby is in trouble? Is Hugh going to have to interview him?* Whatever she tried to tell herself, she knew that she couldn't get out of seeing him this afternoon. She opened the door as quietly as she could, desperate to hear what Hugh was saying.

'Their stories don't tally. I don't think any one of them has told me the truth. I'm not even sure they have a clue what truth is,' Hugh said to Jodie's granddad in his low, booming voice.

Jodie's granddad had a much softer voice and was more difficult to hear from upstairs. She just caught the words, 'closing ranks,' and 'messed up families,' and then she heard the words she was dreading from Hugh. 'I'll have to question Bobby later on today.'

Jodie crept to the landing. She could hear the resignation in her granddad's tone. 'Of course, but I'm not sure how much he remembers.'

She could hear anger in the old policeman's voice as he answered. 'I've never been able to get that bastard and I'll have no evidence unless Bobby can give me some. It's bloody frustrating.' Jodie went quietly back to her room and closed the door softly. She didn't want to hear any more.

Jodie didn't go downstairs until mid-day. She was putting the kettle on when her granddad came back in from the garden.

'How much did you hear?' he asked her.

'Of what?' she asked, trying to sound puzzled.

'Of what Hugh said,' he replied. 'I heard your bedroom door shut just before he left.'

Damn it, she thought. Her granddad didn't miss a trick.

'Most of it,' she replied. 'I'm worried about him, about how he'll cope with re-living it.'

'Don't worry,' her granddad replied. 'He doesn't remember much.'

They didn't say much to each other as they sat in the lounge for lunch and the time seemed to drag for Jodie as she waited to visit him. She dreaded it.

When the time finally arrived, Jodie was nervous. Nothing could have prepared her for how weary Bobby looked. The strain of the last few days had taken its toll on his physical appearance. The dark rings under his eyes spoke of sleeplessness and pain. A part of her wanted to hold him close and feel his soft cheek against hers again. She took his hand like a long lost friend, gripped it tight and then let it go, suddenly too aware of the closeness.

'Hi,' she said, nothing more. The longing in his eyes made her look away awkwardly and by the time she had moved up a chair and sat down, the longing had been replaced by sadness. She felt wretched doing this to him, but she couldn't afford to show him what she felt. They only talked trivia until her granddad suddenly got up.

'I'll be back in a minute,' he said and left the room.

Jodie felt stranded; she hadn't wanted to be left alone with him like this, not yet. Bobby's first words to her when they were alone struck her as odd.

'How are you?' he asked.

She laughed before replying. 'I should be asking you that.'

His eyes seemed to search her heart, which she found disconcerting. 'I'm not sure about that,' he said.

'What do you mean?'

He moved his hand and placed it on hers, gripping very slightly. She pulled back, afraid of the slightest suggestion of intimacy. He spoke to her gently.

'I may have been foolish and selfish and blind over the last few months, but I am not totally insensitive.'

She hid her face behind her hair but he continued despite the lack of encouragement. 'I never meant to hurt you.'

'Then you must have a natural talent for it,' she retorted. 'I'm sorry,' she said flatly. 'I had no right to say that.'

'You probably did,' he replied. She could hear remorse in his tone. 'I didn't believe you loved me, because I didn't believe it was possible for anyone to love me.'

It had become too personal and she replied quickly, unemotionally. 'It can never be the same between us again.' As she spoke, she gently removed her hand from beneath his. He'd hurt her too much and she wasn't about to give him the opportunity to hurt her again. She got up to go.

'I have to go. Ask Granddad to pick me up at the flat would you?'

He didn't answer but she saw the pain in his eyes as he nodded. She said goodbye and left without looking back.

55

When Granddad returned to the ward, Bobby was out of bed staring at the activity in the car park below. He heard the door open, and turned round slowly.

'Jodie's gone to the flat. She'd like you to pick her up on the way home.'

Granddad pursed his lips, and was about to say something when he was interrupted by the ward round. He left the room briefly as the consultant picked up the chart at the foot of the bed.

'How do you feel now?' the consultant said to Bobby.

'I still feel weak, but my head hurts less, and I've stopped feeling dizzy.'

The consultant put the clipboard back on the end of the bed. 'Good, then you can to go home tomorrow.'

He saw the sister point to the notes, and the consultant looked up at him, and back at the notes, then shrugged, 'See if the social worker is available.'

It made Bobby feel like a social misfit. As the consultant walked away, the sister turned back just long enough to tell him that she would be back to talk to him in a minute.

When Granddad returned, Bobby was sitting in the chair with a far-away look in his eyes.

'What did he say?' Granddad enquired, with a sound of hope in his voice.

'I can go home tomorrow,' he said, with a tone of resignation.

Granddad pulled a chair up close and sat down. 'You can come home with me.'

Bobby was uncertain. *How will I be able to bear to be so close to the only girl I've ever loved, when she is steadfastly building a wall of protection to keep me out?* He got up and stared out of the window.

'Is it Jodie you're worried about?' Granddad asked. Bobby simply nodded. Granddad replied to the nod with a hint of anger, 'Jodie's home is with me, but she can always go to the flat. As far as I'm concerned your home is with me too.'

Bobby turned his head back towards Granddad. 'I can't do that to her. It's too much, too soon for her.'

'You're very gracious to her, but you have no choice,' Granddad replied.

His heart ached more than his body. *I still want her back*, he thought. He would wait as long as it took. He didn't feel gracious, he felt impatient and hurt.

Granddad walked to the door. 'I'll talk to the sister and arrange to collect you tomorrow. Oh, by the way, Hugh will be in at some stage today. Try to remember as much as you can. He really wants to charge your father, but your family's statements don't tally and he has no firm evidence.'

Bobby shook his head gently. 'I really don't remember anything after I ran into the room.'

'Okay, well I'll see you tomorrow.'

Hugh arrived soon after Granddad left, and Bobby's admission that he could remember nothing after entering the room clearly left Hugh dejected.

'Thing is, Hugh,' Bobby said, 'now I know the whole story it makes sense.'

'Nothing justifies the way he treated you,' Hugh said with feeling, and then added, with his eyes fixed on the floor, 'I feel as if I failed in my duty to you.'

Bobby reached out a hand and placed it on the old policeman's arm. 'It's not your fault, he's a slithery old snake.' He was unsure if he should continue, but decided he could trust Hugh; after all, he knew the business of most of the villagers, and the truth would come out eventually.

'My father never loved my mother,' he said blandly. 'His current secretary was his childhood sweetheart. They broke up and he got my mother pregnant ... with me.'

Hugh nodded slowly, 'I see. Didn't give you much chance

then, did it?'

Bobby shrugged.

'Anyway,' Hugh said as he got up to leave, 'If anything comes back to you, give me a call.'

Bobby nodded and Hugh left.

With the help of painkillers and sleeping tablets, Bobby slept through the night. His mind was active as soon as he awoke. He didn't relish the idea of being in the house with Jodie, but if he was honest, anything was better than home. His mother's visits had been brief and she was clearly embarrassed that he had found out the truth. Her visits had been full of awkward silences, but at least she had tried. Not that he had been short of visitors or cards; the villagers visited, and cards arrived constantly from college friends and folk club contacts.

When Granddad arrived the next afternoon, Bobby was surprised to see Jodie accompanying him, and in a much more pleasant mood. Bobby smiled to himself. She kissed him on the cheek but there was no love in it. He was packed and ready to go. They waited briefly for medication and instructions from the sister.

'Here's a sick certificate. Don't go back to college for a week and make sure you rest.'

'Don't worry,' Granddad said, 'I won't let him do anything stupid.'

As he got up to go, Granddad handed the sister a box of chocolates and a thank you note.

'Look after yourself,' the sister said to Bobby as he left.

It seemed strange to Bobby to be leaving hospital. He had a strange sense of belonging nowhere. In reality he would probably feel more at home at Granddad's house than he did at his father's, but he felt a strange emptiness. The simple act of leaving hospital seemed tiring, and he was quiet on the way back to the cottage. Jodie carried his bag up to the room they had prepared for him.

'Is it alright if I rest a while?' he asked.

'Do what you like, you live here,' Granddad said.

Bobby nodded and smiled. As he lay down on the bed, he fell instantly asleep.

He didn't know how long he had been asleep, but it was dark when he woke up, and the only light in the room was from a street light shining through the open curtains. He eased himself off the bed and walked over to the window, leaning on the windowsill for support. He stared across the countryside, thinking of his father on the other side of the fields. All hope of reconciliation was gone. He had no strength, physically or emotionally, and he felt vulnerable.

When he reached the top of the stairs, he caught sight of Jodie leaning on her granddad, talking to him. Not wishing to disturb them, he turned around, but the stairs creaked and gave him away.

'Come down,' Granddad urged, and seeing Jodie smile he went downstairs.

'How are you feeling?' she asked. It was a bit too polite, but at least she'd asked.

'I've felt better,' he answered honestly. As he sat beside the blazing log fire, he rested his head wearily on the wing of the chair.

'Would you like coffee?' Granddad asked.

'I'll make it,' Bobby said, getting up from the chair.

'You have to rest,' Granddad said firmly, and walked resolutely to the kitchen. Bobby sat back down. He had dreaded this moment; the first time he was left alone here with Jodie. It would be so easy to feign tiredness and shut her out, but they had to live here, to relax in the same room, so despite his tiredness, he forced himself to make conversation.

'I feel bad about him running around after me,' he remarked, as if it was casual and spontaneous. She looked at him with kindness, he thought, but who could tell with Jodie. She shook her head and he watched her dark hair flick from side to side.

'You've been very ill.'

Is that compassion I can see in her eyes, or is it just wishful thinking? he thought.

She jumped up and sat in the chair opposite him.

'I want to say something before Granddad comes back.'

He nodded gently, encouraging her to continue.

'I'm sorry I was so cold to you yesterday, but I don't know how to relate to you now. It feels awkward.'

Bobby felt relief tinged with sorrow. It was excruciatingly difficult for him to relate to her too. 'I understand,' he replied. 'When you came to the hospital this afternoon I thought that we can only be friends, I hope we can make it work by seeing each other that way.'

Jodie leant back in the chair with a momentary wistful look. 'That's good,' she said, before adding, 'Oh I almost forgot, I started a landscape painting the other day, and I'm a bit stuck. Will you tell me what you think?' She didn't wait for a reply and fetched the painting, returning at the same time as Granddad. She held it up for Bobby to see. He looked at it close up and then from a distance, inclining his head slightly as he thought about what to say.

'It looks uninspired to me,' he said softly, not wanting to offend, but wanting to tell her the truth.

She looked offended, and he reached out and touched her arm briefly.

'I've seen you do much better. I'd start again.'

He looked down at the floor, wishing that she hadn't asked him.

'That's more or less what I said,' Granddad piped up.

Bobby felt weary again and lay back in the chair, closing his eyes.

'Soup will be ready in a few minutes, and then you look as if you need to rest again,' Granddad suggested.

Bobby sighed deeply. 'I think you're right.'

That night as he lay in bed he heard Jodie and her granddad talking quietly on the landing, obviously unaware that he was still awake.

'Do you think he'll be all right? He's so subdued,' she said, clearly concerned.

What would his reply be? Bobby strained to hear.

'It takes less time to heal a broken body than to heal a broken heart. You know that Jodie.'

He'd forgotten that. Deep inside she understood suffering, pain and loss, and somehow it gave him hope that one day she would forgive him. She knew what it was to have a broken heart, and he deeply regretted breaking it again. He wept silent tears onto the pillow that night as he clutched the gift that he still wore around his neck, and he hoped with all his broken heart, that one day he could win hers again.

56

Bobby woke in the middle of the night. He pulled the covers over his head and tried to quell the ramblings that tortured his mind. Every hope, every fear and every dream marched relentlessly through his head. He sat up and clutched his head, willing the clamour to stop, but with no success. He fumbled for the switch on the bedside light, got out of bed and wrapped his dressing gown around himself, before venturing downstairs to put the kettle on for a cup of tea. As he turned round to get milk out of the fridge, he came face to face with Granddad.

'Make that two,' Granddad said with a grin.

'I'm sorry, did I wake you?'

Granddad shook his head and disappeared into the lounge to plug in the electric fire, then sat down and waited until Bobby had set the mugs down on the table. Bobby sat down in the opposite corner of the settee.

'How are you feeling?'

Bobby held the mug tightly, warming his hands. 'I feel numb, just empty exhaustion.'

He stopped briefly and Granddad nodded to him to continue.

'I almost don't care what happens to me anymore. When I was in the hospital, I was afraid that if I fell asleep I might die, but a part of me was afraid that I might live. I've felt like that before.'

He looked up, aware that it must sound strange. 'That seems ungrateful for life I ...'

Granddad interrupted his apology. 'But at least you're finally telling me the truth.'

Bobby took a deep breath and a sip of hot tea and began again. 'All my hopes and aspirations are gone.'

He stopped again, looking up briefly as he fought the

strength of the emotions welling up within. *What was Granddad thinking? Why was he so silent?* He continued.

'I feel as if my mind can't make the connections. Every thought seems disassociated from the one preceding it and the one following.'

Every muscle in his body was tense and his face was taut with anguish. He put down the tea and looked up, turning his face towards Granddad as he heard him move. Granddad moved closer.

'That day, when you wandered here as a free-spirited, wide-eyed boy I wanted to keep you, but I had no right.'

Bobby tried to hide the pain of the memory of that day.

'What happened that day after your father took you home?'

Bobby curled up in the corner of the settee and shook his head violently. 'I don't remember,' he replied quickly.

Granddad nodded slowly. 'Tell me about the first time he hurt you.'

Bobby shielded his face with his hands. 'I don't remember. Really, I don't remember,' he cried, painfully aware that his desperation revealed the truth.

Granddad spoke gently, as if to a frightened child, 'Camus once said that, "crushing truths perish from being acknowledged." Why not acknowledge the crushing truth?' The serenity in his tone calmed Bobby.

Bobby's eyes were heavy and swollen with the pressure of tears as yet uncried. 'You don't know what you're asking,' he said, shaking his head lightly.

'I think I do. This is not your shame, it's your father's.'

Bobby picked up a cushion and hugged it to himself like a vulnerable child with a teddy bear. In a split second he made the decision: he would speak the unspeakable; he would crush the crushing truths. He spoke quickly giving himself no opportunity to change his mind.

'I was about three years old, maybe four. I sat on my mother's lap as she read me a story, *The Ugly Duckling*, I cried

273

and she told me that it was only a story and stroked my hair. Dad went wild. "You're turning him into a sissy," he said as he pulled me from her lap by my arm. It hurt my arm and I tried to tell him, so he slapped my face. I was terrified. I had heard him raging at my mother at nights when I was in bed, but never at me. I screamed, so to shut me up he grabbed me and banged my head on the wall shouting, "Be quiet you bastard".'

'I remember staring at my mother in terror, my eyes pleading with her to intervene, but she walked away. I felt alone and betrayed. I never felt like a child again inside those walls.'

He stopped a while, taking a few deep breaths, but his stomach churned as he relived the incident in his mind.

'It must have been a year or so later that I ran away, though I never thought of it as running away. Every few weeks my dad's temper would flare up, but this time he had been angry for ages. From my perspective it was worse than one quick outburst.

'About a week earlier, he had come into my room and accused me of waking Elaine up. He slapped my face when I was barely awake and I cried myself back to sleep.'

The clock on the mantelpiece chimed 2am. Bobby looked up, catching a glimpse of Granddad, who nodded for Bobby to continue.

'The next morning he started on me as I got ready for school. I was an animated but gentle child. I remember leaning over the pram and letting Elaine hold my finger in her hand. She was about two I guess. I was singing and she was laughing. I don't know if the noise annoyed him but suddenly he punched me in the stomach so that my body lifted off the ground and hit the wall. The next thing I recall is him holding me by the collar against the wall, I could feel nothing, my whole body felt numb but I didn't cry. I don't remember ever crying after that.

'I was too bruised to go to school so Mum helped me to

bed and I lay there terrified. I must have slept but I didn't mean to. I never really slept soundly again. I spent the rest of the week trying to appease him and by the time I ran away I was exhausted with trying to be good.' he looked up at Granddad with a nervous smile. 'It never came naturally.'

Granddad looked straight at him. 'What happened that night, after you left here?'

Bobby picked up the tea and sipped it, his eyes blinking too fast and his fingers in constant motion. He put the mug down and leant over towards a packet of cigarettes but Granddad put his hand over Bobby's to stop him.

'I can't do it,' Bobby whispered. 'I have flickers of memories of that evening but I'm too frightened to try to remember the rest.' He cuddled the cushion tighter.

Granddad rested his arm on the back of the settee, facing Bobby now. 'Begin from the time you arrived here.'

Bobby took a deep breath and let out a heavy sigh as he sank back in the chair and threw the cushion aside. He closed his eyes and furrowed his brow. 'The first thing I remember is seeing your face coming towards me as I crouched over the pond at the end of your garden. I tensed in fear but then as you came closer I relaxed. Your expression was one of surprise mixed with kindness.'

Granddad raised his eyebrows as if to say, "Go on".

'You asked me if I wanted a drink and I followed you inside though you didn't invite me. I climbed up onto the settee, it was over by that wall I think.' He pointed to the wall by the small window as he looked up. Granddad nodded again.

'The house smelled of pickled onions or something like that.'

'Quite likely.'

'You handed me the drink, and all I can remember is how peaceful it felt in here. I recall chattering on, though I don't know what about, except that soon after you got out a violin and played it to me. I begged you to let me play it. You did, showing me how to bow while you played the notes in the left hand for me. I think I sat on your lap as I played.'

Granddad clapped his hands together and laughed at the memory. 'I'd forgotten that! Go on.'

Bobby forced a smile. 'That's the easy bit. Anyway, then you put me down, propped me up in the corner of the settee with a cushion and went to make me a sandwich. After that you played the violin softly. I must have fallen asleep?' He looked up at Granddad questioningly.

'Yes,' Granddad replied. 'I guessed you'd run away. I rang Hugh, your village policeman, because he's the nearest one to here. He sounded very relieved. He told me you'd been missing since 8.30am. It was 4ish when I came across you.'

Bobby closed his eyes and took short shallow breaths. 'I woke up to find his face staring over me. I tried to close my eyes to shut him out of my dream but then I realised it was real. The next thing I remember is being unceremoniously lifted up under one arm. I was screaming, "No, no, put me down, I want to stay here!" as I kicked my legs and flailed my arms, so he tightened the grip and I felt as if I would be crushed.'

He stopped talking and leant forwards, rubbing his eyes between his thumb and middle finger. Granddad waited. Eventually Bobby huddled back in the corner of the settee, closed his eyes and began again.

'I tried to speak to him in Hugh's car going home but he ignored me. As Hugh dropped us off at home, I can remember the tone of his tone as he assured Hugh that it would never happen again: it filled me with sheer terror. I wanted to run as we stood outside the house while he got the key out of his pocket, but I was paralysed with fear.'

Bobby's breathing became faster and shallower as if he was sobbing but without the tears. Eventually he continued.

'He opened the front door and ordered me inside; every muscle in my body was so tense that I couldn't move. He dragged me inside by the back of the collar, pushed me into the kitchen and told me to "stand there". I stood there for what seemed an eternity. Every time he came near I turned my head in fear and each time he slapped my face. After about three times I didn't dare turn it again but my whole body shook. I thought I'd collapse.'

Bobby physically shook as he recounted the story. 'He pushed me so hard in the direction of the door that I fell over. "Go to your room," he said, this time in a quiet, controlled manner. That was even more terrifying. It was cold, somehow.'

Bobby stopped for a while and took deep breaths. 'I can't do it.' He jumped up as if to go and then, just as suddenly, he sat down with his head buried in his hands and wept; deep heart-rending sobs. 'Why, why?' he cried, over and over again. 'He destroyed me.'

Granddad moved closer and put a hand on his shoulder. It was a long time before he could resume his narration.

'He came upstairs painfully slowly, I heard every step. Then he stood in front of me and took the belt off his trousers; again he did it very slowly as if to savour every moment. It was a calculated action. He fingered it in his hands, I can feel the tension even now; I could hardly breathe.

'He stared straight at me with narrowed angry eyes and thin mean lips as he whipped the belt in the air. The sound was terrifying. Knowing what he would do next, I backed slowly away from him towards the wall. "Face the wall," he ordered, but I couldn't move so he screamed it again, whipping at my feet with the belt. I turned round shaking from head to toe.

He pushed my face to the wall and held me there with one hand. The pain and the fear as the belt struck was indescribable, excruciating. I was screaming inside but no sound would escape. I wanted to run but he held me tight. He took his time between each stroke as if he enjoyed each moment. After four or five strokes he stopped but to me it seemed like forever.

'He leant over my shoulder and I tried to move my head away from the hot breath on my face but he grabbed my hair. "That will teach you not to make an idiot out of me," he snarled.

I stood there shaking, paralysed to the spot. Eventually my mother came casually upstairs, got me into pyjamas and put me to bed, as if nothing had happened. From that day I hated him and I despised her. I lay in bed staring upward; the stinging throb was nothing compared to the loneliness.'

He began to weep quietly now, tears of deep sorrow, not of anger. He leant on Granddad's shoulder and Granddad held him until he was almost asleep.

'You're not alone anymore.'

Neither of them spoke any more, words were unnecessary. When Bobby went back to bed, he lay down peacefully for the first time in years.

'Maybe the crushing truths just perished,' he said to himself as he fell instantly asleep.

57

Sleep occupied most of the next week for Bobby. Each day he painted a little, under the watchful eye of Granddad. Jodie had returned to the flat for the week so Bobby relaxed, but at last it was time to return to art college, and he had no illusions about that morning; his first day back wouldn't be easy. His meeting with the principal first thing heightened the sense of detachment, as it meant that he arrived late for the first session of the day.

It was hard to concentrate and he became increasingly frustrated with himself as the morning wore on. Added to that, Jodie's ambivalence nearly drove him mad. At the first opportunity he went outside for a cigarette. Jerry followed him and, much to Bobby's surprise, spoke to him sternly.

'I'm not going to watch you disappear into a morass of self-pity. Of course you can't concentrate, you're recovering from a head injury.'

Bobby took a long slow drag of the cigarette. He had expected more sympathy from Jerry. 'It's not just the art, its Jodie,' he replied. 'I feel as if I've lost her forever. That was the biggest mistake of my life. I've broken her heart.'

Jerry gave him an encouraging whack on the arm. 'It's not like you to be so pessimistic. Think how stubbornly she resisted you in the first place.'

Bobby thought about the early days, when she steadfastly resisted him; maybe he would have to gently break down her resolve again. Jerry was right; wallowing in self-pity wouldn't help.

'You're right, let's go,' he said, throwing the cigarette to the ground.

They talked of other things, particularly the folk club. 'Kate doesn't want to continue running it,' Jerry said as he pushed open the canteen door. They got coffee and sat down at the same table as Kate and Jodie.

'That's right isn't it, baby?' Jerry said casually to Kate, as if she should have known what he was talking about.

She cocked her head on one side and looked up at him with questioning eyes.

'You're happy for Bobby to resume leadership of the folk club aren't you?' he said.

'With pleasure,' Kate said with feeling.

Jodie looked up at Bobby with concern. 'Not this week though.'

Bobby nodded. 'Yeah you're right. Granddad would have a fit,' he said placing his hand on hers.

She calmly removed her hand from underneath his, so he moved his hand away and picked up the cup of coffee.

'Okay,' Kate said cheerfully. 'I'll do it this week and you can do it after that.'

'Are you sure you'll be okay? Jodie asked.

'I'll be fine.' He winked and she turned away from him in such a pointed manner that even Jerry noticed and put a comforting hand on his shoulder. He was hurt and embarrassed but self-pity, he reminded himself, wouldn't help. Claire, a fellow student, sat down opposite Bobby and spoke to him loudly.

'Why do you bother with her, Bobby? What she's doing is punishing you. You could have anybody,' she declared, flicking back her hair from her face.

He couldn't see Jodie's expression but he knew Claire's words would have wounded her. He clenched his lips together tightly as if trying to hold back the words which longed to escape, but eventually he turned on Claire. His eyes narrowed as he spoke.

'You can't imagine what I've put her through. I drove her,' he said pointing at Jodie, 'to the brink of a breakdown because she cared enough to want to tell me the truth.'

He pushed back the chair from the table. 'I don't blame her if she is punishing me.'

Claire looked shocked but said no more as Bobby got up, unaware that all eyes were on him. He left the canteen without finishing the coffee. Jodie didn't say a word, but after a moment she followed him. As she reached the door she called to him, but he ignored her. She called him again and he turned briefly without looking directly at her.

'Leave me alone Jodie, I'm going home,' he said and then ran to the motorbike, revved up and left. In his anger and frustration, he took the country roads far too fast. All he could think of was how stupid he had been to break off his relationship with Jodie. The bike screeched to a halt outside Granddad's cottage. He stood in the front garden smoking a cigarette to calm his nerves before he entered the cottage. He knew his distress would be obvious to Jodie's granddad. The front door opened while Bobby was still smoking.

'What happened?' Granddad asked.

'It's okay,' Bobby said, 'I'm just frustrated.'

Bobby stubbed out the cigarette and went inside, throwing himself down into the corner of the settee with his arms folded, as he poured out the events of the morning without even taking his jacket off.

'Maybe Claire is right, perhaps Jodie is punishing you.'

Bobby shook his head violently. 'Claire has been chasing me since the day we started college.'

Granddad smiled broadly. 'She may have been using it as ploy to get you, but she could still be right.'

At that moment the back door flew open as if a hurricane had swept in. Jodie burst through the door and rounded on Bobby with energy, which reminded him so much of Jodie as he had known and loved her.

'You really are a quick-tempered idiot sometimes aren't you?'

In her anger she had become real with him, and as he looked at her he felt his heart rate quicken. She slammed the door with a vengeance while he sat wide-eyed, unable to say a word. She took immediate advantage.

'I had to get Jerry to drive me out here just because you were too hot-headed to wait and hear what I had to say.'

Even in her anger he could see kindness, and the inconsistency made him smile. He looked away; he should have been feeling penitent. He could see that Granddad was suppressing a smile, judging by the way his mouth puckered. Bobby looked up at Jodie trying not to laugh.

'I'm sorry,' he offered, whilst still sporting an inane grin.

She threw her portfolio into the nearest armchair with such force that the contents fell onto the floor.

'You're always bloody sorry but you still never think the next time.'

She stopped briefly as he spluttered in a desperate attempt to be serious.

'You were supposed to give me a lift home,' she continued.

Bobby was instantly serious. He put his hand to his mouth as he realised that she was right. He began to say 'I'm sorry,' but she cut him off midway as she continued her tirade. He looked across to Granddad who was smiling, and then burst into laughter, which made her even madder. Bobby tried to calm the atmosphere. 'Your eyes look even prettier when ...'

'My eyes do not look even prettier when I'm angry,' she snapped, interrupting him once more.

'Actually,' Granddad said between laughs, 'she's right Bobby, her eyes don't look prettier when she's angry.'

Bobby and Granddad broke into uncontrollable laughter as Jodie stood with her hands on her hips, until a smile crept across her face and she joined their laughter. After they had calmed down, Jodie sat down awkwardly next to Bobby, who could feel her tension but he said nothing. He wasn't laughing any more.

'I'll make coffee,' Granddad said tactfully. It took Jodie a long time to speak, but eventually she turned and faced Bobby. He could sense her looking at him, but was too embarrassed to return the gaze.

'Claire was right, I'm sorry,' she said softly, almost choking on her words. She leant across and kissed him on the cheek. He didn't look up at her and as her granddad entered the room she shot him a puzzled look. Bobby was paralysed with fear. Granddad put down the coffee.

'What is it?' Jodie asked.

Bobby wasn't hiding his anxiety very well. What had he to lose? He might as well tell Jodie what troubled him. 'I'm afraid of hurting you again.' He looked up at Jodie fleetingly, but was embarrassed by the tears welling up in his eyes. He wiped them quickly with the back of his hand and looked away. He still felt vulnerable and unstable.

Jodie leant against him. 'I won't deny that I was hurt, but I want to try again.'

She smiled at her granddad, a deeply affectionate smile. Granddad raised his eyebrows. 'You've changed your tune very quickly,' he remarked.

Jodie kissed Bobby on the cheek and leant on his chest. 'Well ...' she began, 'I may be easily taken in, but if you had heard Bobby's speech to Claire in the canteen, you'd understand,' she declared. 'I was finally convinced that he knew what he'd done to me.'

58

Two days later with snow inches-deep on the ground, Granddad begged Bobby not to ride the motorbike to college, insisting that it would be safer if they walked the two miles up to the main road and caught the bus from there. They arrived late but full of laughter and behaving like children in the snow.

'I hope the snow isn't gone by lunchtime!' Bobby exclaimed just before the first lecture. Jodie laughed as they strolled into the studio; snow lent itself to mischief.

As soon as lunch break began Bobby skipped outside to make a snowman. It took a while to roll the body but, with Jerry's help, it was eventually big enough. To the delight of everyone, they had come to a halt outside the principal's office. The snowman's head took slightly less time and he was soon grinning inanely into the office window. Bobby supplied him with a scarf, hat, eyes, nose and mouth, which he conveniently had in his pocket. The snowman had even gathered a small audience. His mission accomplished, Bobby went to lunch with Jodie and Jerry.

Kate was already in the canteen having a serious discussion with another student. Bobby proceeded to discuss the finer technicalities of their sculptural masterpiece. Quickly guessing his game, the others went along with it. Kate appeared irritated by their giggling and turned her back on them. Bobby and Jodie left the canteen first and he set about creating an ambush for Jerry.

'Bobby you're almost twenty,' she reminded him.

'I know that, I don't have amnesia,' he insisted.

'Please don't involve Kate,' she begged, holding on to his leather jacket in an attempt to restrain him. 'She won't find it funny.'

He broke free of her grip, sporting an impish grin.

'My aim's not brilliant. I wish I could guarantee hitting Jerry without hitting Kate.'

He shrugged and she smiled to herself. She didn't help him as he prepared the ammunition; helping would be aiding and abetting in Kate's eyes. It seemed an eternity to Jodie as they hid behind the tall bushes that lined the pathway to the canteen. Eventually she heard voices.

'It's them,' she said to Bobby who waited for his moment before bombarding them. Jerry responded quickly with hastily made air-borne missiles of his own as Kate beat a hasty retreat. Just before she reached cover, Bobby hit her on the back of the neck with a well-aimed snowball. She brushed away the snow and shot him an evil glare.

Jerry approached Bobby's hiding place at great pace and seeing the impending danger, Bobby fled until he and Jerry were like spots on the horizon.

'Ah well,' Kate said in a tone of resignation, raising her eyes heavenward, 'at least he's back to normal.'

Suddenly Kate noticed the snowman and began to laugh. 'Is that his sculpture?' she asked with a grin as she turned to Jodie. 'Is that what he meant by "rotund form" and "cold expression"?' she asked with a grin. Kate altered her tone to one of genuine concern. 'Is he all right now?'

Jodie sighed. 'He has good days and bad days.'

'I'd hate to make it worse,' Kate said reticently. 'But I met Simon in town, the guy who works at Colin's studio, and the rumours say that Hannah is four months pregnant.'

'So that is why ...' Jodie's voice faded out.

'His parents were arguing, yes probably,' Kate said, completing the sentence.

Jodie shrugged. 'I don't think he'll be surprised at anything now.'

Kate turned a questioning gaze on Jodie. 'Will he stay with your granddad?'

Jodie shrugged again. 'I guess so.'

As they talked, two rather wet looking individuals emerged

from what appeared to be a snow storm. Kate shot them a patronising glare.

'You'll be frozen all afternoon now.'

Jerry reached out his arms to embrace her but she backed away with a look of disgust.

'Do you realise,' Bobby said to Jerry with an ominous glint in his eye, 'that Jodie hasn't got even slightly wet, yet?'

Jodie backed away from him as he scooped up snow. Her eyes said, "No," but her mouth couldn't quite form the words. She backed still further away, watching him for any sudden movement until, taking one step backwards, she fell into the bush behind her before she could heed Kate's cry of warning. Bobby assumed an expression of grave concern as he went to help her to her feet. Instead, she caught him off balance and pulled him into the bushes on top of her.

'Ah well,' he said laughing, 'a bird in the bush is worth two in the hand.'

At Jerry's suggestion he and Kate walked off to the afternoon lecture, although Kate pushed his wet form away from her every time he tried to get close.

Bobby and Jodie didn't feel cold in the warmth of the lecture room, but she shivered while they were waiting at the bus stop and complained as she tightened the belt around her coat.

'Ah well,' he said with a patronising air, 'stupid actions have consequences.' She hit him hard and he almost overbalanced. 'I am suffering the consequences of *your* stupid actions,' she said indignantly.

'You should have looked where you were going,' he replied mischievously, but as he spoke he leant over, removed her saturated scarf, took off his, which had been tucked inside his jacket, and wrapped it carefully around her neck. He stuffed the wet one into the front pocket of his rucksack. The bus seemed to take forever and she was glad when it finally arrived; she couldn't wait to sit down. They sat near the front and she leant on his shoulder, closing her eyes wearily.

'I can't bear the thought of walking home from the bus stop,' she remarked louder than she had intended.

'I could always give you a piggy back,' he retorted.

She looked up at him out of the corner of her eye, barely raising her head. 'Suddenly walking seems a good option,' she replied.

She laid her head back on his shoulder and he laughed as he recalled aloud how she backed into the bushes.

'Shut up,' she said, but there was no stopping him, much to the amusement of the other occupants of the half-full, single-decker country bus. Once they'd reached their destination they stayed close as they walked the two miles home, and for the last half mile he became more serious.

'I don't know where I'd be without your granddad,' he said suddenly as if he was thinking aloud.

'I could say the same thing,' she replied dismissively.

He smirked. 'No you couldn't. My granddad never did a thing for you.'

She nudged him in the ribs with her elbow.

'Seriously though,' he said, composing himself once more. 'I've thought a lot about it. He told me the truth from the start. I'll never forget that.'

She gripped his hand tighter, turned to face him and looked him in the eye. 'He did something very similar for me many years ago.'

He pulled her close. 'Tell me,' he pleaded.

She loosed herself from his grip and continued to walk on. 'It would take too long now, but I will one day; I promise.'

He put his arm around her, and kissed her. She could never forget her own past, but it didn't consume her any more. Maybe one day it would be the same for Bobby, and days like today gave her hope. He would have good days and bad days, and she hoped that she had the strength to stand by him through them all.

59

Hannah was tired when she arrived home. She had agreed to meet Bobby that afternoon and had kept it quiet from Colin. To her surprise, Colin was sitting in her lounge. She could see anger in his eyes the moment she walked into the room.

'Sorry,' Grace whispered as she stood at the door. 'I didn't realise he didn't know.'

Hannah shrugged, desperately attempting to think on her feet. She patted her sister on the shoulder.

'No problem,' she said, although there clearly was.

I'll tell him straight away, Hannah said to herself. 'I met Bobby for coffee today,' she said casually.

'So I heard,' Colin replied, with tight lips. 'Why?' His tone cut the air with its venom.

She didn't apologise; she wouldn't apologise. Meeting Bobby hadn't been easy.

'Because,' she fired at him, 'the boy is owed an explanation. Because,' she continued without a hint of penitence, 'someone needed to acknowledge his pain.'

Colin rose to his feet, anger rising as he moved towards her. 'So you thought it was alright to show contempt for me by meeting him?'

'What are you going to do Colin?' She raised her eyebrows as she spoke, daring him almost. 'Are you going to hit me, like you hit him and his mother?'

Colin sat back down heavily and she smiled to herself. She could still steer him a little. He said nothing, but she could see him mulling things over. She waited, biding her time. She had to confront him; she couldn't afford to remain silent. She held his gaze.

'You need help, Colin. I can't risk you damaging our child's life like that. I used to think that I couldn't manage alone, but now I realise that I can if I have to. I won't move in with you unless you seek help.' Having delivered the ultimatum, she felt relief.

'What did you say to him?' Colin demanded.

'To Bobby?' she asked, noting that he had changed the subject. She shrugged. 'I explained all about your childhood, your mother's death and your father's alcoholism. I told him that you longed for your father's love too, and he knows that your father only died just before Christmas. Oh, and I told him I was pregnant, but he'd already heard that.'

He stood up and paced the floor. 'So you excused me, did you,' he spat, 'as a poor inadequate wreck?'

Hannah answered like with like, angry with him now, 'No Colin, he knows you're an inadequate wreck. He's been on the receiving end of your anger for as long as he can remember. He sees right through you. He sees his mother as weak, bland and ineffectual, and you as a coward who never faced up to his own reality. He's not stupid.'

Colin looked cowed and hurt. 'Is that what he says?'

She looked at the ground as she answered. 'Yes.'

He sighed. 'And do you agree with him?' The tone was less aggressive now, more anguished.

'Yes,' she replied, quickly adding, 'but I know that you did what you did to hide your shame, rather than with more evil motives.'

He said nothing. She had always been able to pierce his heart; she understood him better than a man wants to be understood, especially one whose life has been veiled in duplicity.

'When I look at him I see you twenty years ago.'

He stared past her out of the window. He was still easy on the eye, still held a charm that she couldn't explain.

'Give him a chance,' she said, 'he's artistic, he's musical, he's wild, he looks like you, he's enthusiastic like you, sensitive like you …' she paused, only briefly, 'and he's tortured just like you.'

He winced but there was no way that she would retract a

single statement. 'You hurt him Colin. You should never have stayed with his mother.'

He didn't dispute it and made no attempt to vindicate himself. She added only, 'He's written a song to you.' She had to keep her promise to Bobby, 'he's playing it at the folk club on Friday.'

'Stupid bastard,' he said.

'And that,' she retorted as she got up out of the chair, 'is exactly how your father would have responded.'

It was a measured insult. She could see the tremors that precede an explosion, and then just as suddenly it subsided, as if he had somehow had a revelation.

'Can't we just begin again?' he asked. 'This child, our child, would be a true love-child.'

Hannah sat down beside him but turned away from him slightly, putting distance between them. 'Only if you get help,' she replied and then changed the subject. 'Do you want coffee?' she asked. She got up before he had time to reply, but felt dizzy as she rose to her feet and stumbled. Colin was instantly beside her and she rested her head on his shoulder. Very gently, he stroked her fair hair, dusted now with grey flecks.

'You rest. I'll make the coffee,' he ordered with a smile, and the gentleness almost moved her to tears. She knew that with help he could still be the person that she had always believed him to be, and she remembered why she had loved him so deeply. She lay back in the corner of the settee and forced herself not to cry. Another time, another place and this would have been her heart's desire but it seemed too late, and too complicated, and she was afraid. For the sake of her child, she couldn't risk his anger. When he returned with the coffee he was calmer. He put the coffee down beside her.

'I'm staying over at the house at Dernham for a few days to sort things out and after that I'll stay at Dad's house until it's sold. That will give us time to make decisions.'

Hannah said nothing, merely leant on him for support. She

was tired and stressed and didn't feel awfully well. He put his arm around her and she felt her body relax.

'Okay,' she whispered. 'So will you listen to his song?'

He sighed, with an impatient, 'All right.'

He was doing it for her, she knew that, but she didn't care about the motives. She had no idea what Bobby had written, but it would have feeling and meaning, and who could know what effect it would have on Colin? He suddenly sat upright.

'What do I wear to an art college folk club?'

'Flared cords and a flowery shirt,' she laughed.

'Written me a song indeed!' he exclaimed. 'He never lets up, does he? He's such a stubborn little bastard.'

'His father's son?' she asked and lay back in his arms.

60

Colin was taller and bigger built than Bobby, and his fair hair was mingled with grey, but the similarity was unmistakeable. As soon as Colin walked through the inner door of the folk club with Hannah, rumours began to circulate. The violent attack on Bobby was known only to his inner circle but the mutual animosity was common knowledge. Tonight, people looked puzzled, anxious even. Colin declined a seat and chose instead to stand near the doorway. Kate walked past him without a word, merely casting a contemptuous glance his way.

Bobby had been sitting outside on the low wall for too long, and was feeling the cold by the time Jodie arrived. She seized the cigarette from his hand and stubbed it out under her boot.

'Time to go,' she ordered.

'Kiss me first,' he requested.

'You're stalling,' she said and took him by the hand.

He didn't resist but he tried to stop and kiss her again under the light that illuminated the lettering outside the folk club; "Village People", it said. The club had come a long way in the months since he had taken the reins. He pulled her closer and gripped her hand tightly as they went down the steps together. Nick, who was sitting at a table at the entrance, called Bobby back.

'Bobby, you haven't signed in.'

'Sorry,' he said, 'I was miles away.'

He took the fountain pen from the inside pocket of his jacket and signed himself in, waited for Jodie, and grabbed her hand again.

'Your dad's just inside the door,' Nick warned him.

Bobby pushed open the door, took a deep breath and walked in with false confidence, still clinging tightly to Jodie's hand. He gave a slight nod and said, 'Good evening, thank you for coming,' to his father and Hannah as he passed by.

His father's reply was an equally embarrassed, 'Good evening.'

Bobby was greeted like a returning hero. He returned their greetings with a nervous smile, a sign of weakness which he knew would not escape his father's keen eye. He wasn't paying much attention as he helped Jodie out of her black maxi-coat until he stood holding it in mid-air with his mouth wide open.

'I should have guessed,' he said as he lightly fingered the emerald ribbon tied into the back of her hair which matched the satin dress. 'You look stunning,' he said as he ran his hand over her bare shoulder. 'In fact you make me look shabby.'

Jerry leant closer, 'Perhaps that's because you are.'

Kate glanced briefly at her watch. 'Are you ready to sing, Barron, or do you intend staring at Jodie all evening?'

'Well,' he began, and she shot him a no-nonsense look so he merely replied 'I'm ready.'

Kate leant in close and whispered, 'Whatever happens, don't let the bastard get to you'.

As she turned to walk away, Bobby took hold of her arm. 'You forget,' he laughed, 'I'm the bastard.'

She looked him straight in the eye. 'You may be the physical bastard but he is the metaphorical one.' She slapped him on the arm and walked over to the microphone to begin the evening's entertainment.

'Okay ladies and gentlemen, let's have your attention. This evening we want to welcome back Bobby and Jodie.' Some of the audience cheered and Kate moved back so that Bobby could take the mic.

'Firstly, thank you to all those who sent me get-well wishes and words of encouragement,' he said, keeping his eyes firmly away from his father's, 'Secondly, welcome to my father, for whom I have written this song.'

He sat on the edge of the stool, tweaked the strings and looked straight into the eyes of his father as Jodie played an introduction on the violin. His father's face was fixed and troubled. All eyes darted between the two as the tension mounted. He watched Hannah look first at Colin and then at him. Jodie had played through the introductory bars twice already, and eventually he looked up at her, waited for the right moment, nodded and began. He played the guitar in classical style as he sang his quiet composition. For once in his life his father held his gaze.

'While your dreams lay unfulfilled
so your heart can not be stilled,
like a bird within a cage you cannot fly.
You forget that you can soar,
soon your wings can move no more,
and all hope would disappear as years go by.

I would willingly forgive,
for my heart just wants to live
and forget the pain you brought me on the way,
but there's no more I can do
than extend a hand to you ...'

He didn't finish as he saw his father move towards the door without even stopping to ensure that Hannah was following. Bobby laid the guitar down and jumped off the stage in an attempt to follow him. The audience fell silent, aware that something unusual had happened. Bobby pushed open the swing door into the corridor just as his father was leaving the main door.

'Dad?' he called after him, pleading.

His father turned only briefly, pain in his eyes and only then did Bobby see tears as his father continued on his way out of the door. As Bobby reached the main door his way was barred by Granddad. He shook his head lightly as he held onto Bobby's arm with strength but gentleness.

'You've triggered something in him, don't push it.'

Bobby smiled; the sort of smile that could easily break into tears. Jodie's granddad never ceased to amaze him. 'I didn't know you were here,' he said softly.

'Did you really think I'd leave you to face it alone, son?'

Granddad smiled, and Bobby saw the kindness and the love in his eyes. He returned the smile as he whispered, 'Thank you'.

'Do you want to go home?' Granddad asked him privately.

'Not likely,' he replied with surprising determination, 'I'm here to sing'.

Granddad pushed open the door into the folk club. Kate had kept the club moving through the crisis and Rustic Reflections were in full swing with a rousing song about the oxen. Jerry approached Bobby cautiously with Kate almost hiding at his side.

'Are you okay?' Jerry asked.

'I'd be a liar to say it doesn't hurt, but I've been a lot worse,' he said.

Just then, he caught Kate's pained expression. *She's close to tears,* he thought. 'All you did was force me to see the truth,' he said.

'But if I'd said nothing, your family …' she choked, unable to go on, so he continued for her.

'My family would still be in the abject mess that it was before, and I would still be hopelessly clinging to the desperate desire for my dad's love, even if I ended up killing myself in the process. Looked at that from that perspective, Kate, you saved my life. Where is the logical Kate that we all know and …'

'Despise?' Jerry offered, which earned him a slap on the arm from Bobby, who led Kate by the hand to a corner of the room and sat down. He stared at the table, fiddling with a coaster, and eventually he looked up.

'The truth was too difficult to face. I almost destroyed

myself chasing after his love, but now I can live. You were just trying to protect Jodie.'

'I interfered,' she replied, wiping away tears.

'Aw, come on Kate,' he said, almost patronising her, 'look at the mess that I dragged her into, you were right to be worried.'

She smiled and put a hand on his. 'Thanks Bobby,' she said as they got up to return to their seats. Then she suddenly added. 'Where *is* Jodie?'

It was only then that Bobby realised that she was missing. He caught hold of Jerry's arm. 'Where's Jodie?'

'I'm not sure but her granddad's missing too.'

'Oh yes,' Bobby sighed with relief. 'She must have gone out the back way. She'll be frozen.' He picked up her coat.

As he approached the back door he could hear her crying, but he could also hear the soothing voice of her granddad. 'I'm telling you Jodie, he's alright.'

Bobby contemplated leaving them alone; after all her granddad knew her far better than he did. He opened the door quietly and stood just outside the door listening to the exchange.

'He wouldn't have done it if he hadn't had some hope of reconciliation.'

He could hear anger in Jodie's intonation and he couldn't listen to her pain any longer. She looked up as he moved within her field of vision and she turned away from him, crying again. He wrapped the coat and his arms around her as her granddad moved out of his way. For a few moments he just held her. Eventually he whispered softly to her.

'Granddad's right. My father still has to come to terms with himself. There was a third verse to that song I wrote to him where the caged bird is set free, but he wasn't ready for that. Maybe, one day ...' his voice trailed off.

She laid her head on his chest, her tears soaking into his shirt.

'So you're okay?' she asked.

'I will be. I'm emotionally exhausted but I do have one problem,' he said with an urgent, pained expression.

'What?' she asked him gently, anxiously.

'How the hell do I get this mascara off my shirt?'

He stood back as she hit him playfully and he took her hand, leading her back inside. 'Let's sing. I know,' he said, slowing her step as he walked backwards in front of her. 'You sing and Granddad can play the violin. Sing anything you like and I'll join in when I can. After that I have a solo I want to perform,' he said with a smile that reached his eyes.

They sang together, and then Granddad left the stage while the Cobwebs played for a further ten minutes. The atmosphere was hushed, melancholic almost, reflecting the events of the night.

The atmosphere hadn't altered when Bobby took the stage alone. He sat on a stool with the guitar and Jerry moved a microphone for him. He produced a small, scruffy piece of paper from his trouser pocket, which he placed on the music rest before announcing, 'I've entitled this instrumental piece *Mourning to Dancing*, and it's dedicated to Jodie and her granddad. Jodie leant on her granddad's shoulder as she watched him. He could see the fondness in her eyes and vowed to himself that he would never let her go again.

He looked at them both for only a brief moment before beginning to play with soft, deeply resonating notes like the sound of that first pedal note of a pipe organ: low, slow and reverent. By progressive addition and subdivision of notes, and steadily increasing the tempo, he gradually shifted the music to a melancholic folk style. After a short while, almost by sleight of hand, he moved the accent of the beat, whilst keeping the tune intact, and began to lift the mood into a fast folk tune.

Jodie had sat up to listen now as the room fell into an expectant silence. The tune was gathering pace and began to play catch-up with itself in a startling, colourful syncopated rhythm in a style that had the feel of a gypsy dance and celebration, and suddenly the club took to its feet clapping in time to the beat. He caught Jodie's eye, urging her, challenging her. Her granddad said something to her and she got up, picked up her violin that was still lying by the stage, and joined him. He dropped the syncopated beat as she took it up and the folk club was vibrant with movement for a good five minutes at a breathtaking pace.

When it came to an end the applause was immense, but, despite the cries of 'more', he couldn't continue. The day had been long and stressful, and they still had to clear away. He got up, turned around, took Jodie's hand, drew her towards him and kissed her, which was clearly enough of an encore to satisfy the club members, who broke into applause once more.

As he took her by the hand back to where they had been sitting, she whispered to him. 'That was stunning.'

He simply shrugged as he replied, 'I couldn't have done that without your granddad. He made me see that if I take the good with the bad, just like your Christmas tree, it makes me true to myself. I saw my life as a cacophony but now I see it like a symphony, many parts of the same thing brought together by the conductor.'

At the close of the evening, as Bobby helped Kate and Jerry clear away, Jodie sat down with her granddad. Bobby winked at Granddad as he overheard him say to her, 'Martin Luther King once said that, "Freedom is never voluntarily given by the oppressor, it must be demanded by the oppressed".'

The End

To stay informed about future books by Gill Wyatt, email her at gillwyatt@heartsease.org.uk or go to her website - www.heartsease.org.uk - and follow the links.

Lightning Source UK Ltd.
Milton Keynes UK
UKOW051210051212

203202UK00004B/83/P